ASHEN

Ashen

Jade Wilson

Destroyed Universe Press

Author's Edition, April 2026

Copyright © 2026 by Jade Wilson

Destroyed Universe Press

This is a work of fiction. Names, characters, places, and incidents either are a product of the author's imagination or are used fictitiously. Any resemblance to persons, places, or events is coincidental.

There was no AI used in the production, marketing, or distribution of this work. All art and story elements were human-made.

Cover Art by Ariah Gilbert

Edited by Jen Jilany at Upstyle Editing

Ebook ISBN: 979-8-9946949-0-9

Paperback ISBN: 979-8-9946949-1-6

For the girl who was brave enough to write this first
And for the family and friends who believed in that version.

Look how far we've come.

PROLOGUE

The throne room was quiet when the knock came. It reverberated throughout the room, drawing Syren IceHeart from his thoughts. He had no idea how long he had been sitting there. Time seemed insignificant, even on the days that his memories were intact.
"Enter," he called. He knew what this was about. The Water Realm mission. They were supposed to return today, but there had been no word from Captain GildedFoot, or any of the 500 soldiers he had sent to the Water Realm.
Matthias StoneElf, the king's advisor, slipped through the lavawood doors, carrying a stack of files and a holodisk. The files alone signaled to IceHeart that this would not be good news.
He gestured for Matthias to sit at the other end of the long table that sat in the center of the vast chamber, with IceHeart's throne serving as the head. The buzz from the failing climate regulator in the throne room was the only audible sound as Matthias bowed and took his seat, placing the holodisk on the table across from the king.
"Sir, the situation in the Water Realm has taken an unprecedented turn. The portal tether has been severed, and our troops have still failed to respond." Sweat beaded on the old man's brow. IceHeart briefly wondered if it was from the sweltering Fire Realm heat or Matthias's nerves. "We have every reason to believe that Aydron has captured or killed them," IceHeart smiled tightly. It was almost surely the first scenario. In all his years as king of the Fire Realm, he had never seen Aydron SwiftStream kill anyone. Not without torturing them first.

"Has Aydron communicated his demands? Surely there's something we can use to persuade him." IceHeart asked, unbothered. You could get away with nearly anything if you paid enough. Still, the scenario wasn't ideal. IceHeart knew he should have vetted the details of this raid more thoroughly, but everything had moved so quickly. He hardly remembered giving the orders. IceHeart fiddled with the corkscrew the butler had left on the table, eyeing StoneElf.

There was no use in showing any concern when it was evident that StoneElf was already anxious enough. *Old man worries enough for the entire realm.* The thought was sharp and cold, like it didn't belong to Syren at all.

StoneElf shook his head and tapped the switch on the holodisk to bring it to life. The face of Queen Tenebrae, ruler of the Realm of Darkness, filled the screen.

Great, what does she want?

Elya Tenebrae, while the queen of the Realm of Darkness, was also the leader of the Eastern Division, the co-lead of the Divisional Council, and she was always in Syren's business. Another person who worried too much. He was doing what was best for the Fire Realm. At least, that was what he was *trying* to do.

A time stamp flashed across the screen, showing that the video had been sent within the hour. A crackle sounded from the device as the audio started: "...Syren, you bastard." Syren smirked. It was just like the shadow queen to use human swear words to degrade him. *Cute.* "...You know the consequences of interdivisional travel for war purposes. You've not only awakened the wrath of Aydron, you've stirred the entire Western Division..." As the queen's voice echoed, something flickered in Syren's mind. *Fear?* It vanished so quickly that he wasn't sure. Then his face curled into a smile. Cold. Crooked. Not entirely his. He motioned for StoneElf to cut the feed. He needed to think.

Aydron SwiftStream, the beloved king of the Water Realm, was his greatest political enemy; a feud that was much older than either of them. Their families had despised each other since the IceHearts took power during the First Divisional War. Mainly because the SwiftStreams were evil warlords who hid behind smiles and handshakes while the IceHearts never cared to hide at all.

None of that mattered, though; even if Aydron decided to start a war, the Western Division wasn't known for its power. The Water Realm had some talented mages, sure, but IceHeart's raid should have all but crippled them, at least for the moment. The other realms in the west only consisted of Wind Realm harpies and the Wisps from the Realm of Time, neither of whom liked to insert themselves in political conflicts unless specifically required. And that was a decree that the head of the Western division – King Lux - would never sign. *Coward.*

That wasn't considering that the human realm had all but dropped out of inter-realm politics except for a few heavily regulated trade routes. For all the rest of the Division knew, the strong pantheons of gods that once spoke for the feeble mortals had closed up shop and gone into retirement. Did the Water Realm *actually* think they could win with such a pathetic attempt at an army?

They did detain our men, though.

The thought ate at him for a minute, but he brushed it aside. It didn't matter; he'd get his men back, and there were even a few soldiers about to complete training. He could use them.

"Is this the best she has?" He chuckled, taking a slow sip of wine. "I expected her to grace me with her presence, at least." The line echoed through him, like someone else had said it.

"Sir, I…"

"Who does she think she is? Acting like there's a threat of a Divisional War when the Western Division is down an entire realm and can't find *actual* soldiers…" The king chuckled to himself again. She always spoke down to him, as if he was a child. He scowled at the thought. He'd grown up without a mother; he didn't need one now.

Having watched the message multiple times with the logistics team before this meeting, StoneElf nervously fast-forwarded the video to a one-minute section near the end and hit play again. It picked up in the middle of Tenebrae's sentence: "…You may think what you did can be easily handled, but the Greek pantheon has pledged to support the Western Division. Your actions alone have invoked the wrath of a pantheon that, up until this point, we thought were dead or had abandoned their realm." There was a brief pause as she let the reality of her words sink in. "I hope you're happy, Syren." The holodisk clicked, and the screen went blank, leaving Syren speechless.

The smug look vanished from the king's face as the severity of the situation hit him. If the Greek pantheon stepped in, the Eastern Division would be destroyed. There would be no stopping them. Everyone would perish. He had heard the stories—the Olympians were ruthless. They made the gods of other realms cower in fear. This was no longer a strategy game, this was a war brewing. He gulped. *No. There had to be a way to stop this.*

"What options do we have?" he asked carefully, trying to hide the fear in his voice. The Fire Realm had the best logisticians anywhere. *They had to have come up with something... anything.*

Matthias leafed through the files and produced two folders, each labeled with code names. He slid them across the table silently, not wanting to sway the king's judgment before he had ample time to survey the options himself.

The king picked up both folders, read the code names for each, and opened the one labeled "Operation Spark." It was a carefully planned diversion, something that no one would ever see coming. Something that would render the Greek pantheon helpless and give the Fire Realm the advantage. It was nearly foolproof. The other one was a half-hearted peace treaty that could work but risked making the Fire Realm appear weak. The king slid the peace treaty folder back to Matthias and laid the diversion plan out in front of him.

He rubbed his chin and asked, "Bennett?" His eyes darkened at the name. "Surely not Scott Bennett?" His chest tightened. He hadn't heard that name in ages. Scott was an old family friend. If he could be called that.

StoneElf nodded, "It would seem that his daughter carries the bloodline of Zeus." He paused and peered over his glasses at the king. "She's the *last* in the demigod bloodline after the Line Severance Decree was signed."

IceHeart thought for a moment. The decree had been signed shortly before he was in charge, but he remembered his brother, Kai, pushing for its approval prior to his death. Something about demigods being a threat to the realm. Now that he thought about it, that was also when Scott stopped coming to the Fire Realm. He didn't even attend Kai's funeral. *Traitor.*

The king nodded and picked up his wine glass. This was getting interesting. "How does her being of demigod descent relate to the situation at hand?" After all, IceHeart thought, if she's the last, what would her removal do to further sway the pantheon from war? It wasn't like they were going to weaponize her. That would not only break the Line Severance Decree, but also any subsequent pacts that the Division had signed related to it. That alone could start a war.

Anticipating the question, StoneElf produced a page that he had requested from the logistics team's historian. A piece of little-known lore that the Greeks had taken good care to stash away. He handed the sheet to IceHeart with a smirk.

The king took the paper and, as he read the forgotten piece of history, an evil smile teased his lips. It was nothing more than a scribbled translation of a verse from an archived tablet—something only a historian and the gods themselves could translate presently—but it was enough to demonstrate the point.

...*The link to the pantheon—and thus to power—lies within the demiblood. Without a lineage, the kingdom falls...*

It all made sense. Why the Line Severance Decree had been so important for the realms, and why the Greeks had taken care to let the last of their bloodlines die out naturally, clinging to the residual power held by their demigod children. If only one demigod child remained, they would be the key to the pantheon's power. And, if the Olympians were preoccupied with protecting their power source, no one could support the Western Division in a war.

Nonetheless, eliminating a demigod bloodline without triggering the gods or the rest of The Division would prove to be a difficult task. Since the Greek pantheon had gone silent, only humans had traveled to Earth aside from traders, and demigod blood, whether inherited or divinely created, was intensely dangerous. If this human held the last drop of Zeus's power, it could be enough to destroy an entire battalion with the flick of a hand. That type of concentrated power could not be taken lightly. They needed to be strategic in their diversion.

"What soldiers are available?" The king questioned, the plan unfolding in his mind. He could send a small team, one that could blend in and still get the job done.

StoneElf sighed and replied, "We have a handful, none of which are ideal candidates." He pressed a button on the holodisk, and a screen appeared, listing the soldiers who had completed training and hadn't been sent on the Water Realm mission. There were five, but he only needed three if he could select the strongest among them.

Looking at the screen, one caught his eye. A sharpshooter and strategist. "Private FangSword?" He paused. *Private* sounded out of place next to a surname of that caliber. Names ending in Sword were reserved for those of noble descent, and none of them remained privates for long. "Is that Finn? The former Captain?" He was starting to think there might be hope for this mission after all.

Looking at his notes again, StoneElf nodded. "Yes. Formerly the youngest captain the Fire Realm has ever seen." He flipped the page and continued, "It looks like he was demoted for insubordination directly before Operation SwiftStream, deeming him ineligible for deployment."

IceHeart remembered. The order had been simple: Clear the village. No survivors. FangSword had stalled, then flatly refused. He had spared the camp and only raided for contraband. IceHeart hadn't wanted to demote him, but had to keep up appearances. The political climate in the Fire Realm demanded that someone pay for the act of rebellion. It was demotion or death, and IceHeart had wanted to keep FangSword's skill set in the ranks.

"One of the saddest days of my reign," he said dryly, swirling his wine. "'The mighty fall the hardest, ' they say." He paused. The memory of the trial flickered—brief, ghostlike. He'd fought within himself for several nights before FangSword's trial, knowing full well he could be losing the best leader the realm had seen in decades. "Still…he's capable. I'm willing to forget his past shortcomings temporarily to have his leadership on this mission."

StoneElf nodded approvingly, checking Finn's name from the list on the holodisk, causing it to disappear.

"And…Private FalconTail," IceHeart continued. "I hear he has shown promise in his training sessions."

StoneElf clucked his tongue disapprovingly. "Yes, while he *did* just finish training, He's not the best fighter. However, he makes up for it with his field knowledge and blind loyalty." IceHeart nodded. It might be a good offset, considering FangSword's past. "He's also a gifted technician. He disarms bombs like they're leisure puzzles."

"I'll take him, too. He can see what a real mission looks like." IceHeart replied as he drummed his fingers on the table. The action was slow and deliberate. He paused, staring at his own hand. Had he been doing that?

Three soldiers were left on the list, but one name kept drawing the king's eye: Axel AxeClaw.

Everyone knew the story. He had been part of a minor crime syndicate out of Vespys, the Fire Realm capital, and had watched his entire unit get executed. Most men would have died with their team, but Axel was different. He had raw instinct and talent, traits that the king knew were perfect for the military. IceHeart had given Axel a choice: Serve the realm, or follow his crew into the abyss.

Axel had been barely of age by Flamease standards, too young for execution, too dangerous to be released. He had made the choice the king hoped he would make. Since then, Axel's speed and cunning had become something of legend. Unfortunately, so had his temper...and his mouth. He was one of the only Claw names in the military and wore his name like armor. Despite being of the lowest class, Claws always did that. They stole every ounce of respect they received. Axel spent most of his time in the reform program because he said what he thought, when he thought it, usually with a smirk.

StoneElf noticed the king's eyes lingering on the one name he had hoped the king would skim over and quickly filled the silence. "Private FlameTongue is an excellent linguist, sire—and QuiverTail has tracking experience, he—"

"Bring me AxeClaw," IceHeart said, his tone flat and final.

"But sir...he hasn't been fully reformed. H-he's volatile."

"And fast," IceHeart cut in. "Cunning. If you can find me someone with knife skills half as good as his, I'll consider them." He drummed his fingers once against the table. "Until then...we'll take our chances."

StoneElf nodded reluctantly and pulled up three more files on the holodisk—the aliases that the logistics team had assigned to the three soldiers. He then slipped out silently to assemble the soldiers. The king studied the aliases, another smile forming on his face. *This might just work.*

The aliases wouldn't be hard for the men to assume—a quick surname swap was more than enough—but looking at them stung slightly. Prior to the Divisional War, the Flamease were proud of their true forms—basilisk blood and golden scales. The type of sharp-edged beauty no one could replicate. Now, like all realms, they wore the human shape. It had been an agreed-upon condition of peace following the war, as the realms worked together to rebuild.

IceHeart's family had fought against the pact, citing an infringement of fundamental rights. They said the price was too steep, even for something like unity. Now, he didn't even think about it. No one did. Flamease children had their common form chips implanted soon after birth, with their parents choosing their preferred hair, eye, and skin color. The only problem was that – like any technology - it could be damaged. If only they could shapeshift like some other realms.

While not ideal, the Common Form Decree would work in the Fire Realm's favor for this mission. With the help of the pre-planned aliases, there would be no way to tell the soldiers apart from humans. It was convenient, but convenience always came with its own cost. IceHeart knew that all too well.

***

StoneElf returned with the soldiers in tow, just as the king switched the holodisk to display the mission file. He noted that they were all wearing human attire, as opposed to their regular Fire Realm tunics. He knew that if they showed up on Earth wearing tunics, they would be flagged immediately, so it was best to try to blend in.

He rose as the soldiers bowed. "At ease," he said, his voice low and hollow. The three straightened, completely silent. The king studied them, one by one from left to right.

Finn FangSword stood first in line with broad shoulders and sharp blue eyes that missed nothing. He held himself like a man used to commanding battalions, even if his title *had* been stripped. His jaw was clenched, his stance precise. A soldier still, no matter what the records said.

Axel AxeClaw leaned slightly to one side, arms crossed, expression unreadable beneath tousled blonde hair. His eyes—amber and cold—spoke more than his mouth ever would. He was talented, but he was dangerous. Worse than that, he was *confident*.

Finally, Connor FalconTail looked like every new soldier—young, nervous, and full of anxious hope. He stood like he was holding his breath in every bone. His green eyes darted everywhere, taking in the room like it might explode. It probably had, in his imagination. Twice.

StoneElf cleared his throat. "The soldiers have been given their aliases; they're ready for briefing."

The king nodded, retrieving the holodisk from the table as it flickered off. "Your mission is simple: Eliminate the demigod's bloodline." He handed the holodisk to Finn, who took it without hesitation. "We have a chance to end this war before it starts. Don't waste it." The words echoed around the room, heavy and ominous.

StoneElf handed each man their bags, which included tent rolls, clothes, and enough food for their brief mission. Finn had a crossbow and quiver slung over his shoulder, and IceHeart had a feeling that Axel had more weapons than the two daggers that were visible. He noted that Connor had no weapons, just some dusty field guides he'd probably borrowed from the archives, tucked against his chest.

They already had human faces, now they had human names, and human clothes. None of it seemed abnormal, though. Despite their human forms being unnatural, they moved like they were born in these bodies; no one would ever suspect they were Flamease. What began as a lie for conformity's sake had been worn for so long it had started to feel like their only form. And maybe that was all truth ever was—something repeated until it was no longer questioned.

IceHeart led them down a stone staircase that was riddled with moss and cobwebs. At the bottom of the stairs, a torch flickered, casting a dim light into large room with beacons lined across the far wall. Nine beacons, one for each of the nine other realms in The Division. Long-dead tech buzzed to life under flame-warm lights. The air smelled of dust, rust, and memory. The king stopped in front of a beacon marked with an 'X', an indication that a travel ban was in place for the realm the beacon belonged to. No one outside of the appointed realm guardians and traders had ventured to the human realm since before the Divisional War, and no human had visited the Fire Realm in twenty years. It was a shame that the circumstances were so dire; Syren would have liked to bask in the significance of the moment for a bit longer.

The human realm kept its portal tethers under lock and key, but the logistics team had planned for this. They hacked and produced a tether code that would land the soldiers within range to conduct surveillance on the target before completing their mission. There were currently no realm guardians from Earth, so Syren assumed that the beacons tracking portal signals were not being closely monitored.

As the king studied the trio, he felt his gaze linger a beat too long. Not enough for anyone to notice, just enough to feel it. Something felt amiss about this whole mission, but it was their only chance. You're being too soft, he thought.

"Three days. That is as long as we can keep the tether open without drawing unwanted attention. Miss the window, and you belong to the human realm." He paused just long enough for a chill to seep through the air. "Don't give me a reason to regret this mission." His gaze fixed on Finn. "Is that clear, *Captain*?"

Finn stiffened at the title. It scraped across a wound that hadn't fully closed. But he nodded. "Yes, sire."

Despite his tone, IceHeart was confident in his team. Axel was fast, ruthless, and unpredictable. Connor could locate a target faster than most people could blink. And Finn? Finn had been waiting for a reason to matter again; that was clear to anyone who saw him.

"Perfect," IceHeart said, stepping aside to reveal the portal.

Finn was the first to step toward the portal, the others following behind him. There was a flash, followed by a faint whirring noise that came from nowhere and everywhere, all at once.

Then an uneven, rocky terrain appeared against a gray sky above them. The air was heavy with humidity, and they could hear the distant chirp of birds. The mission had begun.

For the next three days, they weren't soldiers. They were Finn, Axel, and Connor. Just boys. Just unsuspecting enough to stop a war…or start it.

CHAPTER 1
RAINEE

"It's too late; they're coming for you," a distant voice whispered. The voice was soft, confident, and...familiar. Rainee couldn't place it, but the melodic voice sounded like a long-forgotten memory.
Rainee opened her eyes to find a clearing surrounded by the blurry outline of trees. In front of her, a glowing orb pulsed like a heartbeat. She didn't feel frightened, although the orb seemed to be threatening her.
She started to move toward it but, without warning, the grass beneath her erupted into flames. She wasn't burned, but was suddenly paralyzed. Her eyes wide, she looked up at the fading orb.
"Protect the spark," it whispered, just loud enough to be heard.
While she didn't recognize the voice, something inside her instinctively leaned toward it, like her soul remembered something she didn't.

***

Beep. Beep. Beep. The alarm to wake herself up for school sounded, but Rainee had already been awake for the past twenty minutes. The echoes of the dream still thundered in her head: *Protect the spark.* Whatever that meant.
She mashed her phone screen to silence the alarm and forced herself out of bed. Usually, she would have snoozed the alarm and laid there for a while, but today felt different. The world looked normal, but felt thin, fragile, like she was still dreaming. Like reality was held on by a single frayed thread.

She went through the motions of getting dressed, tugging on jeans and a stylish pullover. She paired the outfit with her favorite shoes—simple leather sandals that had passed "broken-in" and were now veering dangerously close to decrepit. Her normal routine, yet the dream still clung like fog. No matter how hard she tried to clear it from her mind, she couldn't shake it. She didn't usually remember her dreams, which made this one feel painfully real.

As she made her way down the stairs, she could hear her dad whistling in the kitchen as he prepared breakfast–just like every morning. The kitchen smelled like toast and bacon, something that Rainee was sure was a core memory at this point. Eighteen years and her dad had never learned to make anything else for breakfast. Not that she minded much.

She rounded the corner to find her dad standing at the counter with his back to her, lazily jostling the bacon in the skillet with a pair of tongs.

"You're up early," he said without turning to looked at her.

She shrugged and took a seat on the barstool behind him. "Couldn't sleep."

"Bad dream or loud thoughts?" he questioned. She could have guessed he would say that. He had been asking it since she was little. It was his default check-in phrase. She sighed, grateful that at least something felt normal this morning.

Rainee shook her head "Neither. Just heard the first alarm and decided to get an early start today." She lied, unable to tell if he noticed or not.

He nodded slowly, seeming to accept the answer. He placed the bacon on a napkin-lined dish and set it in front of Rainee. "Well then, eat up. You've got school soon."

"No, thanks. I'm not really hungry," she murmured, pushing the plate away.

For a second, a look flashed in her dad's eyes. Fear? No, she must have misread it. Whatever the look was, it vanished before she could place it. *Is he feeling okay?*

He pushed a piece of toast toward her, wrapped in a napkin. "If you don't want the bacon, at least eat this. It's peanut butter toast. You love peanut butter toast." He pointed to the napkin with his tongs.

Rainee sighed and took it. Their eyes met as she took a small bite, and he smiled—seemingly satisfied. *God forbid breakfast be skipped in this house.* Still, the routine felt like a reassuring reminder that this was all real.

As she left the house to walk to school, every part of her felt like she'd just been zapped by a powerline, in the worst way possible. Like her body was radiating something…Stress? Anger? Fear? Whatever it was, it made every hair on the back of her neck stand up.

Protect the Spark. She sighed, wishing this dream would hurry and dissipate from her consciousness. She didn't know what spark she was supposed to protect, or if that was her subconscious telling her to stop worrying so much about what comes after high school. Like some weird "protect your energy" mantra.

Lost in thought, Rainee didn't notice that the crosswalk sign had turned into a red hand instead of a walk sign. Her headphones were blaring a true crime podcast just loud enough to drown out the car horn.

In what felt like nanoseconds, a hand grabbed her bicep and yanked her to the pavement on the other side of the street. The car's mirror grazed her shoulder as it passed. Rainee hardly noticed; she was too distracted by the man gripping her like she belonged to him and the sudden scent of leather and smoke. It screamed "Guy-Who-Makes-Bonfires-His-Entire-Personality." Whoever he was, he was probably a fire sign. Those types were always fire signs.

She looked up into the bluest eyes she'd ever seen. Her breath caught in her throat. And then, just as their eyes met, he dropped her arm.

"You should be more careful," he offered coldly—a warning that echoed through the air and didn't seem entirely directed at her.

Before Rainee could respond, he had moved past her, making his way across the parking lot to her right.

"Thanks, I guess!" she called after him. *I guess not all heroes have manners.*

The remaining walk to school was uneventful. But what could be more eventful than almost dying?

Rainee managed to make it through most of the school day, but her mind was racing. Who was that guy? She had never seen him before. Were guardian angels real? Had she just met hers in a near-death experience? Were they all so charmingly cold?

He was definitely hot enough to be otherworldly. Her mind spiraled down a whirlpool of blue eyes and dark hair. Smoke and leather.

There was no way he was real. She must have jumped out of the street herself and imagined him in a weird adrenaline-fueled hallucination.

She rubbed her eyes and tried to focus on her class, but the lack of sleep was getting to her. World History was far from her favorite subject, but she managed to maintain an A. The teacher was droning on about the political happenings of the late 1930s, something Rainee typically would have enjoyed, but the volume of her own thoughts was louder. She sighed and looked out the window.

She stiffened in her seat as her eyes caught a familiar figure standing across the parking lot. Leaning on a streetlight, arms crossed over his chest, was the guy who'd pulled her out of traffic.

He locked eyes with her but didn't seem fazed that she'd seen him. It was like he was studying her. He didn't move, didn't wave. Just watched. She blinked and rubbed her eyes again, sure that the lack of sleep was messing with her.

He was still there.

Maybe she was going crazy? She tried to focus on the lesson, willing herself to forget the whole thing. She managed to stay focused for about sixty seconds, and when she looked again, he had disappeared. He seemed to be good at that.

CHAPTER 2
FINN

"What the hell was that, *Captain*?" Axel growled as Finn passed the alley that he and Connor had been watching from. Finn knew that Axel didn't use the word *captain* in a reverent sense, but he brushed it off.

    Finn stayed silent. His jaw was tight, and he couldn't shake the feeling of her pulse under his fingers. The way she looked at him. Startled. Captivated. *Innocent.* He wasn't sure if he had saved her out of instinct, or out of fear that something so mundane could take his redemption kill from him. Either way, he wasn't in the mood to answer to a reform case. Claws didn't belong on missions like this. They weren't known for their loyalty. At least, that's what his father had always said, and Axel wasn't doing much to disprove the stereotype.

    Finn kept walking. He wasn't sure where to, but anywhere was better than here with Axel's judgment and Connor's wide eyes.

    Axel's boots thudded on the pavement as he jogged to catch up to him. "You could have blown our cover. She could have realized who—or *what*—you are."

    Finn paused, causing Axel to nearly collide with him. "I know," he said flatly. It was true, but that didn't change what he had already done.

    His jaw ticked. Finn didn't want to bring Axel in the first place. He'd heard stories about his difficult personality, everyone had—but orders were orders. Then again, the orders didn't say anything about bashing his head into the pavement.

    Connor watched from afar, his eyes wide and stunned. Finn noted that the kid looked ready to bail.

"You know?" Axel's voice was low. Flat. Like this conversation had just taken a turn from seething to boring with a flip of a switch. "If you *knew*, you wouldn't have done it."

He crossed his arms and leaned back a little like he had all the time in the world to watch Finn internally unravel. It wasn't hard to throw Finn off right now. He needed blind loyalty, not the devotion to chaos that Axel provided.

"You've always been like this. Torn between loyalty and compassion, like either one matters. Name one time your *morals* saved someone on purpose," Axel spat out.

Finn didn't answer. He couldn't. Axel may not have been his direct report before, but he wasn't making baseless claims, either. He was just pressing the nerve that Finn had tried his best to keep buried.

"You call it honor," Axel continued, watching the way Finn flexed his hand from a fist to an open palm repeatedly. "I call it pretending you're better than the rest of us." Finn peeked over his shoulder at Axel just in time to be dealt the final blow: "You're not."

"You think I *wanted* to save her?" Finn snapped, turning to face Axel. He was slightly taller than the other man, an advantage he was starting to appreciate. "You think I don't know how this works?" He stepped forward, in an effort to intimidate Axel.

Axel didn't budge. He just stared Finn down with a confident defiance that only he possessed. Finn chuckled slightly, his pulse still thumping in his ears.

"That—" Finn continued, gesturing toward the empty street, "—wasn't mercy." His eyes didn't leave Axel's. "I wasn't going to let some *car* do *my* job. That would've been too easy." He searched Axel's eyes. They still looked bored. He was taunting him. "I suggest you remember who's in charge here, Private," he added.

Finn felt his lips curl into a snarl. What he said was true, for the most part. It wasn't *his* fault that their target was an aloof, accident-prone girl, but he'd be damned if anything took the glory away from him.

Axel nodded, his eyes burning like he had more to say. Before he could speak, however, Connor interjected timidly, "Shouldn't we follow her?" He pointed behind him to where Rainee had disappeared around the corner.

Finn blinked as if a trance had been broken. Whatever had rattled him about this ordeal had vanished and his military instinct had returned. He shot one last warning look to Axel and moved to acknowledge Connor.

"Go find a place to set up camp." He looked at Axel. "Both of you. There should be a few clearings that will work for a few days," Finn commanded, tossing the holodisk to Connor. "I'll keep tracking the girl."

Axel smirked. "Going to see your new girlfriend, huh, *Captain*?"

Finn rolled his eyes at the jab. Leave it to someone like Axel to make things childish.

"Maybe try talking to her next time, really get to know her before you kill her."

Finn wasn't listening anymore; he was already moving in the direction of the school. "Come get me when you've found something," he called over his shoulder. "I have a few points to debrief on once we're settled." With that, Finn disappeared around the corner to follow Rainee. No way he was sticking around to hear Axel's next remark.

He was still seething. What gave that lowlife the right to challenge him? He was the one in charge here.

***

It didn't take Finn long to find Rainee again. He watched her throughout the day, stealthily moving to different positions in the shadows and within tree lines, careful to stay just out of her sight. She looked tense, like something was bothering her.

Panic crept in. Had she figured him out? Although he was risking being seen by her, he inched closer, leaning on a nearby streetlight to get a better look.

She was beautiful, that much was obvious. But he would never let something as trivial as looks jeopardize the mission. Besides, beautiful didn't mean safe.

He was lost in thought when she locked eyes with him from the classroom window. His heart jumped out of his chest. *Shit. Shit. Shit.*

She rubbed her eyes, but he stayed where he was, paralyzed. They locked eyes again. He tried to hold his ground. No emotion. No worries. No reaction. Just like he had been taught. She turned back to the lesson inside and Finn took his opportunity to retreat to the tree line. *Why was he so good at blowing this mission?*

"I'm starting to think you're either trying to sabotage this mission—" Axel's voice startled him out of his thoughts, "—or you're just stupid."

Finn could feel Axel's eyes like daggers in his back, and his tone was icy as he added, "Either way, I was lied to about you."

Finn stiffened. He hadn't noticed Axel and Connor standing behind him, and he wasn't sure how much they had seen. *Dammit.* Despite knowing that Axel was partially right, Finn straightened his back and eyed him with a look that dared him to continue.

"I'm conducting surveillance. That's still part of field missions, isn't it?" Finn pushed past the other two boys, walking deeper into the tree line. "And for the record," he added sharply, "I couldn't care less what you were *told* about me."

Axel scoffed from behind him. "Right. *Surveillance.* I forgot that's where you stare at your crush in broad daylight. Very smooth. Very strategic."

Finn didn't stop walking. He wasn't even sure where he was going, but he was acutely aware of Connor following him, so he guessed they would figure it out.

"You know what?" Axel continued, his voice getting dangerously loud. "I don't think you can kill her. Not because you don't have the skills, but because, subconsciously, you've already picked your side." Axel paused, letting that jab land. Finn was trying his best not to break. Not for Axel. "And it's becoming clear that it's not the same side the Fire Realm is on."

Finn stopped so suddenly that Connor nearly crashed into him. Faster than Axel could blink, Finn had turned on his heels and was glaring at him with an anger that would make any normal man cower. Axel, unfortunately for them both, was not a normal man.

"You done yet?" Finn growled.

Axel raised an eyebrow smugly. "All I'm saying is that there's a reason you're here with us and not leading an actual battalion." His eyes flickered menacingly. "The pattern is hard to ignore, *Captain.*"

Finn stepped forward, the tension between them crackling so intensely it was almost audible. Connor, wide-eyed, stepped between them, trying to stop them from causing a scene and blowing their cover. "That's enough! Can we not do this? Please?"

Finn looked away first, knowing that Connor was right. This wasn't the time or place to kill Axel. That was probably later…while he was sleeping.

Finn stormed off, not toward the forest, but toward the school. Anything to get away from Axel. He needed to get out of there before one of them said something they couldn't take back. Or worse.

It wasn't until the bell rang and the din of talking people echoed across the parking lot that he realized his mistake. There, in front of him, watching him from the school steps, was Rainee.

Finn froze. *Unbelievable.*

Of course she had seen that. She may have even heard Axel's loud mouth boom through the parking lot. Finn sucked in a breath as she moved toward him. So much for blending in now.

To make things worse, she looked pissed. "What the hell is your problem?" she threw out as she got closer. He had to admit, her confidence was impressive.

Thinking on his feet, Finn looked around like he was confused. "Are you talking to me?"

She laughed, bewildered. "I don't see anyone else following me."

"I'm not following you," Finn replied quickly. He really wasn't following her this time, but his heart still hammered in his chest.

Rainee raised an eyebrow. "So first you pull me out of the street and then you show up at my school?" She was clearly seething, and Finn had to admit that she looked even more beautiful with her temper hot. "Am I just supposed to believe that it's all a coincidence?"

"I…" he started, desperately trying to find a way to explain without exposing their mission. Her gray eyes looked like storm clouds as her eyebrows furrowed. Finn couldn't think.

"What's your name, anyway?" Rainee interrupted his stammering, her hands on her hips.

He paused, wondering if he should lie. It's not like his alias changed his first name.

"Finn." He sighed with finality.

"I'm Rainee," she said coolly. "And, for the record, if you *are* following me, you're really bad at it." The smile on her lips didn't reach her eyes. "Next time you save someone's life, maybe don't stalk them afterward." Her eyes burned into his. "Kind of ruins the mysterious hero image I pinned for you."

She tossed the last bit at him like an afterthought, then promptly walked away, her dark hair blowing lightly in the wind. He was too stunned to speak. She saw right through him, but didn't see him at all at the same time. She hadn't even touched him, so why did it feel like he had just been punched?

He turned to look at the tree line. Axel was barely visible from here, but his amber eyes were locked on Finn like some sort of wild animal. Not thrilled to walk into another assault, Finn waved them on and followed Rainee, this time staying out of sight. He would catch up to them once Axel had time to cool off.

CHAPTER 3
AXEL

Axel stood in the trees, just out of sight of the absolute chaos that was unfolding in the parking lot. He personally hadn't worked with Finn much, but knew him as somewhat of a legend in the barracks. A legend that seemed more like a joke now.

Youngest captain ever. Axel scowled. *More like biggest dumbass ever.* It was no wonder he got demoted. He probably only got that title because his family paid someone off. Typical Sword behavior.

Connor stood behind him. The kid was annoying, but that was just because he didn't know what was going on. Axel knew they didn't talk about how anything *actually* worked in training. Axel doubted Connor would even know what to do if they had to fight. He didn't seem cut out for battle. Hopefully, it never came to that.

He watched as Finn fumbled through a half-assed apology-turned-introduction, then waved them on to follow Rainee again. Axel rolled his eyes. Finn should just reveal their entire mission at the rate he was going.

You don't save targets. It was an unspoken rule, but a rule, nonetheless. One Finn should know. Finn should have let her get hit by that car, and they could have all gone home—Axel with another reform star earned, Finn rebuilding his reputation, and Connor with some innocence still intact. The longer they stayed here, the less likely it seemed that any of them would get happy endings. Not that Axel believed in happy endings, anyway.

Axel watched Finn for a while, his arms crossed. He'd be damned if Finn's moral compass caused this mission to fail. Axel couldn't afford that. Not with the position he was already in.

He turned to Connor, who was watching him silently, waiting for his next order. Axel was going to have to break him of that quiet obedience. No one deserved that sort of reverence, especially not a Fire Realm soldier; at least, not any of the ones he had met.

"What's the next move, kid?" he said, tilting his chin toward Connor.

The boy looked startled by the question, like no one had ever expected him to think on his feet before. "Uh..." He searched Axel's eyes, which revealed nothing. "We could go back to camp and finish setting up." He shrugged, as if he wasn't sure that was the right answer.

Axel smiled slightly. There truly was only one option and that was it, but he liked making the rookie squirm; it was relaxing. "Say it with confidence next time, kid." He patted Connor's shoulder and moved past him toward the clearing. "You're smart; you should sound like it."

Connor opened his mouth like he was about to say something, but shut it quickly. He followed Axel to where they had left their bags.

Axel had already scanned the clearing and the surrounding area. A creek ran across the eastern edge, providing at least some source for food and water if needed. Plus, proximity-wise, it had already proven to be the logical option since the school was just on the other side of the northern tree line, but it was rocky and would be hell to sleep on—another reason to just let the girl take herself out.

"I'm going to start setting up tents." Axel bent down to retrieve a tent roll from his bag. "I need you to build a fire." He looked at Connor, whose eyes were bright with recognition. He could start a fire in his sleep; most Flamease soldiers could. "It needs to be contained and low-profile. We don't need any forest fires on our watch," Axel half-joked. Earth's flora was a lot more flammable than the Fire Realm's, and he didn't want to burn it down. At least, not yet.

Axel watched Connor run off into the trees to collect materials as he undid the first tent roll and tried to find a less rocky spot to set it up. He spent twenty minutes digging rocks out of the ground and tossing them aside before he finally started building the tent. He hated Earth so far. The terrain was hard to work with, and he had yet to find any large game that would challenge his hunting skills. There were no high stakes here. *How boring.* Back home, they had competitions for provision hunting, and Axel was a pro. He didn't even need a long-range weapon, just his knife, and to be smarter than the beast for half a second.

Connor came back, his arms loaded with timber. He could carry a lot more than Axel had expected. Maybe he wasn't useless after all.

They worked in silence, with Axel's senses on high alert for any signs of danger. After a while, he noticed movement in the trees, and could see Finn just standing there, watching them. He pretended not to notice. He had plenty to say to their *captain* once he was brave enough to join them, but Axel wasn't going to go out of his way.

CHAPTER 4
FINN

Finn watched from the forest's edge as Axel and Connor unpacked camp. He had half a mind to set up elsewhere and leave them to their devices. Maybe they'd be eaten by wolves. He paused. *Do wolves live in this part of the human realm?*

He had no doubt they had seen that final interaction with Rainee, and he knew Axel thought he was getting too close to the target. So, he had opted to gather more information before returning to the lion's den.

It hadn't been hard to find them. He followed the obvious signs of disturbance in the trees to a clearing near the school. He wasn't the best tracker of the group, but he knew enough to get by, and Axel and Connor were not exactly being *careful*.

Finally, he stepped into the clearing, keeping his expression unreadable. Axel looked up from his place by the tent he was pitching and smirked. "Fun date, *Captain?*"

Finn's jaw twitched. If Axel didn't stop with that stupid *Captain* bit, he was going to find a wolf to feed him to.

He didn't respond, just took his backpack off and took a seat next to Connor, who was flipping through an archaic field guide about the mortal realm.

"Anything interesting?" Finn asked, gesturing to the leather-bound book.

Connor looked up, looking stunned that Finn would address him so casually.

"Uhh...well..." he stuttered and flipped frantically back to a page he had already read. "There is this...thing about lingual drift that I found interesting." He handed the book to Finn as he continued, "I've never been outside the Fire Realm, so I wasn't aware that being in a different realm can affect your speech patterns."

Finn hadn't heard of that either, but the book—a tradesman's log that was at least a century old—had it all lined out:

> A phenomenon has overtaken Fire Realm soldiers while in the human realm. While the Common Form Decree requires all Divisional inhabitants to use one of the human dialects, we had successfully refrained from letting human profanities slip into our lingo. However, here on Earth, the soldiers cannot go long without a swear word leaving their mouths. The realm has started to consume them, I fear.

"How the *hell* does IceHeart expect us to sleep like this? There's not a single clearing that's dry, smooth, and secluded," Axel shouted as he grabbed a rock from the ground under his tent and tossed it into the trees.

"See?" Connor nodded toward Axel. "Have you ever known a soldier—even someone like Axel—to speak like that?"

Finn thought about it. He couldn't recall a time he'd heard a soldier, or any Flamease citizen for that matter, swear in the human language unless they were mocking it. He started to count the times *he* had sworn—either internally or aloud—since they had arrived and realized that he had been picking up human swear words himself. It was affecting all of them.

Axel gave up on his endeavor to flatten the tent floor, and plopped down on the other side of the roaring campfire. His eyes flickered in the firelight, and despite his disgruntled demeanor, he looked almost relaxed.

"What are you looking at?" Axel asked roughly.

Finn blinked, unaware that he had been staring at Axel. He shook his head and cleared his throat, sitting up a little straighter from his place across the fire from Axel. "I have a few points I'd like to debrief, if you two have a minute."

Axel raised one eyebrow quizzically, but nodded for Finn to continue. Finn retrieved the holodisk from where Connor had placed it near the tent and held it up in front of him. As he clicked the green button on the right edge of the silver puck, a holographic image of a map sprang to life.

It was a map that IceHeart had included in their mission files. A red dot blinked, marking their current location.

Finn placed the holodisk on the ground and grabbed a nearby stick to use as a pointer. Gesturing to a rectangular building, he said, "This is the school. My guess would be that Rainee spends quite a bit of time there during the day. This is fine for surveillance—"

"If she doesn't catch you ogling her, that is," Axel interrupted.

Finn gritted his teeth and continued, "—but it wouldn't be a good place to complete the mission. There are too many witnesses present, and we have no way of knowing who is human and who is pretending to be human."

The irony wasn't lost on him. *They* were the ones pretending to be human, after all. What were the chances that there were other inter-realm travelers—or even divine beings—in their midst? Highly unlikely, but not impossible, so they needed to be prepared.

"However, her house is—" He circled a small subdivision diagonal to the school with the stick. "—here. Her home is a more secluded place to strike."

"Finn?" Connor's questioned, his voice shaking a little. Finn looked at him, causing the younger boy to shy away as if the attention was uncomfortable. Connor took a breath, then persisted, "H-how do we know she's the right target? She looked like a normal girl to me."

"Yeah." Axel agreed, leaning back on his forearms casually. "What kind of descendant of the gods lets themselves get hit by a car? The bloodline might be diluted, but not enough for something like that, right?"

Finn smirked like he'd been waiting for this exact question. "I reviewed the plans before we got here; she is definitely the right target." He pushed down the acknowledgment that their points had merit as he hit a button on the holodisk with his foot, trying to pull up Rainee's report file.

"Look…" he started, but the holodisk wouldn't budge. He leaned down and forced the button down with his finger. The device beeped in warning, and four words flashed across the screen in bright red lettering: STAND BY, TARGET UNDER REVIEW.

"What the hell?" Axel blurted, sitting up.

"I-I don't know, the mission file is supposed to be here. I've never seen this happen before," Finn replied, retrieving the holodisk from the ground and turning it over in his hands. "It must be a glitch, let me try rebooting it. If it does it again, I'll contact IceHeart directly." He tried a few more buttons then added, "This could delay our mission."

"Rebooting it could take a few hours. Do we have that kind of time?" Connor said. "I can try to run some diagnostics on it. I've rebuilt a few holodisks for fun."

Finn was surprised. He had heard Connor was good with tech but wouldn't have guessed holodisk repair was in his repertoire.

Finn nodded and tossed the disk to Connor, who immediately went to work. "Good call. Let's get dinner started while you work on that. We need to stay sharp if we're going to hit our three-day deadline under these circumstances."

Axel sighed and locked eyes with Finn. Finn could tell by the shit-eating grin on his face that he was about to say something stupid.

"Guess your girlfriend gets to live another day, Cap," Axel muttered, kicking a twig into the fire.

Finn didn't take the bait. Not this time. But the firelight just barely caught his jaw twitch. Finding a wolf was sounding more tempting by the minute.

CHAPTER 5
SYREN

The throne room felt...off. It was colder than usual—the lamps that regulated the temperature in the palace seemed to be malfunctioning more and more—but there was something else. An emptiness that IceHeart was having trouble placing. Was the room missing something...or was he?

His head throbbed faintly, and he shifted uncomfortably on the throne, his fingers gripping the armrests in a way that made his wrists ache. He'd never found lavawood to be the most comfortable. Not to mention it was gaudy and horrendously out of place with the rest of the decor. Why had he chosen it? His memory blurred briefly, but he brushed the fogginess aside and refocused on the silence of the throne room.

Someone had spoken earlier— familiar and urgent—but the memory of the voice was already fading. Before he could concentrate on the thought, a knock sounded from the heavy wooden doors to his left.

"Enter," he commanded, rubbing his temple. His voice sounded hoarse, as if he'd been screaming, but he couldn't remember the last time he'd yelled.

The door opened and StoneElf appeared, carrying a holodisk and a stack of files. IceHeart was sure he'd been carrying the same effects since the days when he was advisor to his father.

"Sire." StoneElf bowed. IceHeart waved him on, itching for this to be over so he could have a few moments to piece his thoughts together. "I have a few updates on Operation Spark, if you are keen to hear them?"

IceHeart nodded and took a file to leaf through as StoneElf set up the holodisk on the ground. As he scanned the information, it seemed he was reading it for the first time. Yet somehow his approval stamp appeared at the top of the page. He found himself struggling to remember the specifics of this mission. It wasn't the first time today, either. He had been trying to decipher Aydron's ransom demands before this, only to realize he didn't remember sending men to the Water Realm at all.

The holodisk flickered on, revealing a human girl with a red warning label, DANGEROUS, DEMIGOD, watermarked across her file. Rainee Bennett. He remembered that she was Scott's, but he didn't know why that made him so angry.

IceHeart lifted a hand gently, urging StoneElf to pause. "Just as a reminder, StoneElf...What is the primary objective of this mission again?"

I feel like I'm losing my mind. He heard himself think, but the words got lost as he stared at the girl's picture. *Bennett.*

StoneElf hesitated and a crease formed between his brows, "Are you feeling alright, sire? You look...tired."

IceHeart forced a smile, masking his inner uncertainty. "Perfectly fine. Just too many long nights recently." He waved his hand at the paper on his arm rest. "What, with Aydron breathing down my neck and all."

StoneElf nodded slowly. Nonetheless, he quickly briefed him on the mission's main points and Rainee's role in it.

"The men have successfully found the girl; they're just waiting on an opportune time to complete the mission." StoneElf concluded, flashing a few surveillance photos onto the screen.

IceHeart rubbed his chin. Something was not sitting right with him about this mission. Not just that he didn't remember it, but also that he didn't understand it, even after StoneElf provided his explanation. This seemed more likely to start a war than end it. He sighed and chose his words carefully, not wanting to give StoneElf another reason to worry about his mental status. "Can you have the logistics team and the historian review the identity of the demigod again? As well as any alternative scenarios."

Why does this feel so wrong? he wondered to himself, as the pain in his head grew in intensity.

"Sir, the plans were reviewed several times before being presented to you. I'm not sure how logistics will handle questioning this late into the mission cycle." StoneElf explained hastily. It was apparent he was sweating, and not due to the heat. Although he was undeniably a good advisor, he was incredibly nervous and non-confrontational by nature. He was often the one trying to prevent confrontation of any kind.

"I understand the reluctance, and forgive me, but I need to be sure that this is the best-case scenario. We don't want any surprises down the pipeline." Syren rationalized almost *too* believably.

StoneElf nodded in agreement, his worries pacified for the moment. "Very well, I will put a review on the descendant's file and have the logistics team confirm her identity and any possible alternatives before moves are made." He typed on the holodisk. "This will most likely delay the mission. Should we extend portal tethers?" StoneElf muttered to himself, typing a sequence into the holodisk.

As he finished typing, a watermark notifying the viewer that Rainee's identity was under review appeared. StoneElf closed the holodisk and stuffed it into his pocket, preparing to leave to attend to the rest of his orders.

"No extension needed," IceHeart said with a shake of his head. "I expect an answer in the next few hours." StoneElf opened his mouth to object, but IceHeart continued, "You are excused to attend to those matters." The king nodded, shooing the man away. StoneElf clapped his mouth closed, bowed, and started to shuffle toward the door with his anxious energy reignited.

"Oh, and Matthias?" the king called before StoneElf could open the doors.

"Sire?"

"Don't alert the men about this development. I need them to stay focused." IceHeart eyes darkened, his brain suddenly feeling foggy. "It seems like they may already be getting distracted," IceHeart continued, remembering one of the photos of Finn with his arm tucked around Rainee's bicep, yanking her out of oncoming traffic.

His jaw tightened as annoyance washed over him at the thought of them failing. The feeling faded just as quickly as it had come on, and he shook it off as he watched StoneElf leave.

His head throbbed sharply, a familiar warning sign that often served as a precursor to the gaps in memory that seemed more frequent as of late. The migraines would sometimes steal days from him, leaving him waking up with no recollection of decisions made or time spent. And they were rarely decisions that he would fully agree with.

Beneath the throbbing, his thoughts began to muddle, and a fog crept in as he struggled to summon the memory of approving Operation Spark. Just beneath that, a voice, sharp and angry, rose like smoke: <Stop asking questions.>

CHAPTER 6
AXEL

Axel watched from his spot beside the fire as Connor fidgeted with the holodisk. He'd been at it for over an hour, occasionally mumbling something about ping ratios and pixel degradation. Axel didn't know the first thing about technology, so he let the kid have his moment. Finn had moved a few yards away to set up his tent, leaving Axel alone with his thoughts.

He scowled. Finn had hardly spoken on this mission, other than when he was making a fool out of himself or preaching about morality. He acted like he had nothing to prove, when that was his only reason for existence since his demotion.

Pretentious asshole.

Connor let out a frustrated sigh and dropped the holodisk beside him. "I've tried everything. Manually resetting the drive, reinstalling the mission file software, even replacing the light source thinking it was screen burn. Nothing worked. Rainee's file won't even open now."

Axel didn't look up. He didn't have to. He already knew where Connor's mind was, because his was there too.

"I thought it was a glitch?" he said quietly.

"It's the most persistent glitch I've ever seen, if so." Connor shook his head.

Axel's eyes flicked toward Finn, who hadn't looked up. He was either too focused or was pretending not to hear them.

"You saw that warning label just like I did, Axel," Connor continued hesitantly. "What if something's wrong? What if there's something we aren't being told?"

Axel was silent for a minute. He watched the campfire embers flicker into the darkening air, his thoughts seeming to move with them, returning him to long-buried memories.

"You're catching on, kid," he said, jostling himself back to the present.

"What?" Connor asked, one eyebrow raised.

Axel sighed. He should have kept his mouth shut. Let the kid have his idealistic fantasies about the Fire Realm. Everyone had them at one point.

"Axel?" Connor prodded further, his tone gentle but unrelenting.

Axel rolled his eyes and nodded toward the holodisk. "The missions, the files, the life they tell you to live. It's never as black and white as they'd make you believe."

Connor hesitated, then stammered, "Well, yeah…I guess. Every system has its flaws, but there's always a plan. A strategy. IceHeart wouldn't just send us here for no reason, right?"

Axel didn't answer. He just stared at Connor. But he wasn't really seeing him, not anymore.

"Right?" Connor insisted, his voice higher this time, like he was begging Axel to pull him back from an edge he didn't realize he was standing on.

Axel exhaled slowly. "You really think this all has a reason? That we're not just pawns in a game we'll never get to see the end of?"

"If it doesn't…" Connor started, then faltered. "If it doesn't have a reason, then why are we here?"

Axel shook his head. *Poor kid.* He was piecing together the truth every soldier learned eventually—there was never a reason. Not one that made sense from the inside. Orders came. You followed them. You fought. You bled, maybe even died. And someone else called it "strategy."

"Not everything's supposed to make sense, kid," Axel said, with a smirk that didn't reach his eyes. "Hell, I can't remember the last time *anything* the military told me to do actually made sense."

Connor slumped back against the log behind him with a furrowed brow. Axel wasn't proud that he had to be the one to drag the kid toward the truth; but damn, if he had let it go the first time, he could have kept his rose-colored glasses on a bit longer.

Axel thought Connor was going to leave the conversation there. Then, without warning, Connor's expression turned into a glare.

"You're just cynical," he snapped. "None of that is true, and you know it."

Axel chuckled, though it sounded more like a scoff. "If anyone knows how this arrangement works, it's me." His gaze dropped to the ground, haunted by memories he wished would leave him be. He forced himself to breathe. "I *was* the mission once," he said quietly. "I *was* the file under review." Then his eyes met Connor's in a gaze that was intense, cold, and…*scared*. "They'll spoon-feed you their truth until they physically can't anymore. But by then, it's too late. You're already in too deep."

Connor didn't respond. His attention was on the fire, like the warmth would somehow transfer to the emptiness creeping up inside him as his ideals shattered. Axel knew the feeling, but it didn't make it easier to watch the kid suffer through it.

"What happened?" Connor murmured, barely loud enough for Axel to hear.

Axel paused, flooded by a million memories. The flames from the fire danced in his eyes, casting them in a brighter gold than usual, like the flames were a part of him.

"Before or after they broke everything I had and threw a half-assed second chance my way?" Axel replied.

Connor's brow furrowed. "You mean you weren't always military?"

Axel had forgotten how young Connor was. He had already been a soldier for three years by the time Connor started training. Connor had only known Axel as a soldier. It surprised him that the rumors weren't still spreading through the barracks, but it was also comforting, in a way.

"Not even close," Axel responded. He scanned the clearing, as if what he was about to say was top secret, then continued anyway. "I was born into the Brass and Flame Syndicate out of the capital. It was all I ever knew, really. Would probably still be there, if the military hadn't captured me and used me as their rehab story."

Connor's brows stayed knitted together as he studied Axel like he was waiting for him to say he was joking. "You were a Flameborn?"

Axel nodded slowly, his mind elsewhere. "Probably the worst of the group, depending on who you ask." His jaw clenched. *If there is anyone alive to ask.*

"I was good at what the syndicate was known for. I was fast. I was cunning. Nothing more than a shadow. An omen of death." He paused there. Usually, there was some disbelief that followed that part of the story, but Connor was just watching him intently. Not like he was listening to a story, but like he was trying to picture Axel inside it.

Axel cleared his throat and sat up straighter. "The raid happened suddenly. None of us had time to prepare. The military had been scouting us for weeks. We had always thought we were smarter than them. Turns out we were wrong."

He looked away from the fire, but it wasn't smoke burning the back of his throat as he continued. "They wiped out my entire sector. My family, friends. Anyone I had ever known in the syndicate. Maybe the whole syndicate, but I'm not sure."

The flames danced higher, illuminating Connor's enthralled expression. Axel was glad his life was entertaining to someone.

"I was seventeen. They gave me a choice: Die with my people or join the military." Axel flinched, remembering the smell of blood and ash around him, as if reliving the day all over again. "But what seventeen-year-old would choose to be executed?"

The words hung in the air like fog. Axel met Connor's gaze, expecting fear, disappointment, or maybe both. But his face revealed neither. Connor looked...reverent, like he had gained respect for Axel, in a way his day-to-day demeanor would have never allowed.

"You didn't choose the military, it chose you," Connor said finally. "And yet, you're still here. Which means you must believe in something."

A small smile crept up on Axel's face. *This kid just doesn't quit.* But part of him was happy that Connor was prodding him; it gave him something to focus on aside from Finn's incompetence.

"I believe in survival, Connor. Nothing more. Nothing less."

Connor nodded slowly, unconvinced.

"That's still something," he offered, looking at Axel sincerely.

Axel didn't respond. It was of no use. Blind optimism ran deep in this one, and he wasn't cruel enough to strip the kid of it just yet. He leaned back on the log behind him, admiring the stars. He'd never seen stars before, only read about them in a human story book he'd had as a boy. He couldn't even remember how he got that book; he just remembered that it was his favorite. The stars were beautiful, but something about them made him feel uncomfortable, like being in the calm eye of a storm.

"You should get some sleep, kid. We've got a long day tomorrow," he threw out, not looking at Connor. Finn had already moved inside his tent, oblivious to Axel dropping his lore-like backstory to their rookie.

Connor stared at him for a moment longer, then stood up and dusted off his jeans.

"For the record, I don't think survival is the only thing you believe in. Not really." He moved toward his tent. "But don't worry, I won't tell anyone else," Connor said over his shoulder as he ducked inside.

Axel stared at the fire for a while longer. Occasionally, the review warning would flash in his mind, making his chest ache. To be a target and not even know was a feeling he knew all too well.

CHAPTER 7
RAINEE

Rainee trudged downstairs. It was Thursday, so her first class was later than usual, a luxury she was happy to take advantage of. Her dad had already left for work, but had left her a piece of peanut butter toast and two strips of bacon wrapped in foil on the counter. She sighed, amused; she couldn't even skip breakfast when he wasn't around. But she also smiled. These dreams had been draining her, and she needed the fuel more than she wanted to admit.

  She set her backpack down on an empty barstool and took a seat. It was rare that she was alone in the house, with Thursday mornings being the only real exception since her dad always left for work at the same time. She unwrapped her breakfast and took a small bite of bacon. It tasted normal. She chewed slowly, letting her thoughts wander to the guy she had met yesterday. *Finn.*

  She hadn't planned to confront him; in fact, her entire body screamed at her to run far away. But something made her feel drawn to him. She supposed her fight-or-flight response was fight.

  She couldn't get over the look Finn had given her—startled, guilty even—yet at the same time, something in his eyes seemed confident and completely at ease.

  Psychopath. She sighed. She shouldn't psychoanalyze strangers on an empty stomach. She reached for her toast, brushing the foil wrap just enough that something behind it caught her eye. Moving the foil aside, she saw a small velvet box, the edges worn by time, but still mythically beautiful. That hadn't been there yesterday, and she couldn't recall having seen it before.

Maybe her dad had found it while he was cleaning—a long-forgotten piece of jewelry of her mom's—and left it out for her. Her dad wasn't one for flashy gifts or theatrics, so it made sense that he would simply place it on the counter for her to find. She looked around, like maybe he would somehow appear and explain himself, but the house remained quiet.

A sadness washed over her. Her mother had died shortly after she was born, so she never got to know her, but the ache was still there in every experience she didn't get to have with her. First day of school, proms, senior recitals, and driving lessons. They all felt normal…but with a piece missing.

She opened the box to find the most beautiful necklace she'd ever seen. A pure white ornate stone wrapped in winding silver filigree; it was like nothing she'd ever seen before. It wasn't glittery, more like…lightning captured on a still surface.

She touched it softly, her finger barely grazing it. Immediately, a soft current ran through her, and she pulled back instinctively.

Weird, she thought, but she chalked it up to the box sitting near the warm food before she picked it up. Probably some sort of static electricity.

She took the necklace out of the box to examine it further. It was stunning, and looked like it was brand new, not something that had belonged to someone else. It must have been stored well. She unclasped the chain and slipped it around her neck, re-clasping it behind her. She had never really liked jewelry, but she could make an exception for this one. She felt something inside of her jolt as soon as the pendant touched her skin, making her a little uneasy, but she brushed it off. She was probably overthinking it.

Grabbing her backpack and the remainder of the toast, she hurried off to school.

***

She entered the school just before the bell, a skill she had mastered at this point. The hallway was buzzing with people hurrying to their classes while wolfing down their late breakfasts, but something, rather *someone*, caught her eye.

Finn was standing by the administration office with two boys that she didn't recognize. They were watching the front doors, as if they'd been waiting for her.

Despite her obvious discomfort, she couldn't help but notice how attractive they all were, each in their own way. The blonde guy to Finn's right was staring at her, but not in a creepy way. Just watching. His golden eyes caught the light perfectly, and he looked like something straight out of Greek mythology. And the redhead, he was cute in a "little brother" way. He had kind green eyes and looked like he was just happy to be alive.

She sighed. *This is the opposite of not following me.*

Finn raised an eyebrow like he might have been able to hear her thoughts, which prompted her to swiftly disappear around the corner to avoid their watchful gazes.

Who were they? And why were they so interested in her?

CHAPTER 8
FINN

Finn leaned against a brick wall outside of the admin office. Their aliases were thorough as usual, and included faked system records, transcripts, and transfer details for each of them. Otherwise, there was little difference between their aliases and their real personas. They each had new last names, because *FangSword*, *FalconTail*, *and AxeClaw* were not exactly common human surnames.

So, Finn Mason, Connor Shay, and Axel Taylor were who they'd be for the next 48 hours or less. For some reason, the name change felt right.

When Rainee walked in, he had just happened to be looking at the doors, wondering when—or if—she'd show up. When she ducked into the fluorescently lit hallway, everything else around him stopped. It must have felt the same for Axel and Connor, because they paused their conversation and looked toward Rainee. It was like gravity had shifted in her direction the minute she entered the building.

She saw him right away. And she looked less than pleased to have caught him *anywhere* near her for the fourth time in two days.

"She looks pissed," Axel muttered between clenched teeth.

"Because she is," Finn replied. "She thinks I'm following her, and now you two show up with me? She's accident-prone, not stupid."

They all watched as she rounded the corner, purposely avoiding them. Finn couldn't help but notice that Axel's gaze lingered a bit too long, but he let it go. Honestly, he couldn't blame him for staring. She *was* beautiful.

That didn't matter, though. They had work to do, and Axel's antics weren't about to get in the way of Finn's focus.

CHAPTER 9
RAINEE

Rainee hurried to her first class, hoping desperately that she could get away from the prying eyes of those boys. She had never been more excited to get to Calculus in her life. She chose her usual seat by the window and started removing her notes and textbook from her backpack. It wasn't long before she felt someone slide into the desk beside her.

She didn't even have to look. She could feel his presence like a branding iron on the back of her neck. But when she finally did turn, it wasn't Finn sitting there, it was the blonde one.

He looked over at her and smiled, and it seemed genuine. "Hi, I'm Axel," he offered.

She looked away and didn't answer, didn't engage. Whatever they were trying to do wasn't going to work. She paused. *Is this how human trafficking starts?*

"You know," he started casually. "It's a little rude to snub the new guy. I just got here after all."

Her temper hit its edge. She turned in her seat to face him, her eyes smoldering. "Look. I don't know what game you three are playing, but it's not working."

Axel blinked. He looked…startled. Then, he chuckled, an amused grin tugging at his lips. "Game?" he asked. "Trust me, if there's a game going on, I was not aware. Was I supposed to bring gym shorts or something?"

She glared at him, unconvinced by his attempt to be coy.

He held up his hands in defense. "I get it. New kid, weird circumstance. Not exactly the best first impression. But I'm just here to get through the day like everyone else."

He smiled, genuinely smiled, and something inside her twisted. Not in anger, but more like she felt herself being charmed by him.

"You and your friends staring at me like I'm prey isn't exactly reassuring…or subtle," she half-joked.

He smirked. "'Friends' is a strong word."

It was her turn to blink. His mouth twitched like he hadn't meant to say that out loud, but something told her it was the truth.

Before she could respond, the teacher called for attention at the front of the classroom. Axel gave her a wink and turned forward to focus on the lesson. They didn't talk or even look at each other for the rest of class, but she had to admit she felt drawn to him. As hard as she tried to focus on the lesson, on anything *but* the guy sitting next to her, her mind kept drifting. Back to the smirk. Back to the glint in his golden eyes. Back to the warmth that hadn't left the air between them.

She wanted to believe that he was being honest, even if it was just so she had an excuse to get closer to him, but she couldn't shake the uneasiness in the back of her mind.

CHAPTER 10
SAPPHIRE

"I should have suspected a move like this from Syren," King Aydron SwiftStream said, his back to the rest of the people in the war room. He was staring at communication logs from across the division. One of them was a clearly hacked tether from the Fire Realm to the human realm. Despite the stiff political tension in the room, Sapphire had grown bored with this conversation hours ago. No one had offered up a single plan. She sighed. Some strategy guys *they* were.

She raised her blade in the air and cleared her throat. "Father, if I may," she said, anticipating his dismissal. Aydron turned and looked at her quizzically. "Earth is an easy portal jump away. I have no problem—" She searched for the word, waving her knife around. "—intercepting those Fire Realm pawns and protecting the descendant," she concluded, twirling her blade between her fingers.

She knew he was going to argue with her, but she had already planned for that.

"Sapphire, you aren't strong enough..." he started.

"Okay, then Tobias can go, too," she interrupted. "Between the two of us, I'm sure we can handle some bottom-of-the-barrel assassins." Her eyes rolled, changing to a dark crimson color to match her mood. Cold. Angry. Tired of being underestimated.

Tobias was her older brother, and the strongest mage in the Water Realm. He was also golden heir to the SwiftStream dynasty, something she would never be.

Across the table, her brother gawked at her and she smiled tightly, though her eyes stayed locked in a cold glare. *Gods, he was insufferable. The spoiled brat.*

"No," her father said. His tone was final. "We can't risk the prince on a mission this small. We'd lose the war *and* our heir in one swoop."

Sapphire smiled. This is exactly what she had expected, and wanted, her father to say. With a fake pout she replied, "Oh well, I guess you'll just have to send me. The best assassin the Water Realm has. How will I ever manage?" The sarcasm dripped from her lips like venom.

Aydron sighed, wiping his hand down the length of his face and closing his eyes. Sapphire smiled. If she couldn't be his favorite, she could annoy him, at least.

"Fine," he agreed through gritted teeth. "But you will take two guards with you." His glare searched her face, daring her to object. "You are still a princess, and a very powerful political tool if you should wind up in the wrong hands."

"Of course," she said innocently, batting her eyelashes.

They both knew she didn't need guards. It was just a formality. Sapphire wasn't one for needing protection. *She preferred to do the protecting. And the fighting.* And the other violent things that no one else would do.

With a flick of his wrist, Aydron dismissed the war council, sending the advisors and logisticians scrambling to gather their things.

"And Sapphire," the king added before she could leave the room.

"Father?" She asked, already fearing the response.

The king turned back to the realm map on the wall and threw out, "If you speak out of turn again, I can promise you will not like the consequences that await you."

Sapphire nodded, the boldness that she had possessed a moment ago snuffed out by fear of what her father might do now that there were no witnesses.

"Yes, father."

"Good. You are dismissed." Aydron ordered without turning to face her.

Sapphire gripped her knife as she stepped out of the room and into the cool stone corridor, her heart pounding. She turned towards her chambers, willing her breathing to settle by reciting the things she needed to bring with her in her head. Distracted, she didn't notice her brother leaning against the far wall of the corridor until he cleared his throat, making her jump.

"What was that?" Tobias snarled. His hair, which usually was slicked back, looked like he had run his hands through it and tried to fix it, to no avail.

Forcing a bored look, she replied, "I was only trying to give you the chance to use your powers to help the kingdom instead of whatever you use them for now." She didn't wait for his response, just continued down the hallway in the direction of her room. She didn't care what he thought. Someone needed to treat the prince like a human instead of a deity for once.

She heard his footsteps behind her, and she sighed. She wasn't in the mood to fight with Tobias, but if he insisted, she had no problem dismantling him.

"Are you trying to get us both in trouble, Sapphire?" He questioned. His tone was even, but Sapphire could hear the panic beneath his facade.

She eyed her brother, who was now keeping pace with her. "When was the last time *you* were in trouble for anything?" Tobias didn't answer, just stared at her, his jaw working. Sapphire offered a bitter smirk and added, "Exactly."

His voice lowered as he said, "He's not stable since the attack on the mage's quarters," Tobias looked around, checking for eavesdroppers. "Since mother…"

Sapphire stopped suddenly, "Don't…" Sapphire murmured, not looking at him. Their mother had been in the mage's quarter when the Fire Realm attacked. She had been one of several casualties despite having a more than capable guard detail.

"I'm only warning you, sister. If you think either of us is safe when he's like this, you underestimate our father. Please be more careful with your words."

He gave her one more worried look before the mask was back in place and his usual smugness covered any hint of humanity. He nodded once and turned back towards the war room. She stood there for a while longer, his words echoing in her head. She hadn't taken into account that current events might serve to make her situation more dangerous, but Tobias was right. Their father was unpredictable at best, and outright ruthless at worst.

Pushing his warning aside for now so she could focus, she hurried to her quarters.

***

A few hours later, she had her rations and equipment packed. She'd packed lightly, not wanting to overstay her welcome in the human realm and hoping she could kill those firebugs and be back in time for dinner tomorrow.

Her father hadn't come to say goodbye, which wasn't surprising given that he hardly recognized her as his daughter. Anyone born after Tobias was irrelevant, especially if they were female. If she died, it was one less mouth to feed, and one less person to yap at him about how to run things.

She stepped toward the portal with two guards flanking her on either side. She knew both of them well, and she knew that her own skills outmatched theirs by miles. The king could have at least sent the good guards.

She stepped through the portal and found herself tumbling into a forest clearing. It looked empty, except for a couple of tents and a fire that had been recently extinguished. *What luck.*

She searched the camp, finding little evidence that the assassins had been here recently, other than a corrupted holodisk tucked under the edge of the furthest tent, and a Fire Realm field guide simply entitled *Humans,* that was half-buried in the dirt beside the fire. *How cute.*

After a few minutes, she managed to open the holodisk files and stumbled across the exact information she needed: the soldiers' aliases. The files were glitchy and unstable, but she took a mental note of each name and picture before closing the disk and putting it back under the tent. She couldn't let them find anything amiss.

She tucked her supply bag behind a nearby tree, just out of sight of anyone leaving or entering the camp. She adjusted her shirt and smoothed her hair with her fingers, slinging her prop backpack over one shoulder.

"You two can go. Meet me here in a few hours," she dictated to her guards. "Be prepared for the return trip. We'll be leaving as soon as I return with the boys disposed of." They nodded and disappeared into the underbrush.

Sapphire pulled out her own holodisk, ensuring that the alias she had prepared passed the checkpoints necessary for identity creation. She smirked, seeing the screen light up green and her new name flash across the screen: SAPPHIRE DRAKE. *Perfect.*

She slipped the disk back into her pocket and headed toward the school. She knew this route like the back of her hand; she'd been keeping surveillance on the area for years, just in case she ever had to make the trip herself, on behalf of the Western Division.

As Sapphire entered the school, people had already started to disperse to their classes. She didn't mind; less people meant less witnesses. That is when she saw them. None of them looked directly at her, but there was no mistaking them. They stood out like sore thumbs to a trained eye like hers.

Fire Realm scum. They probably smelled like smoke and ambushes.

She watched them whisper amongst themselves, check the class schedules in their hands, and hurry off in three different directions. At least they weren't stupid enough to crowd their target.

She entered the administration office and sorted the last bit of paperwork she needed, grabbing her own class schedule. Her alias passed without a second glance from the receptionist. Sapphire Drake was a transfer student from one of the other elite schools in the area, just a girl looking for a better shot at a volleyball career and escaping toxic school politics. She smirked—the story resonating with her. There was no escaping the *actual* political hierarchy she was in, just by being Princess SwiftStream, but maybe her alias would have better luck.

She had strategically aligned all her classes with Rainee's. She planned to befriend her, like any human girl would. Sapphire could be *very* convincing.

She rounded the corner into the first class, Calculus, and abruptly froze in the doorway. Sitting in the seat beside Rainee was the blonde firebug, Axel.

She gritted her teeth and took a seat further away. She'd have to get close to Rainee at some other point in the day. For now, she simply observed.

Axel was attractive and charming, and she hated that. No criminal should have that kind of pull. But it was obvious by the look on Rainee's face that his magnetism was mutually sustained, even though Rainee was throwing snarky comments at him like hand grenades. *She might actually become a good friend.*

***

Sapphire followed Rainee all morning, always just slightly too late to reach her before the boys did. There was always one of them sitting in the seat right next to her.

From observation alone, she'd decided a few things: Firstly, Connor was the least threatening. In fact, he just looked scared and innocent. He would probably apologize if you so much as pouted at him.

Secondly, Finn was more difficult. He was quiet and stayed in his head. However, she had no doubt that she could disarm him in a heartbeat. She could start right now, without him knowing that she was chipping away at his armor.

Lastly, there was Axel. Axel was the type that you couldn't read from a distance. He was cool, collected, and devilishly charming. He hid his emotions and his intentions better than anyone she had ever known. Anyone except for herself, of course.

She saw something in Axel. Recognition. An understanding that this world was cruel even to the best of people. But there was no use crying over it. It was always there, just behind his eyes and charismatic facade. She hated that they had that in common.

Lunch period came, and while Sapphire wasn't looking forward to human food, she saw this as her opportunity to intercept Rainee. As soon as she entered the cafeteria, she spotted her—and Connor—in the line-up for the salad bar. She chuckled a bit, knowing that Connor had probably never eaten anything but meat. The Flamease were notoriously carnivorous.

She threaded her way through the crowd, grabbing a tray and joining them at the salad bar. Connor was chatting about something tech-related, and Rainee looked like she was trying to find a way to politely bail.

Perfect. Sapphire could work with this.

She walked around Connor, purposefully catching the heel of his boot with her shoe and tripping. Her tray and salad crashed to the ground. The crash echoed throughout the cafeteria and for a heartbeat, the whole room froze.

"O-oh, I'm so sorry. I was in the way," Connor stuttered, offering his hand to help her up. The chaos around them resumed; no one was worried about the new girl.

Sapphire put on her best smile and took his hand. "No worries, I'm too clumsy for my own good."

Rainee picked up her tray and handed it to her. "Sorry I couldn't save your salad. Luckily, there's plenty more," Rainee offered, trying to lighten the situation.

How sweet.

Sapphire brushed herself off and replied, "Oh well, maybe the salad just wasn't meant to be today. At least I've learned to pay attention where I'm walking, though."

She smiled, and Rainee smiled back. A sincere smile, not just a polite one. Connor still looked uncomfortable. Good, he could stay that way, for all she cared.

"I haven't seen you around before. I'm Rainee," Rainee added.

"Sapphire," she replied with a small nod. "I just transferred from Ridge Front." It was believable. The prep school was just far enough away to avoid questions, but close enough that people had heard of it.

They all walked to a table together, Connor still looking like he wasn't sure what was happening, and Rainee slowly letting her guard down. That's how you do it, red. Let her come to you, she thought, as she snuck a glance at Connor. But she couldn't get smug. There was a lot that could still go wrong before Rainee fully trusted her.

As they ate, Sapphire could feel someone staring at her. When she turned, Axel and Finn were a couple tables behind them, their eyes piercing through her.

"So, Sapphire, you just transferred?" Rainee asked, taking a bite of her salad.

Sapphire returned her attention to Rainee and smiled warmly. "Yeah! I have a chance to be scouted for volleyball this year and Ridge Front wasn't giving me enough playing time." She spewed out what little sports vocabulary she knew, hoping it would be convincing enough.

"So, you play volleyball?" Connor asked. She hadn't expected him to be listening.

"Yeah, for most of my life, actually," she offered nonchalantly, mimicking the verbiage she had picked up throughout the day.

Connor's eyes narrowed slightly, and for a second, she was sure he saw through her facade. "Don't you typically have to be pretty coordinated to be good at volleyball?"

Sapphire chuckled amusedly, but deep down she was panicking. "You know, I guess all my coordination gets spent on the court. Not a lot left to transfer into my day-to-day."

Connor nodded, seemingly satisfied with her response. Before he could continue his interrogation, Sapphire cut in.

"I'm sorry, I don't think I caught your name earlier?" she said in a way that almost sounded accusatory.

He fidgeted like he wasn't expecting the question, and replied, "C-Connor…I'm also new here."

She nodded. "Noted," she said, before adding, "Did you two know each other before you transferred?" Sapphire asked, gesturing between Connor and Rainee.

The questions seemed harmless enough, but she caught the way Connor stiffened. *Got him.*

"Oh, no," Rainee answered politely, swallowing her food. "Connor and I just had a class together before lunch and he happened to sit beside me. Seems like I may be a magnet for new kids."

To anyone else, it may have seemed like Rainee was just referring to her and Connor, but Sapphire caught the way her eyes wandered over Sapphire's shoulder to the table where the other two boys sat. She must have already deemed their presence suspicious.

Amateurs.

Sapphire was poised to ask something else, but the bell rang. She stood up, tray in hand, and smiled at both of them. "It was so good to meet you, but I should try to find my next class before the second bell rings."

Rainee stood with her, a sparkle in her eye. For the first time, Sapphire noticed the pendant on her neck. A tiny, silver-wrapped stone that caught the light in an odd way. It was beautiful, and also unsettling. A faint sense of recognition flickered inside of Sapphire. Where had she seen that stone before? And why did it make her nervous?

"Can I help in any way? I've been at this school long enough that I know where everything is," Rainee offered, pulling Sapphire out of her thoughts.

Sapphire nodded, knowing this was the outcome she had secretly hoped for. "Yeah, I..." She set her tray down and pulled a piece of paper from her pocket. "I need to get to Room 270 for Physics. Do you know where that is?"

Rainee smiled. "What a coincidence! That's where I'm heading next. I can show you once we take put our trays back."

"That would be great, thanks!" Sapphire responded, matching Rainee's tone.

Hook, line, and sinker.

Together, she and Rainee walked through the hallways, laughing about silly things that had the potential to become inside jokes—the foundation of every good friendship, even the strategic ones.

Sapphire was acutely aware of Axel trailing them. He was far enough behind them to avoid Rainee's eyeline, but close enough that Sapphire could feel him. *It must be his turn again*, she thought.

CHAPTER 11
AXEL

Axel watched Rainee and a girl he'd never seen before clean off their lunch trays and move together toward the hallway. Something didn't feel right. He couldn't place it, but something was off with that girl. She was too put-together and somehow knew the perfect things to say to get Rainee to let her guard down.

"You've got the next class with her, Axel," Finn said, looking toward the hallway.

Axel nodded absently, still watching the new girl. He didn't have any proof, but something inside him told him that she was dangerous. Call it instinct or paranoia, but she was too polished to be just a girl that coincidentally ran into Rainee and intercepted her from Connor. Okay, that last part wasn't surprising. A smart dog could intercept a mission target from Connor. Nonetheless, he needed to get Rainee away from her.

He paused. What the hell was he saying? Why did he care who she made friends with, even if they were dangerous? It made his job easier if someone did it for him. Less blood on his hands, and less redemption for Finn. Plus, unlike Finn, he wasn't opposed to unconventional means of completing a mission. Yet, his blood boiled slightly when he thought of someone else hurting Rainee. He must be sick. No mission should mean this much to him. No *target* should worry him like this.

"Axel," Finn said gruffly, snapping him back to reality.

Axel shot him a glare, then slipped off toward the next class. Physics. Whatever that was.

As he entered the classroom, he noticed Rainee and the new girl sitting in the front row, chatting casually. Rainee smiled at something the other girl had said—a smile that could stop the world if she wanted it to. Axel paused and took it in for a moment. He could see why Finn was having such a hard time staying casual around her. She *was* beautiful.

As he took his seat, two rows behind the new girl, he noticed something that made his mental radar spike. The girl, while seemingly normal on the outside, wore a small ring on her right middle finger. The crest looked eerily familiar to Axel, but he couldn't place it, which only unsettled him more.

As the bell rang and class began, Axel slumped in his chair with his arms crossed. He tried to pretend that he was listening to the teacher, but he couldn't take his eyes off Rainee.

She leaned in and whispered something to the other girl, who snickered under her breath. Axel rolled his eyes. This interloper was sure putting on a top-tier performance. She remained open and approachable, and kept her movements and emotions visible, casual, and vulnerable. No one was that poised without practice. Maybe it shouldn't matter. Maybe he shouldn't care. It wasn't his problem if Rainee trusted the wrong people. But watching her guard fall so easily for this obvious plant was infuriating, and made his chest feel tight. She wasn't stupid, that much he gathered from their conversation this morning, so why was she acting like it?

Despite his growing irritation, he tried to refocus on the blackboard. There was a diagram demonstrating the velocity calculation for…

Rainee leaned in again and he couldn't help but look at her. She was smiling, covering the side of her mouth closest to the teacher, hoping she wasn't too loud.

He didn't realize how hard he was staring at her until a piece of hair fell into Rainee's face, and as she turned her head to brush it away, their eyes locked.

His heart thudded, and he looked away…*too fast*. There was no way he was going to be able to play that one off if she ever confronted him. *She's not going to like that.* He could still feel her eyes on him, but he made a point to look anywhere except in her direction.

The bell finally rang, and Axel had never been so relieved to hear an annoying high-pitched noise in his life. He practically flew out of his seat, eager to get away. In his rush to leave, he collided with Sapphire, knocking a notebook from her grasp.

Not entirely a degenerate and trying desperately to blend in, Axel bent down to pick up the notebook and admitted, "Sorry about that. I just have to get to my locker before my next class."

Lies. He wasn't even confident that he had a locker at this school.

The girl smiled, but her eyes looked annoyed as he tried to hand the notebook back to her. She didn't accept it immediately; she just stared at him like he was about to be her next meal.

He cleared his throat. "I'm Axel, by the way." He kept his voice calm and his eyes level. He was several inches taller than she was, and he wasn't afraid to intimidate her if he needed to.

"Sapphire," she finally said, her gaze never leaving his. He was aware of Rainee glaring at him, but he couldn't afford to look at her right now. It would be too much of a distraction.

After what seemed like an eternity, Sapphire took the notebook from him, but not before her ring flashed in the light. A silver wave outlined in royal blue and gold.

Axel froze. He remembered now, the ring had the same crest that he had seen many times before. In the portal room…above the portal to the Water Realm. It was unmistakably the SwiftStream crest.

Shit.

Without another word, Sapphire turned and left, Rainee in tow. Axel's blood had turned to ice. Not only did they have company from another realm, but she was a SwiftStream. He had to find Finn and Connor. *Now.*

***

It didn't take him long to find Finn in the hallway, and the minute they saw each other, Axel was already moving toward him.

"Axel? What—" Finn asked, but before he could finish his thought, Axel was grabbing him by the collar of his shirt and dragging him toward the stairwell.

As the stairwell door shut behind them, Axel made sure it was jammed by shoving the doorstop under it from the inside. Then he turned to Finn, who was looking more confused by the moment.

"What the hell, Axel? You can't just…"

"We have a problem." Axel's eyes flashed with panic. Finn's brow furrowed, and he nodded for Axel to continue.

"That girl who showed up today, Sapphire. I got a weird feeling about her earlier, but this…"

Finn rolled his eyes. "Axel, I really don't have time to hear about your crushes."

Axel grabbed Finn's shirt and slammed him against the concrete wall behind him, hard enough that the impact echoed in the tight stairwell. "Enough!" Axel snapped, his face dangerously close to Finn's. "Just listen to me for once."

Finn went silent. *Finally.* Axel watched the other man's eyes grow genuinely worried.

"The girl's a SwiftStream. She's wearing their crest," Axel revealed, releasing Finn's shirt.

Finn's eyes grew wide, and his face paled. "What?"

He paced the couple of strides it took to cross the stairwell, raking his fingers through his hair. This wasn't just a mission anymore. This was war. And they were not equipped for that in the least. Even Axel knew that.

"Do we know why she's here?" Finn asked.

Axel scoffed. "No, I didn't get a chance to inquire about enemy spy plans in the two minutes between noticing the crest and her darting off to another class with Rainee. But I don't think her presence is in our favor."

"Go find Connor," Finn commanded, sounding much calmer than he looked. "I'll meet you back at camp to figure out our next move. This could mean more than just a compromised mission. This could cost our lives and those of the entire Eastern Division."

Axel nodded, his blood pumping. He quickly unjammed the door and darted off toward the gym to find Connor.

Connor was running by the gym door just as Axel opened it. Axel quickly grabbed him by the sleeve of his school-issued T-shirt and yanked him into the hallway.

"We're leaving," Axel said simply, dragging the smaller boy toward the courtyard. If anyone had seen them leave, no one attempted to stop them.

"Axel? W-wait, what are you…" Connor stuttered as Axel pulled him harder toward the tree line.

No time to explain, kid.

As Axel burst into the clearing, dragging a confused and terrified Connor behind him, Finn was already there holding a rucksack that Axel didn't recognize.

Axel shoved Connor down lightly near the extinguished fire and motioned to the bag. "She's been here, hasn't she?"

Finn nodded, tossing the bag aside. "Doesn't seem like she took anything, but I checked the timestamp on the holodisk—"

"And?" Axel prodded. He already knew that the answer wasn't one he was prepared to hear.

"—and the file was last opened twenty minutes after we left camp," Finn said, sitting down across from Connor.

Axel paced in circles around the fire pit. "What files were still accessible after the glitch?"

"Ours," Finn breathed, one hand in his hair.

That explained why she didn't look surprised or at all concerned by him, even when she clearly noticed him following her and Rainee. How long had she been watching them before she was even on their radar?

"Will someone please explain to me what is happening?" Connor broke in, his eyes fearful.

Finn motioned for Axel to explain. *Of course, "Captain."*

Axel sighed. "Sapphire is actually Sapphire SwiftStream. She's a spy."

Connor nodded, but he didn't seem surprised. "I knew there was something off with her story. My boot was nowhere close enough to the aisle for her to trip on in the cafeteria." He paused, his eyes shifting rapidly as the information sunk in. "She planned the whole thing to get Rainee away from me."

Axel wasn't sure why the last part of Connor's realization made something in him flare. *How dare she try to take Rainee.* He had no time to dwell on the thought before a twig snapped behind him.

Half-expecting Sapphire to be there waiting, Axel spun around, already seething. He forced himself to breathe. He knew that once he tore into her, he wasn't going to stop until someone was dead.

But it wasn't Sapphire. Two men, dressed in all black and wearing blue leather armguards stood on the other side of the tree line. Axel didn't need to speak to them to know who they were. Sapphire had brought backup. *Smart girl.* It did little to relieve the rage building inside Axel.

The guards didn't hesitate, the minute they knew they'd been spotted, they rushed the boys, swords drawn.

Who still uses swords? Axel thought as he charged them.

He dodged the first attack, pulling a blade out of his boot in the same motion. It had been a while since he'd seen real hand-to-hand combat, but he was pretty sure it was like starting a fire. Based on instinct, can't be forgotten. He circled the guard, trying his best to disorient him. This was his specialty. To be faster, slyer, waiting for his opponent to strike, then make the decisive move. He watched the guard, looking for tells about his next attack. As expected, the guard wielded his sword with precision and poise. But that didn't matter to Axel. Weapons were merely an accessory. He often preferred being weaponless. Unarmed combat made him feel absolute and powerful.

The guard's jaw twitched, and Axel lunged right as he swung the sword in his direction. Axel made a jab toward his assailant's ribs and grazed him. It wasn't enough to kill him.

"Connor!" he heard Finn shout through his battle haze. For a split second, Axel lost his focus, scanning the clearing for Connor amongst the chaos. The guard also faltered, the panic lacing Finn's voice catching them both by surprise.

Axel didn't miss the opportunity. His blade caught the light as he jammed it into the side of the guard's neck and twisted hard before yanking it free. The guard's surprised cry quickly turned to the guttural choking sounds. *Cathartic.*

He didn't stick around to watch the light fade from the guard's eyes. He was moving swiftly toward Connor. *The kid better be okay or I'm killing everyone here.*

Connor had backed himself up against a tree a few paces away, the second guard closing in on him. Finn was already loading his crossbow. Axel would let him take care of it, if he wasn't seeing red. *Not fast enough.*

Axel charged, dropping his knife, and slammed his body full force into the guard. The guard hardly budged, but he was stunned enough for Axel to regain his balance and slip in front of Connor.

Get out of here, kid. He hoped like hell that Connor would take a hint. He was still catching his breath, or he would have yelled it.

Connor didn't move. Axel dodged the guard's sword twice by mere inches before shoving Connor roughly into the woods.

"Get the hell out of here. Get to safety," Axel growled.

The action of getting Connor out of the way took too long, a fact Axel didn't notice until he felt the cold sting of metal on his abdomen. *Fuck.*

He looked from the guard to the sword, contemplating his next move. The guard pulled the sword back, and blood flooded Axel's shirt instantly. He cried out as his vision blurred. But he was determined to finish this. He lunged, his wound stinging as he did, and managed to grab the sword's hilt, immobilizing the guard.

Come on, Finn. How long does it take to load a crossbow? he thought, feeling himself weakening as he wrestled with his opponent

Suddenly, the guard lurched forward, making a noise that mimicked the other guard's dying words. An arrowhead protruded from his neck.

Finally.

Axel released the guard, dropping to the ground as his hands fought to put pressure on the wound in his abdomen.

He was vaguely aware of Connor shouting his name, but he sounded far away. Then Finn was beside him, ripping Axel's shirt off and applying more pressure with his own hands.

Dammit, does this mean I owe him if I survive this? The thought floated into his brain just as quickly as it floated out. The edges of his vision were darkening.

"Axel, look at me." He heard Connor, but couldn't move his head. "Axel!"

The darkness swallowed him.

***

When Axel came to, he was lying inside his tent. His abdomen was expertly bandaged, probably by Connor, he thought. He tried to sit up, but the pain was still raw. He became highly aware of how parched he was. His mouth felt like the sand pits back home.

"Hey, take it easy, killer," Finn said jokingly from the door of the tent. He was sitting there, twirling Axel's knife with bloodstained hands.

Flamease healed faster than most, but they weren't invincible. A wound like this could take a few days to recover from.

"Connor," Axel croaked out, his voice sounding hoarse and quiet.

Finn looked at him with a small smile. "He's fine. Went to steal his clothes back from the gym locker room and wash off a bit."

Axel noticed that Finn's smile didn't reach his eyes.

You could have loaded that bow faster. Then we wouldn't be here.

He gritted his teeth in pain as he sat up fully. He didn't believe in relaxing, especially not after what they had learned about Sapphire.

"You know," Finn said, drawing circles in the dirt with the knife. "You could have been killed." Finn's tone was matter-of-fact, but his eyes were distant. He stared at a fixed point in the dirt.

Axel blinked. Was that...*worry* that Finn was masking? He quickly hid his surprise with a smirk and replied, "Now, don't go getting sentimental on me, Captain. It's not a good look on you."

Finn smiled softly. It was a smile that spoke multitudes. One that said, "you're such a dick" and "I'm glad you're okay enough to be a dick."

Axel stood up, probably against everyone's better judgment, and crossed the tent to Finn. "Don't dull my knife," he said, swiping the blade from Finn's hands. Even injured, he was the fastest among them; a fact he took pride in.

As he entered the clearing, the sun had started to set, and he breathed in the crisp night air. He felt every gust of wind on the bare skin of his torso, but it was welcome: a reminder that he was alive and would probably be okay.

He plopped down by the fire that was already burning, a low groan escaping as his wound jostled against the bandages. He dug through his backpack like he was searching for something to hold his sanity together. He was starving, and human lunches sucked. He pulled out a tin of shelf-stable meat and a pot to heat it up with. *Just what a battle-wounded soldier wants. Questionable meat out of a can.*

He set everything up to cook, then looked at Finn. "Have you eaten?"

Finn shook his head slowly, looking down at the blood still staining his arms and clothes. "I haven't really moved other than to get rid of the bodies."

Something inside Axel throbbed, but it wasn't his wound. It was deeper, in his chest. Knowing how worried Finn had been about him made him feel…something. Like losing him wouldn't have been something the other two would just shrug off. He'd never felt that before.

Wordlessly, Axel threw two more servings of food into the pot and began the delicate process of heating it up without burning it. Even though he preferred the taste of burnt meat. Reminded him of his days in the syndicate.

He finished cooking and silently handed Finn a plate. Finn looked at him, gratitude flashing in his eyes, but he said nothing. Axel was careful to leave just enough for Connor when he got back.

They ate in silence for a few minutes, soaking in the night air. Axel grabbed his canteen from his bag and downed it, trying to quench the thirst of being near death.

"So, this Sapphire thing…" Axel started, pausing to find the words. "What do we do? Have you tried contacting IceHeart?"

Finn stiffened like Axel had just slapped him. "I tried. Nothing's going through," he replied. "I also don't know if that's the best option anymore."

Axel tilted his head. "Care to explain, Captain? My brain doesn't have enough blood left to be reading into cryptic messages right now."

Finn smiled thinly at Axel's taunting, but his mind was obviously somewhere else. "What we're dealing with…" Finn paused, obviously battling something that Axel couldn't see. "It's dangerous. It could get whole realms…divisions even…destroyed. We have to try to contain this."

While Axel agreed they should handle this themselves, it wasn't for the same reasons. Axel knew that if they involved the Fire Realm, any sense of freedom they had with this mission would be gone. They'd be nothing more than soldiers in a line, names on a roster. Expendable. Axel hated that feeling.

"Not to mention—" Connor's voice cut through Axel's thoughts, startling him. He hadn't seen or heard him come back. "—we just killed two Spritan guards. That has to be grounds for some sort of retaliation from the Water Realm." He looked back and forth between the two boys.

Dead men can't retaliate. Axel tightened his grip around the plate in his hands. But he knew all too well that the dead didn't always stay silent, either.

Axel nodded grimly. "If the Water Realm figures out it was us—" He gulped, staring into the fire hauntedly. "—it won't matter what division we belong to. They'll wipe us from existence."

"As it stands, I'm not sure that the Fire Realm would be happy with our situation, either," Finn reminded him.

Axel didn't respond. He'd seen his share of the Fire Realm eliminating people. It had only been a few years since he narrowly avoided being eliminated himself. He wasn't ready to chance that a second time.

Connor sat down across from Axel and dished out the rest of the meat from the pot before adding, "We can't exactly kill Sapphire, either. Isn't killing a royal an instant war crime?"

Finn nodded and set his plate down. "Then we need a way to distract her," he said. "Or to convince her to join us."

Good luck with that one, Cap. Axel was pretty sure killing her was still the best option. He could get rid of her easily. No one would ever know it was them.

"I think we should pretend we don't know anything," Connor offered. "Then, we let her come to us. Let her think she has the upper hand." He looked at Axel, who was feeling somewhat proud of the kid for strategizing so quickly. "Then we corner her. Three against one. Finish our mission and get the hell out of here."

Axel nodded his approval, and Finn sighed. They all knew this would be messy; there was no avoiding that fact.

"Fine. I…" Finn started to speak, but the holodisk beeped loudly. He looked behind him to where it lay under his tent flap, and slowly got up to retrieve it. A screen lit up above the holodisk as he returned to the fire. A few simple words appeared, just enough to cause panic to seep into Axel's mind.

    MISSION DELAYED. EXTEND PROTOCOL BY 2 WEEKS

    Two weeks? What about the portal tether? They had all heard what IceHeart said when they left the Fire Realm. His words seemed to echo in the sounds of the crackling fire: *Three Days...Miss the window and Earth becomes permanent.* Was IceHeart stranding them here?

    They all sat in ominous silence, their minds racing. This mission was getting riskier by the minute, and they weren't sure they'd ever see their home again.

CHAPTER 12
RAINEE

The rest of the school day seemed lighter. Sapphire was a great person to talk to, and she made even the most mundane classes entertaining. Rainee walked home alone, thinking about her day. She hadn't seen Finn—or any of the boys, for that matter—since Physics class, when Axel had crashed into Sapphire.

Maybe they finally took the hint, she thought as she unlocked her front door. Her father's black BMW sat in the driveway, and she faintly wondered what he was doing home from work so early. Usually, he was at the office until at least five thirty.

She walked in, threw her keys and backpack down near the door, and called, "Dad?"

No answer. Then, the sound of shattering glass from the kitchen followed by her father swearing under his breath. Her stomach twisted a little. He'd never been one to drop things. Or startle easily, for that matter.

She stepped quietly toward the sound, peeking around the kitchen entryway like she was about to find an alien eating her father. But it was just him, frantically picking up the pieces of a shattered candle. *Since when do we own candles?* Her nerves were getting worse by the second.

He looked up at her, looking tired, rattled, and...unfamiliar. Where was the clean-cut businessman she knew? The man who would always smile for her, no matter how bad the day had been?

"Dad?" she murmured quietly, scanning him for any sign of normalcy.

His eyes were frantic, causing Rainee to take a step back. His gaze immediately dropped to the necklace around her collar. She was aware of it humming against her skin like some sort of live wire, but she could have been imagining it.

"Where did you get that?" he questioned, standing up. She'd never heard his voice like this. He sounded genuinely scared...terrified, even.

Rainee's brow furrowed. "Did you not leave it on the counter for me this morning?" Something felt wrong.

His eyes widened as he crossed the kitchen toward her. "No, I'd never leave something like that out in the open. It's..." He paused, seeming to regain his wits for a minute. "It's a family heirloom. Very old. Very Expensive. It was supposed to be your graduation gift."

Rainee didn't like the tone shift that had just occurred. Her father had gone from pure, unbridled panic to completely unbothered.

What the hell is going on here?

To make things worse, the humming was getting louder. "Well, can you make your graduation gift stop vibrating? It's not exactly comfortable." She was getting angry. *He's never lied to me before. Not like this. Or...has he?*

"Humming?" The panic had returned to her father's voice. Before she could move, he reached for the necklace in front of her. As soon as his fingertip brushed the metal, he cried out and jerked his hand back like he'd been shocked. "Rainee, I need you to remove the necklace. Now!" he demanded, moving to grab it again.

"What? No!" Rainee twisted, dodging him. Her heart pounded. She wasn't sure why she was so desperate to keep the necklace on, but something inside her told her to protect it with her life.

Protect the spark, her dream echoed.

Her dad growled, a sound that was mutant coming from him. "Rainee, this isn't any time for games. *Take it off.*" He lunged at her again, and she screamed, the sound piercing through the air.

The lightbulbs above the kitchen island all exploded, one by one. Shattered glass rained down around them. The other lights in the house dimmed, as if a power surge had overloaded the circuit breakers.

What timing. Her dad threw his arms up to shield his face from the glass, and she took the opportunity to escape, bolting for the stairs and locking herself in her bedroom. He didn't follow her, but she could hear him pacing below, muttering under his breath. Words she didn't quite understand but felt in every part of her body. They sounded like a different language—one she had never heard before.

She slid down against the door, her pulse still pounding in her ears. The necklace continued to hum against her skin, but she barely noticed. Her entire body felt like one big circuit breaker. She tucked her head between her knees, willing the tingling to stop.

This must be what adrenaline feels like. If so, she never wanted to feel it again.

Everything felt like an overload. She grasped at the necklace, trying frantically to unclasp it or rip it off, but it was like it was fused to her skin. The humming intensified again, taking over all of her senses. A bright light flashed, blinding her momentarily. Then, everything went dark and…quiet. No humming, no thoughts, just the comfort of her own unconscious being.

CHAPTER 13
SCOTT

"You promised me more time," Rainee's dad, Scott, accused, pointing at the divine being now sitting on top of his kitchen table. Hermes sat cross-legged, in his gold cuffs and centuries-old wing-tipped shoes, and shrugged nonchalantly. "*I promised you nothing*," he clarified, adjusting one of the gold cuffs with great care. "*Zeus* said it was unlikely we'd ever need her."

Scott rounded the kitchen island, glass crunching under his feet. He'd called a council with the gods, a full divine council, but all they sent was this wing-shoed bastard. "It's going to be you who fixes it," he growled. "Or the gods are going to be down a smug messenger boy."

Hermes smirked. These were empty threats, and they both knew it. Scott knew he couldn't kill Hermes, but he *could* make him regret ever accepting this council without bringing backup.

"You think the spark's awakening is the worst of your problems?" Hermes retorted. "Have you seen what's hunting your daughter in broad daylight, Scott?" Hermes spat his name out like a curse as he slowly uncrossed his legs and leaned forward, his face inches from Scott's. "We're on the brink of a second Divisional War, and you're worried about your daughter growing up." He chuckled in that melodic, cocky way that only Hermes could. "Do you hear yourself?"

Scott's eyes narrowed. "You're talking about those Fire Realm brats? They're nothing," he said, turning his back to Hermes. The truth was, he knew they were in the human realm. He'd known since the moment the beacons he monitored captured a portal signal, for the first time in years. He'd been checking in on the boys since they arrived a couple of days earlier. They were barely older than Rainee; he hadn't pegged them as actual threats.

"You think the Fire Realm would send assassins and leave them without reinforcement?" Hermes slid off the table, pacing toward the sliding door on his right. "It may just be three boys now, but where the Fire Realm goes, war follows." He clasped his hands behind his back. "You can't protect her from the entire Eastern Division, Scott." His tone was surprisingly soft, but Scott didn't trust the god as far as he could throw him.

"Hermes," Scott replied, balling his fists. "Get the hell out of my house before I chain you up in the basement." He was done; this council was over. It had been no help anyway.

Hermes chuckled. "Very well. But you'll do well to remember that your daughter isn't helpless. There's a reason the council let her live. And she very well may be the only thing that holds this world together."

Then he was gone. No flash, no smoke, he just vanished. *Fucking gods.*

CHAPTER 14
RAINEE

Rainee blinked. Her bedroom ceiling came into focus, and she was vaguely aware of her bedsheets pulled up to cover her. How had she gotten here? Her head throbbed dully as she sat up. She was trying to recall what happened when she noticed her dad sitting in the chair across the room. Hadn't her door been locked?

He looked distraught, but not angry. He was clutching a photo so tightly it was like he was forcing himself into the memory it held.

"Dad?" she whispered, still a little groggy.

He didn't look up and didn't speak. He couldn't be this broken up about their argument, could he? Rainee slid out from under the sheets and quietly padded over to where her dad was sitting. She reached out and touched his arm lightly, and he flinched like he was being yanked from a dream.

"Dad?" she asked again, a little louder this time.

He looked up at her slowly. Like he was scared he might see something he didn't want to see. When he finally met her gaze, all Rainee saw were the tears glistening in his eyes.

"You should still be asleep," he said, a thin smile on his lips. "I'm sure you're tired after that ordeal," he added, looking back at the picture in his hands.

It was a picture Rainee hadn't seen before. A woman holding a baby. A closer look told Rainee that it was her mom and, she assumed, herself as a baby. She had only ever seen her mom in photographs like these, but she always looked the same—Long blonde hair, and a smile that seemed to light up every feature on her face.

"She's beautiful," Rainee whispered, staring at the blue-eyed woman who resembled her. Her heart ached for someone she had never met.

Her father sniffed and nodded. "She was the most beautiful woman I had ever seen. I was love-struck from the minute I first met her."

Rainee paused. She had never heard how they had met, just that they were inseparable from that moment on. "How did you meet?" she questioned. It didn't feel like prying, it felt like a little girl trying to piece together who her mother was.

Scott sighed like he was trying to decide what to tell her, or at least how much to tell her. "I met her on a mission," he said simply.

What? Rainee thought she heard him wrong. "What do you mean, 'mission'?" She didn't think he'd been in the military.

"Rainee..." He faltered, choosing his next words carefully. "This world...It's a lot bigger than you think it is. And it's not even the only one."

She quirked an eyebrow and smirked. "I know what other countries are, Dad." She nudged him playfully, but his expression didn't change.

"Not countries, Rae. Realms," he said, his tone grim.

Her smile faded, and she stammered, "Like...alternate universes?" It was starting to feel like a plot twist that made every problem more complicated, yet also somehow simpler.

He shook his head. "Not alternate. Just...adjacent. Existing on the same plane, just not right here."

"And...you met *Mom* in one of these realms?" She felt like she was playing along with some delusion he had created for himself, but she couldn't force herself to break it. She was too intrigued.

He looked up at her again. "She was divinity, at least partially. I was appointed as her guard. She was never meant to stay in this realm, but in the end, she didn't have a choice."

Rainee's throat went dry. "She didn't have a choice?"

"Celestial beings were forbidden to take mortal partners a few years after I married your mother. They said no more demigods or demigod children. We were grandfathered into an exception clause for that pact." He smiled slightly, like he was remembering her. "Then, the Line Severance Decree was passed, which outlawed any form of demigod bloodlines. She was already pregnant by then, and things got...complicated." He stood up and paced to the other end of the room. "Not *bad*...just harder. We knew that once the realms found out about you, they would either take you from us to use as a weapon, or they'd want you dead. We couldn't take that chance." He went quiet, his eyes glassing over with tears again.

"What happened to her?" Rainee asked quietly. He had never explained how she had died.

He let out a shaky breath. "Because of the broken decrees, she was seen as a criminal in the eyes of the Divisional Council that oversees the realms. They executed her, right before your first birthday." He let out a sound that sounded like a small sob. Rainee had never seen him like this. "The only reason they didn't take us too is because they thought you'd be useful someday. And because you needed a guardian." He looked back at her over his shoulder. "Someday came a lot sooner than I expected, Rae."

The air in the room felt colder. "What do you mean 'someday'?" She was vaguely aware of the necklace humming again, but this time it felt like it was humming from inside her body.

"I never wanted you to be a weapon. I wanted you to be normal. At least, for a little while. They told me I would have more time than this," he said, nearly breaking down completely.

"Who?" Rainee demanded, stepping toward him to place her hand on his shoulder.

He smiled in a way only a man who had withstood the world for too long by himself could: broken. "The gods. The Olympians." He gritted his teeth. "*Fucking Zeus.*"

Rainee stumbled back, the hum from the necklace was getting louder, and it felt like she'd been zapped by a current.

"I tried to protect you, but they outrank me, Rae." His eyes met hers again, and she could tell he was barely holding himself together. "A war is coming, and you're the only one powerful enough to stop it."

CHAPTER 15
FINN

Finn stood near the stream that ran through the clearing's eastern edge, scrubbing Axel's blood from his skin. It didn't bother him as much as it probably should have; he had done this sort of thing many times before. No, what bothered him was the fact that Axel had almost died, and Finn gave a shit about it.

The holodisk in his pocket beeped again.

Another mission amendment.

He didn't rush to look at it. He'd had enough of IceHeart's mind games for one night. Ever since the initial extension had come through, the duration had been growing in length of time every half hour. They were up to four months, as per the latest update.

Might as well get a job at this point, he thought. He doubted that "trained otherworld assassin" counted for much in this realm.

"So, are we still doing this mission or not?" Connor asked from behind him, causing Finn to jump.

He looked down at his arms, and realized the blood was gone and he had been rubbing his raw skin for the last few minutes. He shook the water from his hands and stood up, but didn't turn to face Connor. "Yeah, the mission is still on. It's just...longer. More surveillance." He crossed his arms. "Shouldn't be an issue."

He didn't actually believe that. But Connor didn't need to worry any more than he already was. If anything, Finn and Axel would take care of everything.

Connor didn't answer right away. When Finn finally turned around, the kid's mouth was set in a frown. "You don't have to lie to protect me, Finn," he said quietly. "I'm a soldier, too."

Something in Finn cracked. He remembered his first mission, when things were still new and ideal. He hated to see that reality shatter for Connor. He wished he could have shielded him a little while longer.

Finn sighed. "I wish you didn't have to be." He meant it. He wished none of them had to be there. To fight a war they didn't cause and probably couldn't finish.

"I chose this," Connor reminded him, matter-of-factly. There was still a hint of pride in his voice. It almost comforted Finn knowing that not all of Connor's innocence had been stripped yet.

Finn smiled softly, looking at the ground. "Yeah, you did." That was all he could manage to say. They stood in silence for a few moments before he added, "Have I ever told you about my last mission?"

"You mean…" Connor started.

Finn nodded. "Yeah, the one that cost me my rank."

Connor shook his head. Finn motioned to a spot near the stream and took a seat. The younger boy joined him in a movement that was all too eager.

"The mission was simple, or so we thought," Finn began, bracing himself to tell the story out loud. It hadn't hit him until now that he had never talked about it with another person. Just in his inner monologue, on replay.

"We were sent to the Outer Coves to clear a suspected rebellion hideout. But when we got there—" He sucked in a breath. "—it was all families with small children. There were no signs of a rebellion camp existing there."

"What did you do?" Connor asked, staring at Finn in childlike awe. Finn briefly wondered how he hadn't heard this story from other sources.

Finn had to fight to maintain his composure as he answered, "The only thing I knew to do—I phoned the throne room." Finn looked at the ground, his thoughts disappearing into the memory. "IceHeart personally gave the order to continue clearing the village, civilians and all." He looked up at Connor, who seemed mesmerized. "I couldn't do it. I told my men to raid for contraband, but to leave the villagers unharmed."

"So, you're the good guy then?" Connor offered.

Finn smiled thinly. "I thought I was. I thought the decision I made was the valiant one. But it cost me everything I had worked for. It almost cost me my life."

Connor shook his head, unable to believe what he was hearing. "W-why would they do that? You saved people."

"They didn't want the people saved; they wanted them dead." Finn stared into the distance and let out a chuckle of irony. "The worst part is, they still killed them. They sent another battalion out a few hours after we left. Not a single civilian survived." He looked at Connor seriously. "Morality isn't what saves people out here. It's luck and timing."

Connor was silent for a while, soaking in Finn's words. Finn let the silence linger; he wasn't sure if he could get any other words out.

"You still saved them," Connor said abruptly. "Even if it was only for a few hours."

Finn smirked bitterly. "That's not really how saving works, Connor."

"Why not?" Connor pushed again. "If you save someone from being shot but then two days later they drown, you still gave them an extra two days."

Finn froze. He hadn't thought about it like that. He was impressed that Connor's toxic optimism had broken through the mindset that had been a part of him since his demotion. Usually, it was just slightly annoying.

He searched Connor's eyes and found nothing but sincerity, not that he was expecting to be deceived by him. Not yet. Connor hadn't lived enough life to know that deceiving people was sometimes necessary. All he knew was truth, which Finn was grateful for in that moment.

"You really believe that?" Finn said. "That what I did still counts as saving them?"

Connor smiled. "I do. You did everything in your power to do the right thing. What happened next was out of your control." Connor stood up and looked back toward their camp. "The blood isn't on your hands at that point."

Finn smiled back. "I wish it felt like that. I really do."

The holodisk beeped again. This time Finn took it out of his pocket and let the screen flicker to life.

BEACON SURGE DETECTED.

He looked back at Connor, whose face had gone pale. "Does that mean what I think it means?"

"It means—" Finn said, switching the holodisk off and getting to his feet. "—this mission just keeps getting more interesting."

He started toward camp, his mind racing. If the beacons within range of the holodisk were surging, either the gods were involved or Rainee had discovered her power. Either way, it meant she wasn't as innocent as she looked, and Finn could deal with that. Whether it took three days or four months or ten years, he was completing what he had been sent there to do.

CHAPTER 16
SAPPHIRE

Sapphire stood in the tree line about fifty yards from the boys' campfire. Close enough that she could track all their movements, but far enough that they couldn't see her. It was probably for the best; she was absolutely seething. She had noticed that none of them had shown up in their last three classes, which was suspicious enough in itself. But, between her guards going radio silent, the stench of blood still clinging to the clearing, and Axel's torso being bandaged like he was cosplaying a mummy and ran out of gauze, Sapphire could connect the dots.

How dare they. I have half a mind to start a war.

It wasn't just the fact that they so easily disposed of her entourage, it was more so that none of them seemed phased by it. Connor was joking with Axel about something and seemed…content? He should be shattered. These had to have been the first real kills he'd seen in his career.

Finn leaned against a tree a few yards away, his hair still glistening from washing the blood out of it. He wore the same stoic look he always had, which was annoying. She'd expected him to be more panicked. His leadership was at stake; shouldn't he be worried?

And Axel. *Screw Axel.* He should be dead. What kind of semi-immortal asshole casually survives being run through by a sword? A *Spritan* Sword, nonetheless. He should be bedridden, at least. Even with the Flamease's ability to quick-heal, he shouldn't be able to walk or talk or…smirk the way he was.

She shook her head. *Focus, Sapphire.*

She needed a way into their camp that would allow her to distract them without making herself too vulnerable. She smiled. She had just the idea. Taking a deep breath, she stepped into the firelight's edge, just enough to catch Finn's eye.

His mouth curled in a snarl. "I wouldn't get any closer if I were you. I don't mind digging another grave tonight."

The other two looked up at her at the sound of Finn's threat. She briefly caught Connor glancing back at Finn with a look that bore both confusion and fear.

She raised her hands, palms forward, in a gesture of surrender. "I'm not here to fight. Not tonight," she said, barely loud enough to hear over the roar of the fire. "We all have our own missions, but I'm calling for a truce. For tonight only." She locked eyes with each of them, feigning sincerity. "I'm hungry and my guards are dead. Give me tonight to mourn that loss."

Axel scoffed. "You expect us to fall for that?" He rolled his eyes. "What? We let you in for tonight, then you kill us in our sleep? You have a lot of nerve. Even for a SwiftStream."

She glared at him, her eyes dark. "I wouldn't need to wait for you to fall asleep, hot shot," Sapphire retorted, but she couldn't help but smirk back at him. His charm was incredibly disarming, and he seemed to be aware of that fact.

He started to get up, his temper rising in true Axel fashion, but Finn motioned for him to stay on the ground. "Let her talk. I'd like to see what other lies she can come up with." Then he made eye contact with her. "We don't have any spare food, but there's a stream nearby. Spritans eat fish, right?"

Impressive. Someone's been doing their homework.

She nodded. "Thank you, I'll make my way over there later. But for now…" She sat down at the head of the fire like she belonged there. Axel flinched slightly, which made her happy. The more she intimidated him, the less of a threat he was. "I take it your holodisk picked up the beacon signal earlier?"

The boys froze, looking over at her distrustfully. She figured if she handed them information that wasn't classified for either party, maybe they would give her some new information by accident.

Finally, Finn nodded. "I can't tell if it was portal-related or demigod-related. But something big happened." He crossed his arms. "Why? What do you know?"

How cute that he thinks it could be anything other than demigod-related. Rainee-related.

She thought back to the necklace Rainee had been wearing that morning. She had finally remembered where she had seen it before. Similar ones were on display in the throne room back home. The Water Realm had a memorial hall for those who were lost in the First Divisional War. Several demigods had fought and lost their lives. Anyone who had seen those necklaces or other divine artifacts would recognize them.

"I don't know much, admittedly," she said nonchalantly. "Other than it wasn't portal-related."

Connor looked at her with an eyebrow raised. "And how are you so sure?"

Oh, sweet boy. Under other circumstances, Connor was the type that she would take on as an apprentice. In fact, he reminded her of her younger brother, Sebastian. Innocent and hopeful. It was sad that most people didn't make it through the cynicism of daily life in the realms with those characteristics left intact.

"You know she carries demigod blood, right?" she questioned with an eyeroll. "Or do I have to be the one to brief you on that, too?" It came out colder than she anticipated, but none of the boys flinched. Not even Connor. She was surprised. She had expected a reaction from at least one of them. Instead, Finn just nodded. Something in his eyes looked different. Like he was living somewhere else.

"We suspected as much by the watermark on her profile. They usually don't write *demigod* on just anyone's file," Axel retorted, shifting to sit up straight. It was obvious he was still in pain, but he masked it well. *Admirable.*

Axel's eyes stayed on her. Watching, calculating. He was studying her, watching for tells, signs she was lying or deceiving them. *Oh, honey. You won't find any of those on me. I threw those giveaways away years ago,* she thought with a smirk.

She turned back to Finn; it was best to address the leader of the group directly. "And what exactly were your orders regarding...demigods?" It was a long shot, and she knew it, but there was no better segue than what they had given her in this conversation.

"You first," he said, tipping his head back. "What's your business with Rainee?"

The way he said her name betrayed him. She wasn't just a target; she was a person, and he saw that. Sapphire knew that thought must be eating away at him.

It must be tough to have morals in his line of work, she thought. She would empathize with him if her empathy hadn't been ripped out of her years ago by her own father. She stiffened her jaw, refusing to slip into those memories right now.

"I'm here to protect her—" she said softly. She looked between the boys, who were all completely silent. "—from you." Briefly, she thought she had said too much, but the feeling in the air hadn't changed. Connor shifted uneasily beside her, but something told her that he did that all the time. Finn seemed unfazed, lost in thought. Axel just smirked. They probably suspected as much. They were stupid, but not that stupid.

She half-expected to be ambushed or at least verbally berated. But none of them moved from their position. Still, Sapphire's hand stayed where she could quickly grab the knife at her hip. She was outnumbered, but she had been thinking about how to fight them since she first saw them.

Why aren't they reacting? Her unease grew by the second. What had she missed? And why did they all appear to be…conflicted? Except Connor, who just looked tired.

"You'll be here awhile if that's the case." Finn broke the silence.

She raised an eyebrow. *How cryptic.* "And I assume you aren't going to tell me how long that is? Or why?"

Finn shook his head. "Nope."

"I could just kill you all right now and go home," Sapphire said, lacing her threats with velvet. "Make it easy on both of us."

Finn was silent for a moment, eyeing her. And she could sense Axel's smirk widening, even without looking at him.

"Then why haven't you yet?" Finn asked quietly.

She swallowed, trying not to look phased. Then she smiled like both a huntress and a seductress. Poised. Amused. Calculated. "I enjoy playing with my food first, boys."

Then she stood, spun on her heels, and made her way back to the tree line. "Happy hunting, firebugs," she called over her shoulder. "I'll be seeing you around."

None of them followed her. Good. That's what she had hoped for. They didn't need to see her panicking, trying to figure out her next move. She'd have to surprise them somehow, isolate them, and pick them off one by one. Or, call in more guards from the Water Realm.

No. She knew that if she involved her father, she'd get a whole lecture about how she hadn't been ready, just as he'd predicted. She wouldn't risk that. She couldn't give him or Tobias the satisfaction of knowing that she had failed.

CHAPTER 17
AXEL

Axel stared into the fire. *Happy hunting* echoed in his mind. He had hated Sapphire before, purely because of her ties to the Water Realm, and now her smugness made him want to tear her throat out.

Except he couldn't move. He was still wounded and, while he might yet be faster than Connor and Finn, he wasn't certain that he could outrun Sapphire in his condition.

As he watched her leave, he thought he caught a moment of her character breaking as she reached the tree line—a slump in her shoulders told him it was all an act. Then the darkness swallowed her before he could be sure.

"She's bluffing," Axel said, breaking the silence. He wasn't really saying it for conversation, he just needed to hear it out loud.

Finn walked over and took a seat by the fire. He was quiet, like always, but Axel could see the wheels turning in his head. He was strategizing. That's one thing that Axel admired about Finn— he knew how to plan, and could think four or five steps ahead of the enemy. Axel would never give him the satisfaction of admitting it, though.

"About protecting Rainee, or being able to kill us at any time?" Connor asked. Axel looked back at him, deciding how to answer. There was no doubt that Sapphire could kill them under the right circumstances, but he wasn't too sure the current climate was ideal for that to happen.

"Either or," he said. "I think she *could* kill us if we were caught off guard. But now that we know who she is—" He leaned back against the log behind him, wincing slightly as his wound shifted. "—she's going to have to be really creative. Three against one isn't an easy fight." He left it at that. *Even though, right now, it's more like two against one.* He thought back to the fight with the guards and how Connor had froze. Axel was struck by the need to train him, but that was a problem for later. He knew that if Sapphire had been with her guards earlier, they wouldn't have stood a chance. He grimaced. That wasn't a feeling he was fond of: vulnerability.

Finn finally looked up, his eyes locking with the fire, the glow flickering in them ominously. "You two should get some sleep. I'll keep watch. I have a feeling she's not done."

Axel started to protest, but he was in no shape to keep anyone safe right now. So, instead, he stood up slowly, gritting his teeth against the pain, and moved toward his tent. Tomorrow he would be in much better shape, as long as the healing process continued the way it had already started.

"And Axel—" Finn said, making him pause and turn around. "—at some point, I'm going to need you to show me how to use that knife of yours." His back was to Axel, but Axel could tell he was serious. Finn was never one for close-range weapons, but it was an expertise Axel was willing to share if it meant the outcome was them all staying alive.

Axel didn't respond, just nodded and ducked into the darkness of his tent, a smug smile forming on his face.

CHAPTER 18
RAINEE

Rainee's dad had left her alone shortly after their discussion. Something about "time to process." But how do you process something like learning your mom was a demigod who was killed for loving your dad and having you? She wondered if she would ever love someone enough to risk her life for them, but decided she had bigger problems on her hands than theoretical romantic dilemmas that she may or may not live to see.

It was Friday morning. She sat on her bed, still wearing her pajamas. She hadn't slept much the night before, and she had thought about skipping school entirely for a day. But she needed a normal activity to feel like her world wasn't falling apart. She needed to feel like a human, not a demigod, not some divine weapon. Just Rainee.

Her alarm sounded again. Her "last warning before you're late" alarm. Usually, her dad would have hollered up the stairs to move her along by now, but he was quiet this morning. It made the house feel empty. As if only echoes lived there. She silenced the alarm and forced herself to stand, catching a glimpse of herself in the mirror. She looked tired, but that was expected. What she hadn't expected was the necklace around her neck to be glowing softly, like she had backlit it with some fairy lights from the dollar store.

She looked at it for a second longer, then turned away. *Nope. Not my problem today.*

Next, she rifled through her dresser for a hoodie and yanked it on, making sure to tuck in the necklace. She had tried to take it off multiple times throughout the night, but it had either shocked her or the clasp remained fused together as if by some magnetic force each time she tried. If she couldn't take it off, she could at least hide it, even if it did pulse against her skin in a way that made her feel uneasy.

    She finished getting ready and went downstairs. Her dad was nowhere to be found. No breakfast. No note. She checked the time; it was possible he had an early meeting, but she had a feeling he was just avoiding her. *Thanks, Dad. Very helpful.*

    She opted to skip breakfast, looking around like he might jump out and force peanut butter toast down her throat if she stepped foot outside with an empty stomach. But the door shut behind her, and when she locked it, he still wasn't there. His BMW was gone, and the street was quiet. When he had said *leave you alone to process*, she didn't think he meant *alone* alone.

    She forced her feet to move toward the crosswalk. She half-wished a car would zoom past her, one she could throw herself in front of on purpose this time. No Finn to save her. She rolled her eyes. She'd never get that lucky. He was probably already watching her, just out of sight. *What a weirdo.* But something inside of her felt warm when she thought about him saving her. She had never properly thanked him for that. She had been too busy trying to avoid him and his friends. Or whatever they were, because Axel hadn't seemed too sure that they *were* friends.

    The walk sign lit up, and she jammed her hands in her hoodie pocket as she crossed the street, the spitting rain not doing anything for her mood. She finally entered the parking lot just before the bell, her head down to shield the rain from her eyes. She went toward the stairs to the main building, eager to get inside, and nearly collided with someone in the process. She felt him even before she saw his face. *Axel.*

    Sure enough, when she looked up, she was met with golden eyes and his signature smirk. He was wearing a leather jacket, black shirt, and his eyes glinted with something she couldn't quite place. Was that pain?

    "Oh, sorry. I wasn't watching where I was walking," she admitted, too stunned to come up with a witty remark on the spot.

    He smiled. That damned smile that made the rest of the world freeze for a moment. The same one he'd given her in Calculus yesterday. "I could tell by the aimless stumbling." His eyes

shone. "Thought maybe you had a wild night and didn't think to invite me." He opened the door for her, and they stepped inside. "To which I say, 'ouch'."
    She rolled her eyes at his hypothetical, wishing that it was closer to the truth. The door clicked shut behind them and she jumped.
    "You okay?" he asked, one eyebrow raised. *Shit.* She was hoping he wouldn't notice how off-kilter she was today.
    She put on a fake smile and nodded, "Of course. Do I not look okay?"
    "Is that a trick question?" he replied, walking beside her down the hallway. She couldn't help but notice that he was limping a little, and the weight of his backpack seemed to be bothering him. The nonchalant one-strapped carry was gone, and he was extremely stiff.
    She didn't answer, instead she shifted the question back to him, "Are *you* okay? You're limping."
    His face went a little pale, but he smiled. "I asked you first. Don't change the subject."
The words sounded harsh, but something inside Rainee sparked when he looked at her like he was now—eyebrow raised, devilish charm, the kind of guy that screams trouble, but you can't seem to escape from. She didn't realize she was staring at him until the bell rang and she looked away. He didn't even blink; his eyes were still studying her.
    "Yeah, I'm fine. Just didn't sleep well last night," she offered, pushing her way around him to get to class. Luckily, it didn't seem like they shared their first hour today.
    She could still feel his eyes as she walked away, like he was trying to memorize her features. While it felt a little weird, she felt comfortable. No one had ever studied her like that before, even for brief exchanges such as that one. She entered her classroom and took the only available seat, next to Connor. He smiled when he saw her, and this time she tried to be nice to him. He seemed like a good kid.

CHAPTER 19
AXEL

Axel stood in the middle of the empty hallway, still watching in the direction that Rainee had disappeared. She looked rattled. Not that he cared, but he still wanted to know what could shake her so badly if it wasn't him.

"Axel?" Finn's voice cut through his thoughts. *Dammit.* He had hoped Finn would already be in class like the good little soldier he was.

Axel had taken a few extra minutes to get ready that morning, with the bandages needing to be changed and his muscles stiff from battle. He'd waved the other two ahead with a promise that he'd catch up with them later in the day. He hadn't planned to run into Rainee. That was just luck.

He turned and looked at Finn, wincing as pain shot through his ribcage. The wound was a little better this morning; it didn't feel like his guts might fall out if he twisted the wrong way, but it was definitely still painful. He wondered why he wasn't healing faster.

"You okay?" Finn's voice wasn't warm, just concerned. A captain worried about his soldier, nothing more. It was almost more comforting for Axel that way.

Axel nodded, painting a grimace on his face. "When have I ever been okay?"

"Well, just try to stay low today." He nodded toward Rainee. "She already suspects something is up; she doesn't need to know people are getting stabbed in the clearing out back." Or that we've decided to start a graveyard out there, Axel added in his head. It was strange how oblivious the majority of humans seemed to be.

Axel nodded once, looking away. "I'll try not to bleed through this shirt. It's the only one I have left anyway."

Finn didn't blink, his eyes stayed locked on Axel. "Good." He glanced at his torso briefly and added, "If it gets worse, get out of here. I don't want to explain to the principal why you're bleeding all over campus."

Finn clapped him on the shoulder, eliciting a sharp wince from Axel, then he turned and headed toward his classroom. Axel stood for a second, a small smile on his face. As much as he hated Finn's leadership style, Axel had decided it was best that Finn was the captain for this mission.

Axel shifted the weight of his backpack and started walking to his class. The pain was manageable but constant, and he knew that today was going to be harder than most. Especially if Rainee was actually going to talk to him today. He secretly hoped she would but pushed the thought down as he sauntered into the classroom.

He had a class with Rainee right before the lunch hour, but she didn't seem to be in the mood to talk to anyone. She had even shut Sapphire out, from what he could tell, which had earned him a disapproving glare from his least favorite assassin. As if it was his fault that Rainee wasn't interested in being friends today. *Petty.*

Despite the clear signals Rainee was sending, Axel still managed to steal a few glances in her direction, studying her features, the way her hair parted naturally in the middle, and the way she looked put-together despite wearing the most basic clothes he could imagine. She really was impressive, whether she knew it or not. He shook the thought away quickly, *Focus, dumbass. She's the target, not some conquest.* Those were the type of thoughts that got soldiers executed for treason if left unchecked. He'd already been acquitted of that charge once; he wasn't looking for a round two.

The bell rang. *Lunch time.* He exited the classroom before Rainee, hoping to find an empty table to commandeer so he could discuss some sort of plan with Finn. This mission was starting to get complicated in a way that made him wonder if killing her in public was really such a bad thing. They didn't live here; what could the humans really do to them?

He found a table, the only one without an occupant, and sat down carefully, so as not to chafe his wound. He played out strategies in his head, yet kept getting distracted in each scenario. That wasn't like him. He wasn't the distractible type…usually.

Someone sat down at the table across from him with a lunch tray, but he wasn't paying enough attention to realize it wasn't Finn until he looked up and met dark gray eyes and a frown.

"No one is sitting here, right?" Rainee asked, motioning to the spot she was already occupying. Something told him she wouldn't move even if he said it *was* taken.

He shook his head slowly, scanning the room quickly for Finn and Connor, and didn't see them anywhere. *Great.*

"So," Rainee said, pointing her fork at him. "You going to tell me what happened to you, or am I going to have to force it out?"

Her remark caught him off guard and brought a grin to his lips. There were few people who could challenge him like that and keep their tongue, and Rainee had solidified herself as one of them, for now. He erased the smile and leaned forward, the pain making him grimace. "Just because I let you sit here doesn't give you the right to ask questions." *Or to read me like a book, dammit.*

Her eyes narrowed. "I don't remember needing your permission," she retorted. Something in Axel jumped as if an electrical current had hit him. If only she knew how dangerous he really was to her. She'd never speak to him that way.

"I'm fine." He smirked at her. "Just a surface wound. I tripped." *Onto a sword.* It wasn't his best lie, but lying was better than the truth in circumstances like this. What Rainee didn't know wouldn't hurt her.

She raised an eyebrow. "You tripped?" She didn't look convinced. "Like off a cliff, or something? You look like hell, Axel." The way she said his name made his stomach do flips, but not in a disgusted way. He hated that it wasn't in a disgusted way. She said it like she *actually* cared if he was okay. Maybe she wasn't as smart as he had thought.

He opened his mouth to reply with something equally snarky, but Finn and Connor plopped down on either side of him, killing the tension. While he was grateful for the distraction, he almost wanted to see how far Rainee would have pushed to get the truth out of him.

"Rainee," Finn said with a nod in her direction. "Axel," he added, with a look that said it all: "Too close." Axel didn't argue. He was getting too friendly and *almost* enjoying himself.

He took the opportunity to fade into the background a bit, but he noticed that Rainee's gaze never really left him for long, even while she was talking to Finn or joking with Connor. Axel was always there in her sights. Honestly, he liked it that way. Getting to her without trying. His smirk widened at the thought.

After a few pleasant exchanges, Rainee stood, grabbing her tray off the table. "I need to get to class to go over some homework questions. But I'll see you guys around, I'm sure." The last line was pointed. She knew they'd been watching her, and she was letting them know that she'd noticed. "Oh, and Axel," she said, looking back at him with a playful grin that made Axel's heart pound. "Try not to trip off any more cliffs, okay?"

That was it. That comment sent his brain into a frenzy. He shouldn't care; she was just trying to get to him. But why was it working?

"Care to tell me what that was about?" Finn asked, his tone gruff. Axel couldn't tell if it was due to disappointment, or if it had been a hint of jealousy that he heard.

Axel looked over at him, his eyes feigning innocence. "Explain what?" He smiled. "She asked about my injury, and I told her I tripped."

Finn rolled his eyes. "I pegged you for a better liar." Axel didn't respond. He'd pegged himself as a better liar. But staring into Rainee's deep gray eyes as she saw right through him, that was the closest to being disarmed he had felt in his life. He'd take a hundred sword fights over that feeling any day.

The school bell rang, and Finn got up, casting one last warning look at Axel. "You're getting too close to this. We're not supposed to be her friends. Or whatever you were trying to be."

Finn was right, but he wasn't just going to give her the cold shoulder. There was a certain level of closeness needed to complete this mission. Axel just needed to find the line and walk it without crossing it. His specialty. At least, it always had been in the past.

CHAPTER 20
FINN

Finn watched Axel throughout the day. He was acting strangely. Finn had initially chalked the weird behavior up to him being injured. Wounds could alter soldiers' brains, and the quick-healing process wasn't gentle. However, he'd never seen the healing process cause people to become more likeable. Especially not people like Axel. It was usually the opposite.

The way he bantered with Rainee was dangerous. Finn could tell from across the cafeteria that she was starting to break down his walls, and who knew what the dumbass would tell her if that happened.

Axel hadn't talked to Rainee since lunch—at least not that Finn had seen—but the way she would try to catch his eye or smile at him in the hallway made Finn uneasy. She shouldn't be this comfortable with them, especially not with Axel. Now, as they walked back to the clearing, Axel was oddly quiet. He didn't even offer a snarky greeting when he met Finn and Connor in the parking lot.

Good. He needs to keep his mouth shut for once. But the eeriness wasn't lost on Finn, and he almost wished Axel would say something obnoxious, just to fill the space.

He didn't have to wish for long, because Connor began jabbering excitedly about his electronics lecture. Finn didn't understand everything he was saying, but the kid's excitement was palpable.

As they stepped into the clearing, the air shifted, and Finn froze. Sitting near their campfire, waiting for them, was a man that Finn recognized from Rainee's log files: her father, Scott.

The stranger locked eyes with them, then gestured for them to sit down. "We need to talk," he said. The fire was already lit, and he had open-cuffed gold chains dangling from his right hand. Finn could tell by the markings that they were binding chains. He'd seen them used on some of the Fire Realm gods during certain highly publicized trials. Fire Realm gods were notoriously messy and petty, airing their skirmishes for the entire realm. They were less like religious deities and more like immortal sources of entertainment.

Finn briefly wondered why Scott would be in possession of equipment like that. There wasn't anything notable about him in Rainee's log, just the normal dad debrief. He was an accountant, Finn remembered. Did they pass god-binding chains out to every human dad now? That seemed like a blatant waste of resources.

Still, Finn wasn't going to test his luck, and it didn't seem like the other two were in the mood to either. He once again found himself wishing Axel would break the silence with his attitude, but he just dropped his bag and took a seat on the log to Scott's left.

Finn and Connor followed suit, with Finn sitting on the ground across from Scott. The older man's eyes never left the fire as he said, "I know what the three of you are."

CHAPTER 21
SCOTT

The fire crackled, drowning out any other noises in the forest clearing. Or maybe that was the blood in Scott's ears. He couldn't be too sure. He hadn't felt adrenaline like this in years. He wasn't used to it anymore.

After a long pause, he looked up at Finn. Or, at least, who he presumed to be Finn, based on the limited information he could access on their holodisk. The information had been mostly locked, and his hacking skills weren't what they once were. Plus, holodisk technology had become far more advanced since he had stopped realm traveling. But the boy in front of him carried himself like a leader, someone who knew how to speak for his team. If the circumstances were different, Scott could see himself liking him.

"Are you going to tell me why you're stalking my daughter?" Scott asked finally. He narrowed his eyes, chest thumping. "Who sent you?"

Finn searched his eyes, clearly trying to decide what to tell him. Scott shifted slightly, purposely rattling the chains in his hands. He didn't know if any of them had divine blood, but he wasn't going to take any chances by bringing standard chains.

"I have no idea what you –" Finn tried

Scott smacked one end of the chain on the ground, interrupting Finn's lie. "You have exactly three seconds to answer my questions with something other than excuses before I show you what these chains are good for, boy."

The sound of the chains on the ground seemed get the point across, because Finn responded, "We were given orders from King IceHeart."

"Kai?" Scott questioned. *That bastard should be dead.* Last Scott had heard, Kai had died on a diplomatic crusade that had failed decades ago. Hearing his name out loud sent chills down Scott's spine.

Finn shook his head, his eyes flashing with confusion. "Syren."

Scott almost laughed. Syren IceHeart had been a boy, no taller than his shoulder, the last time Scott had traveled to the Fire Realm. Now he was ruling a realm. What a turn of events.

"And what does he want with *my* daughter?" Scott growled. He had half a mind to confront Syren directly. He wasn't afraid to cause tension between their realms, if it meant Rainee remained safe.

Finn didn't respond, and the silence was all the confirmation Scott needed. "Does he want to use her as a weapon? Because let me tell you…"

"He wants her dead." The blonde sitting to his left interrupted.

Scott froze. "What did you just say?" He gripped the chains harder. This was worse than he thought. Images of Rainee's mom being dragged by her arms toward a realm portal cycled in his mind. *No. They won't take her too.*

"What Axel means—" Finn jumped in, trying to dig them out of the hole Axel had put them in. "—is that we were ordered to end Zeus's lineage. We were unaware that referred to your daughter until we were already here."

Scott scoffed. "Didn't seem to change much," he said, eyeing Axel. "I know you three have been getting close to her. Trying to gain her trust." His eyes burned black like charcoal in the light of the fire. "Give me one good reason why I shouldn't chain all three of you up and leave you for dead."

Axel smirked in a way that questioned who Scott thought he was to threaten them. "You wouldn't get the chains on before one of us took your head off."

Scott saw Finn shoot Axel a glare that screamed "Shut up." But it was already too late. The challenge had been cast and Scott was boiling. He looked at the redhead to his right, who was cowering silently. He looked like nothing more than a kid. Scared, dragged into something he didn't fully understand. *Damn Flamease military*. It seemed like they were recruiting soldiers younger and younger these days.

Scott glared back and leaned toward Axel, his left forearm resting on his leg. "You don't know who I am, do you?"

"A dad with a god complex?" Axel retorted. Scott stood, quick as lightning and clamped one of the cuffs around Axel's wrist. *I'll teach him to mouth off to me.* The shocked look on Axel's face was enough to calm the racing of Scott's heart, even if only a little.

Scott yanked the chain toward him, and he heard Axel yelp and grab his torso. "You'd do well to listen more than you talk," Scott snarled. He noticed the bandages peeking out from Axel's shirt, now soaked in fresh blood.

What would have given him an injury like that in the human realm?

Panic set in as Scott wondered if there was something he had missed. He'd been so busy with Rainee and watching these brats…Was it possible that there had been other threats that had slipped through undetected?

He nodded toward Axel's injury. "Where did you get that? That's a battle wound."

Finn spoke first, his hands up in surrender. "We'll tell you what we know." His eyes flickered in the firelight. Calm, composed. "But we have to agree to be civil."

Scott had another moment of reluctant fondness for Finn. He was everything a good leader should be. Confident, loyal, and willing to go to war for his team. He reminded him of himself.

"Civil," Scott said with a nod as he dropped the chain. However, he didn't unhook the cuff from Axel's wrist. He might still need to remind him of his place throughout the night. "You have ten minutes to explain before *civil* goes out the window."

Scott took his seat by the fire, gesturing for Finn to do the same. He noted that Connor hadn't moved, and was staring at Axel in little-brother-esque horror. If things went south, he'd be the hardest for Scott to kill. Not because his skills outweighed Scott's, but because he had no business being there.

Axel had sat himself up, clutching his abdomen in a silent attempt to smother the pain. Scott felt a tinge of regret; he hadn't meant to hurt him that badly. *Yet.*

"We were sent here with orders to kill the last descendant of Zeus; that much is true." Finn's voice startled Scott, bringing him out of his spiraling thoughts.

"Why do I sense a 'but' coming?" Scott asked, eyeing him suspiciously.

Finn's eyes flickered. Was that uncertainty or just exhaustion? The wind picked up at that moment. A cool breeze rustled the fire and sent small embers skyward across the clearing. "Our orders weren't clear. I've lost track of the revisions that we've been sent in the past twenty-four hours." Finn shrugged. "I couldn't tell you what our actual business here is anymore…or why IceHeart wants Rainee dead."

"Yet you're still carrying out the orders?" Scott questioned. His head was starting to ache. "Ever thought of regrouping on your own turf?"

To Scott's surprise, it was Connor who spoke up, "It's not just the mission communication." He looked up at Scott with an innocence that spoke volumes, and continued. "It's the entire holodisk. All the programs and files are choppy…corrupted. I'm not even sure we could open a portal right now with the state that it's in."

Scott stiffened. He had noticed the disk was hard to operate, but it had not occurred to him that it was corrupted. That didn't sound like a simple technology issue. That sounded like interference.

"I'm not even sure a tether to the Fire Realm is still intact," Finn added, searching the ground. "We were originally supposed to finish the mission today, and I haven't heard a single direct communication yet. No regroupings, no recall orders. Not even a damn voice message." He looked up, his mind calculating. "The tether would have broken naturally in about an hour, if it hasn't already."

Scott sucked in a breath. This went far beyond his daughter. Syren had left these boys to rot, whether intentionally or not. But with no way for them to relay mission details, Scott had an idea.

"Maybe they left you here on purpose," Scott pushed. Did he believe that? No. But planting seeds of doubt could be his only way to ensure Rainee's safety.

Connor looked between Axel and Finn, but neither of them gave anything away. Scott could tell by the twitch in Finn's jaw that the thought had crossed his mind already. He just wasn't going to admit it out loud.

"How…" Connor started, looking up at Scott with a fear that hit him deep in the chest. "How do you know so much about the Fire Realm? Hasn't the human realm been out of communication since the First Divisional War?" Connor finished, then shied away.

Scott smiled. Even in the face of danger, the kid was always learning. "It's true," Scott admitted, turning to Connor directly. "Humans stopped participating in realm politics on a public scale centuries ago. Despite that, it didn't stop the underground operations. The gods and the council still appointed realm guardians from Earth until recently, and the realms still trade commodities back and forth; the public just isn't aware of what goes on behind the scenes." He paused there, watching Connor's eyes turn bright. Scott had dreamed of telling his story in full someday; he had hoped it would be to Rainee, but he didn't think that would happen any time soon.

"Realm travel never went away after the war; they were just very selective in who could use it." He shrugged. "I'd know. I had those clearances once." He watched all the boys shift closer, even if they weren't willing to show their interest, it was obvious in the way none of them spoke. Another torrent of wind hit, causing smoke to blow in Scott's direction. "I've been to the Fire Realm many times in my younger days. Back when I was a realm guardian serving Zeus's temple." His eyes were cast downward, focusing on the memory. "Kai IceHeart was a well-respected diplomat and acquaintance of mine. Syren was his little brother who always tagged along."

Axel scoffed. "Well, Syren's in charge now. Little brother or not, he calls the shots."

"That's because—" Scott inserted, glaring at Axel. "—Kai died the year the Line Severance Decree was signed. The year they outlawed new demigod bloodlines and tried their best to eliminate the existing ones." A somberness overcame Scott. Kai had been an asshole, but he was also a good leader, and he almost wondered what the Fire Realm could be today if he was still in control. "He had gone out to the Fire Realm's Outer Isles to try to garner support from The Fire Realm's gods to help expedite the decree process. At least, that's what he'd said he was doing." Scott paused. Even Axel was looking at him in disbelief. "No one really knows. He never came back. At least as far as I know."

He let the words linger. He hadn't spoken about the Fire Realm with anyone except Hermes in decades, and something like nostalgia burned his eyes, or maybe that was the campfire smoke. His Guardian days were well behind him, but he'd never forget the friends he had made. He would have included Syren and Kai in that sentiment, despite the falling out. So why was Syren targeting his family? Why now?

"What's changed in the Fire Realm?" Scott asked, looking at Finn. "Why…after all these years…is Syren willing to start another Divisional War over my daughter?" The mention of another war made all the boys stiffen.

Finn's brow furrowed. "No, he's trying to prevent one." Scott could see Finn's mask breaking as he stood up and started to pace. Soldier or not, Scott was dropping view-changing evidence of conspiracy in the Fire Realm. He could tell Finn was coming to grips with learning they were the villains in every story except their own. "He…the tension in the Water Realm…He said this was the only way to stop the war."

Scott let Finn spiral for a minute, turning his attention to the other two boys. Axel was staring blankly into the fire. From what Scott had gathered about him, this probably didn't surprise him in the least, but it was still a hard pill to swallow. Connor had retreated into himself, his knees tucked against his chest with his head resting on them. Scott was worried about him the most. Young soldiers tended to have the hardest time having their ideals torn down around them. Scott also knew this wouldn't be the last time it happened to him.

"And how do we know you're telling the truth?" Axel asked. "You're so desperate to save that Rainee you'd feed us whatever line we needed to make us switch sides."

Scott stood, chuckling a little. "Fair point, but if you're so sure I'm bluffing, why not test that portal tether out?" He took a step toward Axel, who flinched. Scott bent down and undid the shackle from his wrist, gathering the rest of the chain in his hands.

None of them answered him; they stared at each other in silence. Scott dusted off his jeans and started for the edge of the clearing. "Oh, and if you need more gauze or a stitch kit, stop by the house. I have plenty." He meant it. He had no idea how this night had ended this way, but he was pretty sure he'd just planted the seeds of an unlikely alliance. *IceHeart be damned.* His soldiers worked for Scott now.

CHAPTER 22
AXEL

Axel could feel the blood soaking through his shirt. *Dammit. My last shirt.* He still wasn't sure what had just happened, but based on the way Finn was pacing and the tightening in his chest, he concluded that something had shifted in all of them. Connor was still curled up, staring across the clearing. *Poor kid.* He would have let Scott yank him around a bit more if it meant Connor could have remained ignorant of what had been said amongst them.

He tried to stand up, but his abdomen throbbed. He sank back down against the log. *Screw it.* He painstakingly pulled the shirt off over his head and tossed it to the side. He'd wash it in the stream later. He winced at the movement, but the cool air offered a sort of relief to the stab wound and his aching muscles.

"You okay?" Finn asked. He had stopped pacing and was staring at the blood soaking the front of Axel's bandages.

Axel waved him off. "It's fine. The worst of it has healed." *He hoped.* He hadn't examined it since that morning, when it was still a deep gash.

"Maybe we should get a stitch kit," Connor said softly, watching the gap in the trees where Scott had disappeared through. He looked back at Axel and added, "I know you heal fast, but a wound like that could still take another week to fully heal without stitches."

Axel growled. He knew the kid was right; he always seemed to be right lately. But there was no way in hell Axel was going to ask Scott for help. Not after what had just happened. His wrist was still sore from those chains.

"He did offer," Finn chimed in.

Axel shot a glare in Finn's direction. "Yeah, well—" Axel grumbled, holding up his bruised wrist. "—he also godbound me to a log. So, forgive me if I'm not in the mood to engage with that man again."

"Your *mouth* is what got you chained to that log," Finn reminded him. "If you could have given him the silent treatment you've been giving me all day, you might have avoided that."

Axel scowled. Right again. But he still would rather bleed out than admit that.

Connor stood up, glancing between Axel and Finn. "Well, if you won't go, I will. I can probably still catch up to him," Connor stated matter-of-factly. Axel was surprised. The kid wasn't usually one to take initiative. "I'm not going to let you die or get an infection just because you're stubborn."

Axel would never say it, but he was grateful that someone cared enough to try to keep him alive. He hoped this version of Connor—the one who was optimistic and willing to do anything for his team—stuck around. Traits like that rarely outlived the cynicism that bled in later. Part of him wanted to hug the little twerp. The other part of him wanted to get up and get the stitch kit himself. He wasn't one to be taken care of. He didn't need, nor deserve, the pity party. He stood up slowly, settling for the middle ground.

"I'm not going to let you go alone." Axel grunted as he forced himself to his feet. Fire tore through his abdomen, and he briefly wondered if he should have stayed on the ground. "Who knows what that maniac is capable of, one-on-one."

Connor nodded and bent down to pick up Axel's shirt. Axel took it and reluctantly slipped it over his head, wincing again. It was already bad enough that they were going to show up at Rainee's house, he didn't need to show up shirtless *and* wounded. He'd never hear the end of that one from her.

He looked at Finn. "You coming, or sulking?"

"I'm..." Finn paused, looking away. "I'm going to do a perimeter sweep just to make sure there aren't any more spies around."

Axel smirked. "Sulking it is, then," he said as he made his way to the edge of the clearing with Connor in tow. They didn't need Finn anyway. Even though he was injured, Axel was confident he could hold his own. He hoped that they could catch Scott before he reached his home—maybe he could keep their presence hidden from Rainee. Just maybe.

They had no such luck. Scott was nowhere to be found on the way to the Bennett house; he must have parked in the school parking lot and driven home. *Just perfect.*

As they made their way up the street, the pain in Axel's torso seemed to be getting sharper, and sweat beaded on his forehead. *Come on Axel, just a bit further.*

"Axel. You don't look great," Connor said, looking at Axel worriedly. Axel could only imagine. The blood wasn't clotting, and he had felt the color drain from his face a few steps ago. But he had to keep going; they were less than a block from Rainee's house.

He shook his head. "I'm fine." But he didn't feel fine. His head felt fuzzy and his legs were unstable. The next few steps were a blur. He could see Scott getting out of his car in the distance. He heard Connor call after him, and he tried to grab the kid, tell him it was fine, he was fine. But he hit the pavement instead. The world was ringing. How did he keep finding himself in these situations?

CHAPTER 23
RAINEE

Rainee paced in her bedroom. She had been waiting for her dad to get home, but it was already seven o'clock. She was bursting with questions about her mother, and about herself now that this power had surfaced, but he still wasn't home. Maybe he really was avoiding her.

She was about to call him when she heard his car door shut. She rushed downstairs to meet him, but instead was greeted by shouting from the driveway. *Is that Connor?*

Without thinking, she flung the door open to reveal Connor and her dad kneeling beside an unconscious Axel. She didn't notice the blood at first. All she could see was the worried expression on her dad's face. Her heart pounded in her chest. *Please be okay.* She didn't have time to wonder why she had thought that before her dad scooped Axel up and carried him toward the house.

Connor ran off in the opposite direction. Probably to get Finn, if she had to guess.

"Dad?" she questioned as he pushed past her to get inside. "What's going on?"

He looked at her, but his mind seemed to be racing. "First aid kit, now!" He laid Axel down on the couch. "I'll explain what I can while I patch him up."

She hurried to the bathroom and dug through all the cabinets and drawers until she found the white box her dad kept on hand, full of stitch kits and bandages. She had always thought he was overprotective for that, but now she was grateful for it.

She brought the kit back to the living room, where her dad had already ripped Axel's shirt to get a better look at the wound.

Axel was pale and motionless, and his skin was moist with sweat. She couldn't help but notice his toned chest and the tribal flame tattoo that wrapped around his right shoulder.

Focus, Rainee, she thought as she handed over the kit. She tried to avert her eyes, but her curiosity got the best of her. Axel's wound was deep and triangular, like he'd been stabbed. She wondered how an injury like that could have happened around there, but pushed the thought aside as she watched her dad work with a sureness she had never seen before. It seemed like he could dress wounds in his sleep.

"*Fuck*," Scott muttered, reaching for a pair of surgical scissors. "It's necrotic. This isn't a typical sword wound."

She wasn't sure what he meant by that, but continued to watch as he cut away blackened tissue and wrapped it in gauze. He looked at her as he was packing the wound, his face serious. "Are you sure you want to know what's going on here? Because I'm willing to forget this happened." He reached behind him for more dressing. "And I'm sure Axel would like us all to forget it happened, too."

She hesitated. Something in her father's voice made her feel uneasy. How would the knowledge change things for her? For the boys? For her dad? Finally, she gulped down her fear and nodded. "I want to know." She looked at Axel's face, her stomach churning. "Please."

"You may have noticed—" Scott started, his hands flying over Axel's injury with learned precision. "—that Axel and his friends aren't…normal." She didn't respond. She knew they were a little weird, but that's not what her father seemed to be implying. He reached for the stitch kit. "Do you remember when I told you there were other realms?"

Her brow knitted. Where was he going with this? "Yes…" she whispered, her mind racing.

"Well," Scott said as he started stitching the wound. "Axel is from the Fire Realm. And so are Finn and Connor. They're what's known as Flamease."

She blinked. The information felt heavy, but it felt comforting to know that her intuition had caught that there was something odd about them, before her dad told her the truth.

"What are they doing here, then?" she blurted. She felt she already knew the answer, but needed to hear it before she'd let herself believe it.

Scott sighed and shook his head. "Rainee…"

"Please," she interrupted; afraid her dad was about to shut down, right when things were finally starting to make sense.

He nodded without looking at her. "They—" He paused briefly. "—were sent to kill you. They're assassins." The last part was barely audible, but she heard it nonetheless.

Assassins? Her mind reeled. In what world was she important enough to have assassins sent after her? And in what world were *these* three considered assassins? The last thought almost made her laugh. They were horrible at their job. Finn had actively saved her life the first time they met. Axel, while he looked dangerous, could barely walk this morning. And Connor…Oh, Connor. If it were up to him, no one would die. Ever.

"But…why?" She hadn't realized she was crying until she started to speak. The crack in her voice betrayed her. Her insides felt like they were twisting.

Scott had just finished suturing, his speed almost god-like. He looked up at her. "The power you have is something that could tip the odds in a war that's been brewing for some time." He rose from where he was kneeling, setting the needle and scissors on the coffee table. "Now that it's coming to a head, some will want to use your power, and others—" He looked at Axel. "—will want to destroy it."

The necklace vibrated against her skin. She didn't have to ask what power. She knew. She'd been thinking about the fight she had had with her dad in the kitchen. How the lightbulbs had exploded. How her skin seemed to radiate electricity now. Those were things that she may have just ignored under other circumstances, but they seemed like glowing beacons in the current context.

She didn't respond to her dad's revelation; she was trying to brush back her uneasiness. So, instead she gestured to Axel, whose color was returning slowly. "Is he going to be okay?" She didn't know if she wanted him to be okay. If he was really sent to kill her, maybe dead was the better option. Still, something inside her was begging her dad to say yes.

Scott nodded. "He should be. The Flamease have a natural healing ability. I'd expect it to take hold now that I've cleaned the wound."

She looked up at him, but he didn't feel like her dad anymore. He felt like something more. Something she couldn't quite place yet. "If they're trying to kill me—" She was finally brave enough to say the words out loud. "—why are you helping them?"

"I'm not saving him to help them." Scott said. "I'm saving him to gain their trust." He moved around her, grabbing a large gauze patch to place over the stitches. "You'd be surprised where your allies come from this early on."

She watched in silence as he finished dressing the wound. His words made sense, but she still wasn't sure what they needed allies for. She wasn't sure he fully knew, either. She also couldn't shake the fact that Axel had never felt like a threat to her. Their whole group was a little weird, but she had never feared them. She had felt annoyed, confused, and sometimes angry, yes. But she had never truly questioned her safety. She wasn't sure she *would* fear them, even now that she knew who they really were.

CHAPTER 24
FINN

Finn had walked the perimeter of the clearing about four times. There was nothing unusual, not even a sign of Sapphire being around, which he found odd but dismissed.

Axel and Connor hadn't come back yet. Maybe Axel's blood had attracted a wolf. Wouldn't that be Finn's luck? His team eaten alive and him, stranded alone in an unfamiliar realm. Right when he had started to actually care about something again.

A few days ago, he may have welcomed being alone, but now his fellow Flamease soldiers were the last sense of normalcy he had.

He pulled the holodisk out of his pocket and flipped the switch to summon the portal home. The disk whirred, then a warning beeped and the message NO TETHER appeared.

He shook his head and stuffed the disk back in his pocket. He'd tried several times to summon the portal, all with the same result. They were stuck here. No one was coming to save them. Although by this point, he didn't know if he wanted to be saved.

He kicked a twig on the ground, sending it flying into the trees. He couldn't help but wonder if maybe this had been the plan all along. Who would send a demoted soldier, a criminal, and a kid who barely knew how to shoot a bow to another realm, on a mission that could cause a war? It didn't make much sense once he thought about it.

Then he thought about Rainee. The look on her face when he had pulled her out of the street, the way his heart had pounded in his chest. He knew in that moment, whether he admitted it or not, this mission was more complicated than they had been led to believe. He knew that she was powerful—he could feel it radiating from her—but the look in her eyes was what had shaken him. The defiance. The independence. Like "how dare you touch me." But beyond that, there was curiosity, like maybe her life had gotten interesting for the first time.

He returned to the dying fire. The air was just chilly enough to keep him alert. *Why are Connor and Axel not back yet?*

He knew that stitches could take a while, especially on a wound from a Spritan sword. But this was excessive. Finn had neglected to check the swords the other day. That had been his first mistake: assuming that Spritan guards would carry normal swords. His second mistake was not realizing how much worse Axel's condition had become. It was hard, when all he did was smart off and act tough.

Idiot.

Finn had dug the swords up during his perimeter check, just to be sure. And to confirm it, he saw gold flecks and a faint glow emanating from them. They were dire tip blades. Axel would have died without intervention. Finn just wished it had been someone other than Scott Bennett to offer help.

He looked around the clearing. Still no sign of anyone. He had a bad feeling that something had happened. Which meant that Rainee probably knew about them. How could she not? Her dad knew. What was stopping him from telling her, especially with a mortally-wounded Axel in their house? Not exactly subtle.

It wasn't about the mission anymore; Finn was just worried about her reaction. Not that she wasn't already noticing something unusual about their presence, no thanks to him.

Finn sighed and turned in the direction that Connor and Axel had gone. He guessed he needed to go check on them. As he started through the trees, he nearly collided with Connor, who looked frantic.

"Connor? I was just coming to find you." He glanced over Connor's shoulder. "Where's Axel?"

Connor was still panicking, his eyes wide. "He collapsed," he said grabbing Finn's arm and pulling him toward the parking lot on the other side of the tree line.

"What? Is he okay?"

Connor didn't stop moving. He pulled Finn with more strength than Finn thought the kid possessed. "I-I don't know. Scott grabbed him and took him inside." He paused once they hit the sidewalk leading to Rainee's house. He was panting. "He said he was fine, Finn. I didn't think…"

Finn grabbed the younger boy by the shoulders, grounding him enough to get him to look up. "Listen to me," Finn said, his voice concerned but calm. "You had no way of knowing this would happen. You can't help that Axel is a prideful asshole who refuses to ask for help."

Connor nodded slowly, taking in Finn's words. It was then that Finn noticed the trail of blood that gradually became more prominent the further down the sidewalk it went. *Dammit, Axel. Stubborn asshole.*

They continued down the street, following the trail to a pool of blood, right in front of Rainee's house. Finn wasted no time running to the front door.

"Shouldn't we knock?" came Connor's quiet voice. Even panicked, he was worried about doing things the right way.

Finn didn't reply, and turned the knob slowly. He could hear people talking inside, but the voices were muffled. As he opened the door, he saw Scott and Rainee standing by a couch where Axel lay, unconscious and *maybe* breathing; Finn couldn't tell.

Rainee and Scott both looked up with grave, but not overly concerned, expressions. Finn looked between them, each second feeling like ten. "Is he…"

"Lucky? Yes," Scott interjected calmly. "Dead? Eh. Not today, but I could make some arrangements if I needed to."

Finn's panic started to subside. He could see that the wound was patched expertly, a skill he would need to have Scott show him at some point, especially if Axel was going to be around more.

Finn looked at Rainee. Her cheeks were red, like she'd been crying. How much had happened in the time it took Connor to come find him? How much did she know?

"When were you going to tell me that you were sent to kill me?" she said finally, catching Finn off guard. She never feared confronting him.

Finn stayed silent. That answered his question about whether she knew or not. But he couldn't say he liked the outcome. He opened his mouth, then shut it. What was he supposed to say to that? Sorry? No, it was probably better to keep his mouth shut and let her fury play out. Connor was looking at him and he wished he knew what to say, but there was no sugarcoating the truth. No denying their mission. The betrayal in her eyes made his chest hurt in a way he'd never felt before. He realized that she wasn't just a mission. Not anymore. She was Rainee, and, at that moment, that meant something.

"If you two are going to fight, I need you to take it out back," Scott interrupted. "I have enough bloodstains in my carpet for one night."

Finn looked at him and Rainee. The way he said it made it seem like a joke, but his face didn't suggest that he was kidding. "Look, I'm not here to fight." He looked into Rainee's eyes. "And I'm not here to kill you." He sighed. "In fact—" He looked away. "—I'm not really sure what we're doing here anymore." He wasn't talking about the house. He was talking about the realm. Existence itself was confusing, and he wasn't sure whether he was the assassin or the victim anymore.

"You tried the tether, didn't you?" Scott said, eyeing Finn knowingly.

All Finn could do was nod. They were trapped here. Out of food, no way to communicate, and he was pretty sure Scott had just ripped Axel's last shirt saving him.

"Well, in that case—" Scott started, looking at Finn and Connor in a way that made Finn feel cared about. "—you three need a better place to sleep than that clearing in the woods." Finn's brow furrowed. What was Scott saying?

"Sir?" Finn asked. His instincts were telling him to run, to figure out some way to get back. But his legs weren't cooperating.

Scott looked at Connor, who seemed more on edge than usual. "Go get your things. I have a few rooms and an extra shower in the basement." That perked Connor up. But Finn remained silent, shocked, and a little hesitant. He looked at Rainee, but she was looking at Axel, lost in thought. He wasn't even sure she'd heard what Scott had offered. Scott's eyes locked on Finn. "But if you so much as look at my daughter—" His voice lowered. "—I'll make you wish the tether was the worst of your problems."

Finn wasn't sure if this was genuine, or if it was a trap to get them all in one spot so Scott could monitor them more easily. But part of him didn't care. His body ached from sleeping on the ground, and the stream did little to wash away the smell of dirt and blood. So, against his better judgment, he nodded in acceptance.

CHAPTER 25
AXEL

Axel opened his eyes to the smell of alcohol. He was having trouble recollecting what had just happened. But when he saw Scott standing over him, placing a new gauze patch on his abdomen, he remembered. *Dammit.*

"Welcome back," Scott murmured. "You didn't tell me this was a wound from a Spritan sword. You know you should be dead, right?"

Axel had known. He had just hoped that it wasn't really a Spritan sword, and that the Flamease ability to heal would outweigh the blade's effect. Spritans were known for their expert bladesmiths, those who could craft blades from radioactive materials. He had hoped that the blade that hit him had been non-radioactive. It hadn't looked out of the ordinary. Obviously, that had been wishful thinking.

"I removed the dead tissue the best I could. It should allow your healing abilities to kick in fully," Scott continued. Axel tried to sit up, but Scott shoved him back down onto the couch. "But, if you pass out on me again, I'm not sure I can bargain with Hades again. So, you need to take it easy."

Easier said than done. Axel looked around; he was in a living room, out in the open. And there was no way Rainee didn't know he was here. How was he going to explain this one to her? Fencing accident? Maybe?

He was vulnerable, flat on his back, shirtless, with a gaping wound in his abdomen. Not exactly the hot-bad-boy aesthetic he'd been going for. To make matters worse, her father, the man who probably hated him more than anyone else right now, was caring for him.

"That cliff was pretty sharp, huh?" Axel knew the voice before he saw her. *Rainee.* Part of him was comforted that she was there, the other part was terrified of not having an actual lie to cover this.

Scott cleared his throat. "Well, everything is patched for now." He stood up, dusted his hands off, and added, "I'll be in the kitchen. I think you two need to chat." He eyed Axel knowingly. "Don't bleed on my couch."

Axel rolled his eyes. He didn't want to be alone with her. Not just because he wasn't in the best shape, but because he had no clue what to say to her.

Scott left the room without another word, and Rainee sat in the armchair across from the couch. They were both silent for a while, then Axel smirked. "Stop looking at me like that."

"Like what, exactly?" Rainee asked. Her voice was soft.

Axel rolled his eyes again, but his heart thumped in his chest. "Worried. Like you care. You're not supposed to care." He froze; he hadn't meant to say the last part out loud.

"Why?" she questioned, sounding amused. "Because you're from the Fire Realm?"

She said it like she'd known all along, but Axel knew she hadn't. He stared at her in shock, trying to find the words to say—any lie to get out of this—but nothing came to mind.

"My dad told me. You don't have to pretend," she said pointedly. *Of course he did. Dammit, Scott.*

He nodded. He wasn't about to say anything else on that topic. He didn't know how much Scott had told her. "Look, Rainee..." he started. He wasn't sure what he was going to say, but he continued anyway. "Fire Realm aside..." He took a breath, his ribcage burning. "I'm not someone you want to get close to. I don't have the best track record with people." His chest smarted. He didn't like her getting this close willingly. It wasn't safe.

I'm not safe.

She quirked an eyebrow. "So, you get to decide who my friends are now? I don't remember giving you that power."

"I can't choose your friends for you," Axel stated. "I just don't think I should be one of them."

Be friends with Connor. Or maybe even Finn, but not me. Please, anyone but me.

She smiled and stood up. "I don't really care what you think, blondie," she threw out, walking toward the kitchen. Then she added over her shoulder, "And just for that, we're friends now."

A wave of panic ran through him. No one had ever said something like that to him, even out of spite. He wasn't sure what to do with the feeling. He wasn't going to argue with her, but something still felt wrong. His chest tightened, but not from pain, from something he didn't recognize. He shook it off. Whether his mission had changed or not, he couldn't let himself get close to someone. Friend, lover, or otherwise. *Not again. Not ever.*

CHAPTER 26
FINN

It didn't take much time for Finn and Connor to take down their camp. As Finn packed the last of the supplies into their bags, he paused. Axel's knife sat on the log where he had been not even an hour before. The fire was almost fully extinguished, a few glowing embers casting just enough light to see the knife glinting through the darkness. Finn grabbed the blade, hearing Axel's voice echo in his head: *Don't dull my knife.* The reality that Axel could have died from this wound set in. And he hated himself for caring about that asshole. He stuffed the knife into his shoe and wondered how Axel managed to walk anywhere with it tucked into the side like that.

Vowing to ignore it, he slung the last bag over his shoulder and looked at Connor, who had been oddly quiet since they left Rainee's. He was looking at the ground, toeing a charred piece of wood.

Finn sighed and walked toward him. "You okay?"

Connor looked up. His eyes were tired, but he nodded slowly. It hurt Finn to see that look on someone so young. Given any other mission, he may have had a couple of years before that look really set in. Between the scenario they were in, and Scott dropping lore like some sort of historian, Connor's naivety had never stood a chance.

"Did..." Connor started uncertainly. "Did they really leave us here?"

Finn's heart broke. He hadn't wanted to think about that anymore, but he dug for the holodisk in his pocket. He held it out in front of him, flicking the switch like he had done multiple times already. NO TETHER, the words flashed, just as he'd expected.

Connor nodded, still processing. Finn clapped him on the shoulder in a semi-comforting way and moved toward the tree line. "There's nothing we can do about that now," he called over his shoulder. "Our only goal is to survive." *Even if that means accepting help from whatever the hell Scott is.*

Connor followed slowly, his silence deafening. Finn focused on the path they were taking. The sound of their boots on the pavement. The blood spatters increasing in size as they neared Rainee's house. He was wondering who was going to clean that up before morning, when Connor's voice startled him out of his thoughts.

"How do you know what you believe in?"

The question caught Finn off guard. No one had ever asked him that. He paused, turning to look at Connor with all the calmness he could muster. "You know—" he said carefully "—because what you believe is the only part of you that sticks around through everything." Finn looked at the sky. It was black and starless under the glow of the streetlights. "It's the only part of you that guides you when you aren't sure what's next or what path to choose." He looked back at Connor. "Why?"

Connor shrugged and looked at Rainee's house. "What if..." He hesitated, like what he was about to say was treasonous to the part of him that was dying. "What if I were to believe that we're the bad guys in this story? Or at least, we were." He gave a small shrug and looked at his boots, like the words might bite him if he gave them too much weight.

Finn nearly choked. He had never voiced that fear to Connor nor Axel, but Connor's innocence allowed him to articulate it perfectly.

"I'd say you're paying attention, then," Finn admitted, not taking his eyes off the younger boy. He was glad that his moral compass wasn't the *only* one going haywire for once.

Connor was silent for the rest of the return trip, his eyes on his feet as they shuffled down the sidewalk. Finn made a mental note to check back in with him later as he opened the door to Rainee's house.

Axel was awake, staring at the ceiling with his jaw clenched tightly. He locked eyes with Finn as they entered, panic setting in as he realized that he and Connor were carrying all their gear.

"What are you…" Axel asked, starting to sit up. It was obvious he wanted to bolt.

"Axel, I swear to gods if you rip open your stitches, I'm letting you die," Scott interrupted, rounding the corner with a mug in his hand. He had a fresh shirt on, one that wasn't covered in Axel's blood.

Axel sank back down on the couch, but his eyes never left Finn. Never stopped screaming "What the hell?"

Scott looked the boys up and down and then gestured to the door on their right. "Basement's ready." He hit a few buttons on a keypad, causing the door to audibly unlock. Opening it, Scott led them downstairs. *A security system?* Finn should have guessed that Scott had certain precautions in place for keeping Rainee safe, but the security system had already been there, meaning that there was something he was keeping down there that he didn't want found. Or maybe didn't want it to escape. Finn pushed the thought aside as they descended the stairs. The basement was finished with tan carpet and matching paint. It seemed homey enough, but Finn felt something was wrong. Scott paused in the middle of the common space and pointed toward a hallway on his left. "Two rooms and the bathroom that way." He pointed behind Finn. "Third room over there." He glanced at the boys' grungy clothes. "I can do your laundry if you need." He paused, looking like nothing more than a dad welcoming guests. He eyed Finn like he was studying him. "If you need anything, I'll try my best."

Finn nodded slowly, calculating. The two smaller rooms were closer to the stairs and the shower, but the bigger room was more private. Not that he really valued privacy at this point. There was nothing to hide anymore. They were all open books, whether they wanted to be or not.

Scott started toward the stairs, stopping midway. "And…remember what I said about my daughter." He raised his mug to his lips and took a sip, his eyes lingering, boring into Finn's soul for a moment before he continued up the stairs.

Connor's eyes were wide, but he didn't speak. Finn had a feeling that Scott wasn't really threatening Connor. The kid was the least of his worries, soldier or not. No, Finn was pretty sure that when Scott had said, *Don't look at my daughter*, he wasn't just talking about trying to kill her. He was a dad after all. A dad who had just opened his house to three unpredictable boys from another realm. He was daring them to try something.

CHAPTER 27
AXEL

Axel had finally managed to sit up without tearing any stitches. He was seething. Finn was lucky he wasn't in top shape, or it would be *his* blood Scott was scrubbing out of the carpet. He watched Scott work. Even his domestic side was scary—precise, ready for anything.

"How are you feeling?" Rainee's voice came from the entryway. He looked over at her, his heart beating a little faster. He shrugged but didn't answer. She made her way around the couch and sat next to him. Not close, but close enough. "You still look like hell."

Scott eyed him from where he was scrubbing the floor. Daring him silently. "I'm fine, really," Axel replied dryly. He cleared his throat and looked away from her. He could smell her perfume now, lavender and other floral notes. It was nice. He shook his head. *Focus.*

"Just like you were fine this morning?" she said, nodding toward his bandages. He stared at her for a moment. No one had ever challenged him like she did. No fear, just pure concern. As much as he wanted to hate the feeling it gave him, he didn't.

He sighed, his gaze flickering over to Scott, who had stopped scrubbing and was busying himself with pretending not to listen, making a point not to meet Axel's eyes. "You're not going to stop, are you?" Axel said finally, meeting Rainee's gaze.

"Not until you're honest with me," she said simply.

Honesty? It'd be easier to just kill her, Axel thought. But something in him ached at the thought of hurting her. He brushed it off and sighed. "I said I'm fine, Rainee." He wasn't giving in to this. Whatever *this* was.

"And—" She glared at him. "—*I* said you're full of shit." Her eyes were locked on him and his heart pounded. What game was she playing? And why did it feel like he was losing?

He looked back at Scott, who was looking at something out the window. *Great support; thanks, Scott.* "It's not the worst wound I've had," he offered. Which was true. He'd had his share of near-death experiences.

She stared at him silently. She knew that Axel was deflecting. Axel knew he was deflecting. He just didn't know how to answer a question like that. He wasn't about to unpack his laundry list of traumatic life events. At least, not tonight. At a minimum, he wanted to be wearing a shirt when he opened up *that* box.

She sighed and stood up, and he thought she might drop the subject. Instead, she paced over to the living room window. Scott had cleaned up his bucket and brush, and moved to the kitchen to put them away, but he was still making enough noise that Axel knew he was there, just around the corner.

"The tough guy act is cute, I'll give you that," Rainee said, finally. Axel's cheeks flushed involuntarily. His heart raced, his nerves getting the best of him. That never happened.

"You think you're funny, don't you?" he threw at her, trying desperately to flip the script. "You think you can get under my skin. Get something out of me." He clasped his hands behind his head and leaned back slightly. "Maybe try that with Connor. I don't work that way." It sounded good, but his heart was still pounding. Hopefully, she couldn't hear that it was about to beat out of his chest.

She nodded but didn't say anything, which made him uneasy. She was reading him like a book. That was *his* trick, and it didn't feel great to have it turned on him.

Scott rounded the corner then, tossing something in Axel's direction. A hoodie and jeans. "You should probably clean up," he remarked. "Just don't get the stitches wet."

Axel nodded, grateful for the interruption. He was waiting for Scott to add something dad-coded. A threat, or a joke. But he didn't, he just blinked wearily at Rainee. Axel's own exhaustion was starting to hit him, more than just physically.

He stood slowly, his wound stinging. His head spun slightly, but he stayed upright. Rainee glanced at him, attempting unsuccessfully to ignore his chiseled physique, but Axel noticed how her gaze lingered. He curled his lip. *Checkmate.*

She rolled her eyes and retreated upstairs, but not without another glance in Axel's direction. One that lingered even longer than the last.

Axel gathered the clothes Scott had thrown at him and moved slowly toward the basement door.

"You handled that well, Romeo," Scott said, breaking the silence.

Axel grabbed the doorknob and pulled the door open. "No idea what you're talking about, sir." His heart was in his throat again. Was this whole family psychic? Or was he that obvious? Either way, he was uncomfortable. Scott just smirked as if he was enjoying it all. *Sadist.*

Axel ignored him and descended the stairs as quickly as his injury would allow. Finn and Connor had already gone to their rooms, so he took a second to get his bearings. He noted four bedrooms and one bathroom. One room was locked, and only a faint whirring could be heard behind it. Of the other three, he could tell by the sound of movement within that Finn and Connor had claimed the two closest to the bathroom, leaving him with the larger main suite. *Huh.* Guess all he had to do was almost die to get a little respect around there.

He investigated the room; it seemed standard enough. A king-sized bed, a dresser, and an armchair decorated an otherwise empty room. Perfect, he didn't need anything fancy. He wondered how many cameras Scott had installed down there.

His knife and backpack were sitting on the bed unassumingly. One would never guess how much those items had been through in the past 48 hours. How much *he'd* been through.

He sighed and walked to the bathroom, locking the door behind him. He kicked his boots off with a thud and peeled the bloodstained jeans off his body. He wasn't sure the jeans would be salvageable. More gauze patches sat on the counter, so he slowly pulled the one covering his stitches away from his skin. The stitch work was immaculate. If he didn't know better, he would assume he'd had it done at a hospital. The area around the stitches was already starting to heal. One dressing change may be all that he would need. He stared at himself in the mirror. Rainee was right. He looked like hell. His eyes were bloodshot and had dark circles under them. He hadn't shaved in a few days, so his stubble was thicker than he liked it to be.

    He turned on the shower and then let the steam envelop him, careful to keep the stitches from getting wet. The last thing he needed was for Scott to have to redo them. He sighed, his muscles relaxing for the first time in days.

CHAPTER 28
SAPPHIRE

Sapphire paced around the now-empty clearing. She'd been following some minor beacon spikes a few towns over, but they hadn't been worth her while. Now the firebugs were gone, and she had very little to track them with. Their holodisk was so unstable that she couldn't even proximity-track it when she tried. It was like they had completely disappeared.

This was not the mission she had planned for. But she couldn't go back to the Water Realm when those Fire Realm degenerates could still be tracking Rainee. They could still hurt her.

"Not your brightest day. Aye, Princess?" an unfamiliar voice said from behind her.

She stiffened without turning, and placed her hand on her blade, listening intently. "I'm not a fan of surprises. So, you'd better start explaining yourself."

A twig snapped behind her and she spun, her knife ready, and she was face-to-face with a cocky-looking man wearing gold cuffs and a white tunic. She didn't recognize him. But she didn't need recognition in order to slit someone's throat.

"As much as I like the idea of knife play, I don't think it'll get you very far," he said steadily, eyeing her with an arrogance that pissed her off more than Axel's.

She glowered at him, pointing her knife at his throat "You talk a lot for someone with a knife to their jugular."

He chuckled and took a step back, quicker than Sapphire could react. "And you don't listen enough for someone who's on a recon mission," he said flippantly.

Sapphire's temper was ready to explode. *Who does this guy think...*

"Man, a few centuries of no realm travel and everyone forgets you, I see."

She paused. *Centuries?*

"The name's Hermes," he threw out casually before adding, "Incredibly charming errand boy of the gods. But you—" He eyed her up and down. "—you can just call me 'charming,' if you'd like."

Sapphire lowered her knife, but not her guard. She'd heard of him. But she didn't expect him to be so... *him*. She didn't fully buy it. Still, if he was a god, he was *technically* an ally. Not that it would stop her from stabbing him just because she could.

Hermes smirked. "I'll take your silence as professed adoration."

Sapphire rolled her eyes. *Insufferable.*

"Are you going to tell me why you're here or just flirt with me unsuccessfully all night?" she growled out, not intimidated by him in the least.

He feigned offense, his hand on his chest. "I'll have you know, people used to beg to have council with me." He took another step back, turning like he intended to leave. "I don't give messages to ungrateful princesses." He peeked back over his shoulder. "Even if they are pretty."

Sapphire shifted her stance, crossed her arms, and waited. She'd witnessed his game before, and she wasn't about to play it. "Fine, go. I don't need an ally that withholds information in the name of flirting." He paused, and she held her ground. "I'm sure whoever sent you is well-aware of how important your ego is," she added. One last blow. Divine or not, she couldn't stand him.

He let out a little laugh as he turned back around. "I like you," he said. He took a seat on one of the logs near the fire pit, and the moonlight glistened off his cheekbones like he was made of glitter. "Anyways—" He carried on like he was switching the topic from work to school, not flirting to war communication. "—about the descendant you're watching."

"Rainee," Sapphire supplied.

Hermes waved her off like names weren't really his thing. "Yeah, the girl." He cleared his throat. "She's gotten…acquainted…with those hot-headed assassins. But…" He paused for effect. Sapphire rolled her eyes again. He continued, a little frustrated with her lack of cooperation, "The pantheon has decided they're no longer your concern."

"Not my concern? They're here to kill her!" she whispered fiercely, looking at him like he had lost his mind.

He smirked again. She was going to slit her own throat if this kept up. "Let's just say that the pantheon has…taken matters into their own hands." He smiled. "We are pretty good at—" He looked at the sky, searching for the right words. "—blurring the lines. Whether of knowledge or allegiance, we aren't picky."

The pieces were starting to fit together. The broken holodisk. The corrupted mission files. Her holodisk picking up false beacon signals. "The gods are interfering with the mission?" Her eyes narrowed. "But why?"

He shrugged. "All in due time. But, as for your missing targets, I'd check your spark's house. I hear they've gotten pretty *close* with her father." He stood up and dusted off his tunic, then disappeared without so much as a puff of smoke.

Sapphire stood there for a moment, processing what she had just learned. If the pantheon was already aware of what was playing out in the human realm, she was way out of her depth. Still, what did they want with three Fire Realm rejects?

Hopefully they want them dead, she thought. But she knew it was wishful thinking. If they were still alive with Olympus breathing down their necks, there had to be a plan in place. And it far outweighed anything she could conjure up herself.

CHAPTER 29
SYREN

The headaches had been getting worse over the last few days, and Syren couldn't remember if he'd even gotten out of bed. Every time that he gained consciousness, it felt like he was swiftly forced back into the void. This was the first time since the mission review that he'd been fully awake for longer than a few minutes.

He stood in front of the mirror on his bedroom door, staring at himself. Or, he thought it was himself. He looked different every time he checked. It was the eyes. Hollow pools of obsidian that didn't match the rest of him. How long had they been like that?

He kept thinking about the girl...Rainee. Her father had been a frequent guest in the Fire Realm when Syren was a teenager. His brother, Kai, and Scott Bennett had been fast friends. Scott had stopped coming around after the Line Severance Decree and Syren had never understood why. He had never asked, either. He had had far too many things to worry about back then, with Kai's disappearance and all.

A torrent of pain shot through Syren's head. <Scott Bennett is a traitor. To me. To the Fire Realm. To peace.> The thoughts echoed in his brain and surrounded him like a fog. It wasn't his voice. But then again, it never was anymore.

Syren stumbled forward, steadying himself on the desk beside the door. As he looked up, his body shaking furiously, he realized it wasn't *his* face looking back at him. It was Kai's. <Be silent, Little Brother,> his voice echoed. Syren's vision blurred, and the darkness consumed him.

CHAPTER 30
SCOTT

Scott sat in the kitchen, sipping a cup of coffee as if it was going to fix the dumpster fire surrounding him. He stared out the glass sliding door into the dark backyard, his mind somewhere else. Sometime else.

He had been thinking about Kai since his first chat with the boys. The situation itself was odd, but it felt like there was more than that. Like he'd forgotten to turn the stove off, but twenty years ago. The last time he had spoken to Kai, he had tried to convince him not to go to the Outer Isles. Kai hadn't known that Scott's wife was pregnant at the time. He didn't know that the decree he was fighting for could get Scott's family killed.

Scott had gone to the Fire Realm to try to reason with him. They had been friends for years by that point, and they had always had mutual respect for each other. But Kai hadn't been in the mood to listen. When Scott had revealed the pregnancy, Kai had spat in his face and called him a traitor for daring to produce a demigod child. He had declared his unborn child a threat to the Fire Realm, and had Scott escorted back to Earth. Nothing else was said, despite Scott's protest that they could negotiate.

Scott would be lying if he said that he hadn't reacted when he heard that Kai didn't return from the Isles. He might have even cried. He never got a chance to make the amends that he wanted to. The decree was passed a few weeks after Kai disappeared. His influence was unnecessary; his death was forgotten as if it were meaningless. That was the part that hurt the most.

"Fucking bastard," Scott murmured, sipping his coffee again. Tears stung his eyes, but he didn't let them fall. This was his fourth cup. It was well past three a.m., but sleep was the last thing on his mind. He'd checked on Rainee multiple times, just to make sure she was still there, still breathing. She was. Thank gods she was.

  The basement door creaked. He hadn't set the alarm yet because he knew that he'd be awake. Scott flew to his feet, ready to pounce on whichever boy it was.

  I told them to…

  But, when he saw it was Connor peeking around the corner, he paused.

  "Need something?" Scott asked, trying to keep his voice from shaking.

  It was obvious Connor hadn't slept; it was the circles under his eyes that betrayed him. He shook his head. "I…" he started but then closed his mouth. Scott softened a little. He was reminded that Connor was still just a kid. Probably younger than Rainee, even. Connor looked up at Scott. "I could hear you moving around. I thought maybe…" He sighed, like his words sounded strange to him. "… maybe if we both couldn't sleep, we could at least…"

  Scott smiled and went to grab another coffee mug. "Sure, kid," he said, already pouring them both a cup. "You like coffee?"

  Connor visibly brightened and nodded. He took the mug from Scott and stared at the counter for a minute. Scott could tell he had a lot on his mind, but he wasn't going to pry where it wasn't his place. So, he stood in silence and waited for Connor to offer the first words: a verbal consent to open up a bit more.

  Connor looked up after a few minutes, still quiet, but he seemed to be getting closer. Scott sipped his coffee. Finally, Connor asked, "Have you ever believed something was one way, then you learn that it's actually so much worse than you could have thought?"

  The question felt like a gut punch. Scott suddenly craved something stronger than coffee. Instead, he set the mug down on the counter and looked into Connor's eyes. He was too young for this, and that ache lingered in the air.

  "Yes. More than once," Scott admitted quietly.

  Connor nodded in that slow, deliberate way Scott had noticed him doing when he was thinking. Then he asked, "How do you handle it?" His tone suggested he was searching for something more than an answer to a question, but rather anything to hold on to. To keep him grounded while he spiraled.

Scott sighed. That was a good question. One that even he had trouble fully answering. "You don't, at first," he offered. Connor's expression shifted slightly, worried. Scott continued, "It handles you for a while. Swirls around in your head until you think you'll go crazy if you have to think about it anymore. Then—" He met Connor's eyes again, making sure he heard the last part. "—you wake up one day and realize that it's not worth worrying about anymore. You can't change the facts, only how you see them."

Scott picked up his coffee and took a sip. He was going to need some worn-out robes and more gray in his beard if he was going to play dad-mentor. He'd gone from one kid to four in a matter of hours, and nothing could have prepared him for that adjustment.

Still, it felt right. Like a role he was born to play. The look on Connor's face was all the gratification he needed. He looked at peace for the first time since Scott had met him. Scott smiled behind his mug and tried to hide how much he was starting to like the kid.

"You should get some sleep now," Scott offered, placing his own coffee mug in the sink to deal with later. "I don't know what happens next, but I know that we're both going to need rest for whatever it is."

Connor nodded, pushing his half-full mug toward Scott before starting toward the basement. Before he disappeared, he turned to look at Scott. "Thanks. I…I needed that," Connor said softly.

Scott nodded and watched Connor descend the stairway, wondering how he was going to manage to keep all of them alive at once. He sighed. *That's a "morning Scott" problem.*

He washed the mugs in the sink, his mind racing. He needed to check the beacons again before he went to sleep for the night, but he was worried that checking them would mean getting no sleep at all.

Pushing his concern aside, he crept downstairs, avoiding the step that creaked. He didn't need any of the boys snooping around. Not yet. The lights in the main part of the basement were off, and everything was quiet. Perfect.

He went to the one room in the basement that he always kept locked, and produced a small key from his pocket. He slipped inside, leaving the lights off until the door was closed and latched behind him.

He flicked on the light, the room in front of him coming to life. A large mainframe computer stared back at him. The room was covered in database towers and some realm-based tech that ensured all realm records could be accessed if needed.

His hands moved over the keyboard as if it were second nature, pulling up the beacon pings from the last three days. The first one he had already seen; it had alerted him to the boys' presence:

[Ping 234354. 05052025. Origin: Fire Realm.]

Then, a second one that he had missed, populated:

[Ping 234355. 05062025. Origin: Water Realm.]

He stiffened. The Water Realm had also sent spies, which meant this was getting out of hand faster than he had anticipated. This was no longer a one-off assassination attempt. This was war espionage, and Rainee was right in the middle of it.

Three more pings hit the mainframe before it displayed the end code.

[Ping 234356. 05062025. Origin: Earth.]
[Ping 234357. 05072025. Origin: unknown.]
[Ping 234358. 05072025. Origin: unknown.]

The first one, he was pretty sure, was Rainee's power surge when the kitchen lights had exploded. The other two were more concerning: unknown origins indicated either a system malfunction or some kind of higher interference. He'd only seen an unknown origin once before, right after the Line Severance Decree was signed, and he didn't like the odds that this was anything but a similar case.

He sighed and kicked the box under the console. God-binding chains rattled back at him, bringing him a little comfort. He could still use them if he had to.

CHAPTER 31
RAINEE

Rainee stared at the ceiling, her thoughts running wild. Another dream had stirred her. It was the same as the first one, but it had warned her too late. The assassins were in the house, and her father was patching their wound for them. She checked her phone: 5:17 a.m. Two minutes since she had last checked. Why did time feel like it had stalled suddenly?

    She'd heard her dad finally shuffle to bed about an hour earlier, and she was concerned that all of this might have been too much for him. He had checked on her at least three times while she pretended to sleep. He had peered into the bedroom, paused for a few seconds, then left. He was not okay.

    She sat up, and the lamp on her bedside table flickered. She didn't think she'd ever get used to the energy transfers that occurred whenever she moved. It was like she was a walking electrical conductor. She forced herself out of bed and walked to the mirror across the room. The necklace hung around her neck quietly, unassuming. That didn't stop it from making her feel uneasy. She wished she could go back. Leave the necklace on the counter, let her dad hide it away. But she couldn't. And now it was practically fused to her skin.

    Her hair was a mess, and her eyes were puffy from what little sleep she'd gotten, and her pajamas hung off her in a way that made her look slimmer than she was. It was frightening, like looking at a ghost. She sighed and yanked the door open, deciding that she just needed a sip of water and more sleep.

    As she made her way downstairs, she realized that someone else was up. The sounds of someone clumsily searching through unfamiliar cabinets were unmistakable. She rounded the corner slowly, trying to stay quiet and saw Finn with all the cabinets behind him open and a single glass in his hand.

"You know, I could have helped you find that," she said. He jumped, nearly dropping the glass.

He looked up at her with tousled hair, wearing one of her dad's old painting shirts tucked halfway into a pair of sweatpants that also probably belonged to her dad.

"I didn't want to wake anyone. Just—" He paused, staring at the glass in his hand a little too hard. "—thirsty, I guess." His voice was low, barely audible. She couldn't help but think he looked more handsome this way. It was endearing to see a crack in his usual stoic demeanor.

She smiled softly and crossed the kitchen, closing the open cabinets and grabbing a glass for herself. "You shouldn't drink the tap water, by the way," she threw over her shoulder as she filled her glass with filtered water from the refrigerator. "Who knows what they're putting in the public drinking water these days." She paused and wondered if forever chemicals affected the Flamease.

He eyed her, seemingly amused by her concern for his welfare. "You know, it can't be the worst water I've had to drink." He downed the rest of his glass and set it on the counter. "So..." He turned to face her, leaning casually on the kitchen counter.

She shrugged. "So?"

It was obvious he had something to say, but he was tiptoeing around it with whatever fake normalcy he could conjure. She sipped her water, but his eyes never left her.

"If you're going to apologize, don't bother," she said between sips, a small smirk on her face. "I'm not sure what the etiquette is surrounding assassination plans, but I think you standing in my kitchen in my dad's old clothes makes up for most of it." She winked.

He gave her a genuine smile. "You know it was never personal, right?" he said, glancing at her playfully. "Orders are orders." He said it like he was trying to convince himself.

"And your orders...they included pulling me out of traffic the day we met?" she asked. She already knew the answer, but enjoyed watching him fumble over his words—it was endearing. She took another slow sip of water, awaiting his response.

He chuckled slightly, looking at the floor as he shook his head. "No." He looked up at her, his eyes soft. "That was not in the plan."

She leaned back on the opposite side of the counter.

"Then, what made you do it?" she teased. "Seems very anti-assassin of you."

He tilted his head up slightly, obviously contemplating disclosing the truth versus taking an easy out. But he wasn't Axel. He looked at her again and said, "I wanted to."

She stayed silent, watching him, wanting him to continue sharing his thoughts.

"I saw the car and believed for a second that my job had been done for me. But then, I grabbed you." He looked away again. "It was all instincts...the wrong ones. But still instincts."

She raised her eyebrows, nodding slowly. "The *wrong* instinct, huh?" She knew he didn't mean it like that, that it was all in the context of his orders, but it still stung a little.

"I wouldn't..." he started, looking at her, wide-eyed, trying to backtrack. "I wouldn't say that now. But...at that time..."

Rainee stared at him. "Well, glad you made that mistake. Hopefully, you don't let it eat you alive," she said flippantly. The words felt like poison in her mouth. She moved away from him, back toward the stairs.

He caught her wrist. "It's not like that anymore. I..." He paused, like he might be saying too much. "I'm glad I did it," he said finally. His voice was quiet, resigned. Like he'd just admitted this to himself as the words tumbled out of his mouth.

She stared into his eyes for what felt like hours, then ripped her arm away. "Great. Glad we settled that," she hissed before storming back upstairs.

His initial commentary echoed in her head, her chest aching. She still wasn't sure why it had stung so bad. But for her survival to be referred to as the wrong instinct, it hurt. Especially coming from the one who had saved her.

CHAPTER 32
FINN

Finn stood in the kitchen; his arm still outstretched where he'd grabbed her wrist. He wasn't quite sure what he'd done wrong, other than let his guard down. But now she was mad at him. Or hurt by him. Or both. And, for some reason, that felt like a stake to the heart.

The wrong instinct? Dumbass. Who says something like that? Him, apparently. But only because he didn't know how else to say, "I saw you and knew I was willing to lose everything again, as long as I didn't have to watch you get hurt."

That sounded stupid anyway. He was an assassin. He was *supposed* to hurt her. That was the whole point. So why did the thought of hurting her feel like betraying every single part of him except for the mission assigned to him?

Still sulking, he retreated to the basement, only to find Axel awake, sprawled on the couch in the common room, still shirtless, flipping through a sports magazine.

"You kiss her yet?" Axel didn't look up. "Or are you waiting until after breakfast?"

Finn couldn't have rolled his eyes harder if he tried. But a part of him was glad Axel was up and moving. Alive. He preferred him this way. The extent of his true dick-ish charm was hard to capture in memories.

Finn flopped down in the chair across from Axel and sighed. He wasn't sure how much Axel had overheard, but knew that it was probably enough for him to get the wrong idea. "One conversation with her and I've already managed to piss her off."

Axel finally looked up. "Yeah, you do that sometimes." Finn glared at him. He hated how casual he looked. Axel grinned as if he'd hit every nerve he meant to. He was relaxing on the couch, wearing baggy jeans that hung off his hips. His syndicate tattoo shone in the light. It was a tattoo that Finn had seen several times during raids. He wasn't sure of its significance, but he knew that all the other big syndicate players had them too. It was a flame, drawn in a tribal swirl pattern that wrapped from Axel's right pec to his shoulder blade. Finn could tell there had been attempts to remove it, by the burn scars rippling the skin around the edges of it. Probably some sort of military reform punishment due to Axel mouthing off.

"Do you ever say anything helpful?" Finn said pointedly. "Or do you live for making things more difficult?"

Axel sat up, tossed the magazine back onto the coffee table, and picked up another one before replying, "Helpful is boring." He opened a new magazine, *Business Insider*. "You should be thanking me for keeping this mission interesting."

"So, *no* then?" Finn clapped back. It came across as annoyed, but Finn's smile betrayed him.

Axel let out a small chuckle. "No, not even once." He flipped through the magazine and then tossed it onto the table. He lay back on the couch, staring at the ceiling.

Finn didn't think Axel was going to add anything more to the conversation, but then he sighed. "You get used to pissing people off, don't worry."

Finn raised an eyebrow. He couldn't remember a time when Axel had ever been uncomfortable pissing people off. Dissonance was practically his middle name.

Finn studied him for a moment. He held himself with a cocky indifference that was almost admirable, but that was just surface-level. Finn always knew what lay under the surface. Axel was a wounded animal who kept everything but sarcasm and combat at arm's length. In a way, Finn's stoicism served the same purpose. Keep the feelings out and follow orders. It was basic survival instinct. Instinct that Finn had lost, apparently.

"If you don't stop staring at me like that, *I'm* going to kiss you." Axel said, propping himself on his arms and glaring at Finn. "And neither of us wants that, trust me."

Finn laughed. Axel shrugged, but something told Finn that he would make good on that threat if called for. From what he knew of Axel, he wasn't picky. Still, it *had* startled Finn out of his head, which was probably Axel's goal.

"Who are we kissing?" Connor's voice came from the hallway. Finn turned to see the younger boy rubbing the sleep from his eyes, his auburn hair wild.

Axel smirked, and Finn knew he was going to say something unhinged. "You volunteering, kid?"

Connor's eyes widened. "W-what?"

Finn sighed, a grin tugging at his mouth. *Absolute chaos.* He could tell Connor was about to become a stuttering mess if he didn't say something, so he stepped in.

"Alright," he said, getting to his feet. "That's enough before I have to explain to Scott what the hell just happened here."

Axel cradled his head in his hands and kicked his feet up on the coffee table with a smile that only a menace of his caliber could give. Connor looked like he was about to die of embarrassment, and suddenly, the world didn't feel quite as heavy. Even if this mission had gone completely sideways, at least they could joke about it.

CHAPTER 33
RAINEE

Instead of sleeping, Rainee spent the next two hours pacing her room. Finn's words echoed in her mind, despite her trying to push them aside. She reasoned that he hadn't meant it the way it felt. But she couldn't let it go.
Wrong instinct.
Maybe it was because, even for a second, she thought that him saving her meant something. But that was stupid. They had been strangers in that moment; why would it have meant anything beyond a basic impulse?
She was starting to realize she didn't really know him, or any of them, that well. It had only been three days, and all they had done was stalk her…and move into her basement. She didn't know anything about the Fire Realm either. Were any of them even safe? Axel seemed to have already decided that he wasn't. Connor was just a kid, so he had potential to be harmless. And Finn. She didn't know where Finn fit into that scale. He seemed to be the leader, but he always seemed so…conflicted. Like he was overthinking every step, word, and movement.
She took a shaky breath to ground herself. Whether they were safe or not, they were there. In her home. Her father had invited them in and seemed to trust them. Or maybe he just wasn't scared of them.
That was the other thing. Who was *he?* Mr. I-traveled-across-realms. Casually. As if that made perfect sense. Was she just supposed to accept that? Was there more to tell? Was he even actually an accountant?

She shook her head. That was a dilemma for another day. She hadn't noticed the lights dimming around her until they flickered back to normal. Yeah, there was no way she was going to get used to that. The necklace pulsed, and she sighed. *Can we just go back to Monday?* When she was still just Rainee. Just trying to graduate. Back when Earth was the only realm on her radar and she wasn't the center of some life-altering war plot.

That was too much to ask, of course. All she could do now was get dressed and try to figure out how to live with her new housemates.

She pulled on a hoodie and a pair of jeans, then slipped downstairs. She could already hear her dad in the kitchen, talking to one of the boys while the sizzling of bacon acted as white noise.

She rounded the corner and saw her dad, still in his pajamas, cooking what looked like a whole pig's worth of bacon. Did he go to the store? Or buy a pig farm?

Connor was seated at the table, a plate full of bacon in front of him. He looked up when she entered.

"Morning," she murmured, trying to process the scene. Connor was wearing one of her dad's T-shirts, which looked huge on him, and a pair of shorts with the waistband rolled down. He wasn't scrawny, even though he was obviously just a kid; but he *was* considerably smaller than her six-foot-five father.

Scott turned and placed another plate of bacon on the counter, looking at her. "If you want bacon, you'd better get it before the other two get upstairs." He motioned to the plate. "The Flamease are known for insatiable carnivorous appetites, and I *only* have bacon right now." He smiled like that was a completely normal thing to say at seven o'clock in the morning.

Not only were there assassins (former assassins?) living in her house, but they were also strict carnivores. *Because, why not?*

She just nodded. What else was she supposed to say to that? She grabbed a plate, some toast, and a few pieces of bacon, then sat down next to Connor, who seemed too happy for someone whose life had just been turned upside down. She would know.

Before he could say anything to her, Axel sauntered around the corner. Shirtless, with loose-fitting jeans slung low on his hips and hair that looked too perfectly messed up to be bedhead. He still had a bandage on his abdomen, but he looked a lot less like a corpse than he had the last time they'd talked.

"Axel," Scott said, hardly looking up from his third pan of bacon. "I gave you a shirt to wear, didn't I?"

Axel didn't answer right away, just reached over the counter and snatched a piece of bacon from the plate. "There was one," he said, taking a bite, "Thought it would be better to let the injury breathe a bit." He smirked playfully.

Scott ignored him, but Rainee could see that her dad's face was tired. Too tired to fight with a Fire Realm reject about wearing clothing to the breakfast table.

Axel grabbed another handful of bacon—no plate—and turned to the table where Rainee and Connor were sitting. Rainee looked away quickly like she hadn't just been staring at his abs and his biceps and that tattoo…*Damn him!*

He grinned at her. Of course, he had caught her staring. And, of course, he was enjoying it. "Well, good morning. No witty greetings today, static?" He took a bite of bacon as he eyed her.

She rolled her eyes. "'Static?' How original."

He didn't respond, just grinned mischievously. He had no business being this attractive *and* this insufferable. She opened her mouth to say something else, but Finn flew around the corner, interrupting her.

"We have a problem," he said, throwing a silver disk down on the table. It flicked on, revealing pictures of all of them, stamped with the words TARGET, ELIMINATE.

Rainee looked at the disk, then at all of their faces. "What is that? What does it mean?"

Connor was the first to speak. "Our holodisk…with all the mission orders on it."

"Those stamps weren't on our files last night," Axel added, his face unreadable.

Finn shook his hand, grabbing the disk. "I received the communication this morning." He shifted uneasily as he locked eyes with Rainee. "They've tagged us as: 'Kill on sight.'"

"We're fugitives…" Connor said quietly, still processing.

The room felt heavy. She wasn't sure what this meant, other than they were all in danger now.

She looked at her dad for help, but his expression was grim. "I thought you said communications were jammed?" Scott asked, pausing his bacon-cooking relay for a moment.

Finn shook his head. "I tried sending comms back to them, multiple times. The disk crashed or was unresponsive every time." He looked at Scott wearily. "Then, with the portal tether being broken, I thought for sure…" He paced back and forth, his hand tangled in his hair.

Scott sighed and wiped his hands on the towel tucked into his waistband. "That's what I was afraid you'd say." They all looked at him, waiting for him to continue. "I don't think this is a tech glitch. This is purposeful."

They all froze, the tension in the air thick. No one spoke, but they all seemed to agree: this changed everything.

CHAPTER 34
SYREN

The sky was dark with smoke, but Syren pretended not to notice. The riots had gotten out of control of late, and without a proper military detail to snuff them out, they seemed to consume more and more of the city. He knew the small guard battalions that remained wouldn't be able to hold them back forever.

They had all but given up on getting their troops back from the Water Realm. Aydron had made it clear that there was a price to pay for the stunt they had tried to pull.

The Earth mission had gone silent, with no communication from the assassins in two days, and now their tether was severed. <We warned them,> Kai's voice echoed in his head.

Syren's head throbbed. "Can you... give me a few peaceful moments. For once?"

He could hear Kai chuckle, but the fog in his brain dissipated for the time being. A holodisk beeped on the table. StoneElf had left it with him to review the Earth files again. The girl was the target, without a doubt. He sighed and moved to the table, scooping the disk up like it was nothing.

A surveillance picture flashed across the hologram. It showed *his* assassins gathered in a house, talking with none other than *Scott Bennett*. Something inside Syren surged, and the fog returned.

<Traitors, all of them.>

Syren fought the fog back, determined not to let Kai take control again. A piercing pain hit his temple, making him stumble backwards. Steadying himself on the arm of the throne, he growled,

"Kai, you have to stop this." Another jolt of pain hit him; he cried out. The fog was getting thicker. "Why are we doing this? She hasn't done anything wrong." He gasped.

    <She's the key to the pantheon. Our only hope is to end this war before it starts.> Kai's voice felt like it echoed in the throne room, but Syren was sure it was just echoing off the walls of his skull. Before he could stop himself, he was clicking buttons on the holodisk, sending orders.

    "Kai...please," he pleaded through gritted teeth. It was too late. He felt his eyes glassing over as the screen flashed with the men's personal files, each marked with the words, TARGET: ELIMINATE.

    "Kai...no...Those are our men." Syren tried to reason. He was laying on the warm lava-imbued tile, his vision blurring as he fought to stay conscious.

    <Their act of treason will not go unpunished.>

    Syren tried to protest, but his body was no longer cooperating. He felt the fog consume him.

CHAPTER 35
SAPPHIRE

The recall orders had come early that morning, directly from the throne room. Sapphire wondered if her father knew something was wrong with the mission or if he was just tired of waiting for her. He wasn't known for being patient, especially when it involved his daughter. Or whatever she was to him.

She prepped the holodisk to summon the portal, her backpack slung over one shoulder. The clearing was empty, and a faint mist blanketed the area. Under other circumstances, she probably would have found the atmosphere peaceful.

She typed in the last tether code, something that the Water Realm had implemented to limit unauthorized portal jumpers without completely severing their tether while not in use, then flicked the switch to call the portal.

The device whirred, and a blue-green portal materialized in front of her. She waited, knowing that the destination had to load before she could use it. One...two...She counted the seconds. Finally, the portal rippled, and the portal room of the Water Realm could be seen on the other side.

She exhaled heavily. *Here goes everything.*

She stepped through the portal, the whirring consuming her senses until she crossed the threshold. The air felt lighter on the other side, less dry.

"Welcome back, Princess," said a guard on her left. "Your father waits for you in the throne room." *Of course he does.*

She nodded; no other words were needed. Neither guard asked about the men she had taken with her to Earth. They already had their assumptions.

A river flowed through the portal room, connecting the rest of the palace through intricate canals. Spritans preferred to spend their non-diplomatic time in water, something that they inherited from their water sprite ancestors. Instead of stepping into the water, which would have been a faster way to get to the inevitable meeting with her father, she walked beside the river, studying the currents, observing the occasional servant bustling just under the surface and the quiet babble it produced.

Due to water being a large part of Spritan culture and travel, they had perfected water-repellant clothing and accessories that allowed for efficient water travel. She wasn't sure how it worked; she just knew that she could travel through the river to the throne room if she *wanted* to. But she was in no hurry.

As the hallway started to narrow toward the lapis-gilded doors at the end of the corridor, she could already feel her heart in her throat. Her father's voice carried into the hallway.

"How dare they!" she heard him yell, and could hear the indistinct hum of his strategists trying to calm him down, but she couldn't make out the exact words.

She took a deep breath and rapped on the door.

"Enter!" the king growled. His anger permeated the air as she pushed the door open and slipped inside. She was the picture of stealth and grace, as always. There was no room for anything less in her father's presence.

Aydron SwiftStream was perched on his throne, head in one hand, a document in the other. He looked like he hadn't slept in years. Maybe he hadn't; Sapphire hadn't paid much attention to his personal life. Not that he'd give her that luxury, even if she wanted it.

He looked up, just enough for his crystal eyes to shoot daggers at her. *Lovely to see you, too, father.*

"You're alone," he observed, looking around her. "Did I not send you with guards?"

Yeah, incompetent ones, she thought. But she bowed slightly to him anyway and responded, "There were some complications."

"Define 'complications'," he spat, his voice unwavering. This was it. She had to confess that three fur-brained firebugs had taken out two of their best-trained guards.

The strategists gathered near the throne had all fallen silent, their eyes locked on her. Tobias stood near the window that overlooked the ocean outside the palace, hardly listening. Oh, how she wished she could strangle him.

"They left me, Father," she said, her tone shifting to a small whine. She thought, maybe if she could tug at what paternal instinct might reside in him, she could get out of this. "And those... those firebugs *killed* them."

The king's face remained unchanged. "You expect me to believe that *my* guard detail left the princess unattended, without explicit instruction to do so?" He looked at her with all the weight of a disapproving father in his eyes. "Do I look that gullible, Sapphire?"

She shrugged, not looking at him. "Well, they aren't here, are they?" she offered. She had used up all the cards in here hand. Her father was the only one who had ever run through all her tricks so quickly. She hated that.

He practically rolled his eyes, but his composure remained intact. He sighed and waved the strategists away, before getting to his feet. He approached her with Tobias on his tail like a lost puppy.

"Walk with me, Sapphire," he said, motioning toward the corridor. "We have much to discuss."

She nodded, watching him. The lump was still in her throat. Did he know that the gods were now involved? Is he the one who contacted them? She walked beside him as they wound through long hallways. Where was he taking her?

"As you are well-aware—" he said after a few corridors of silence. He opened the door to the dungeon and started to descend the stairway, much to Sapphire's surprise. She couldn't remember him ever personally or willingly entering the dungeon. "—there was a blatant attack made on our mage quarters last week. We've captured and detained the Fire Realm battalions that were responsible."

The noise from the dungeon was horribly loud. Screams, shuffling feet, and clanking chains. No doubt the prisoners were being treated with the same amount of respect that the Water Realm had been giving the Fire Realm for centuries. *None.*

Her father knocked on the iron door in front of them, a coded knock that was returned from the other side, before the door slid open. He led her and Tobias into a room lined with bars on either side. Sapphire could see hundreds of prisoners, all wearing Fire Realm tunics, filling the dungeon. They looked like corpses. All of them.

"Syren has requested his men back," the king continued, startling Sapphire. He paused to look at her, likely gauging her reaction.

"Did he really think it would be that easy?" Tobias spoke up. She fought the urge to roll her eyes. He was a carbon copy of their father. *Disgusting.*

Aydron smiled, a crooked half-smile that made his eyes darken. "Whether he thought so or not, I can assure you I have far too many plans for his men to just…give them back." He looked at Sapphire again; she was staring into one of the cells where a Fire Realm soldier was muzzled like a dog, his arms locked above him in cuffs. He couldn't have been more than fifteen. His eyes silently pleaded with her, but he didn't move. Her stomach turned. Fire Realm or not, she wasn't a fan of torture without a purpose, and this was plain cruelty.

"He was so kind to gift them to me, after all," he added, continuing down the hallway toward another wooden door.

She followed him reluctantly, each step feeling like she was wearing lead bricks on her feet. She tried not to make eye contact with any of the other soldiers, each of them shackled by either their legs or arms, each of them wearing a muzzle.

The sound of the wooden door scraping against the stone floor made her raise her gaze. Her father was standing there, looking at her expectantly. "You look tense," he noted. He didn't need to say anything else. She felt his judgment like an ice pick to the eye. Cold, pointed. He was testing her.

"Just tired, Father," she said. It wasn't a lie; she just didn't specify what she was tired of.

He smirked, then led them into next room. It was open, damp, and reeked of chemicals. In the center of the room sat a singular soldier, older than the others in the prison. His jaw was clenched tightly, his face bloodied and bruised. His eyes were closed as they approached, but he opened them slowly at the sound of footsteps. Sapphire noticed immediately that they weren't normal eyes. They looked like snake eyes—diamond-shaped and glowing yellow. Then the realization hit her: they were beating the common form out of him. Reducing him to nothing but Flamease trash.

She'd heard of tactics like this before, but had never witnessed it. It was only possible when a certain part of the form, near the head, got damaged. That was why soldiers from other realms always wore proper helmets, unless they were undercover...or being tortured. The Spritans were lucky—they were natural shapeshifters and didn't have to rely on shoddy tech to keep their common form. It also allowed them to change their appearance at will.

Reverting to true form was a Divisional crime that was punishable by death. It was in direct violation of the Common Form Decree that had been signed after the war. Everyone knew that. Forcing a prisoner into their true form would give a viable reason to put them to death with only a minimal trial. Hence, the half-basilisk, half-human staring at her.

The Flamease man smirked, his snake eyes flickering. "Aydron, so nice to see you again," he hissed, a forked tongue barely visible as he spoke. How did he know her father well enough to call him by his first name? His eyes flicked toward her and Tobias, and he smiled coldly. "These your kids?" He looked her up and down. "Beautiful."

Without warning, her father lashed out, landing a blow to the soldier's jaw. The soldier laughed. *Laughed.*

"Captain GildedFoot." Her father greeted the man like he hadn't just hit him hard enough to shatter his skull. "Care to explain to my guests how you landed in this position?"

The soldier raised his head, blood dripping from his nose, his common form slowly losing more of its integrity the longer she looked at him.

"You mean you haven't told them?" the man—GildedFoot—said, looking at Aydron in fake astonishment. "You haven't told them how you trapped us here? Forced us to admit to more crimes than we actually committed?" He looked back at Sapphire, his eyes wide. "Beat my men into their Flamease forms just so you could slit their throats in front of the entire battalion."

He scoffed. "I'm surprised you didn't mention it." His voice was dripping in malice.

Aydron struck him again, nearly sending the chair toppling backwards. "*You* invaded *my* realm," Aydron snarled, placing his hands on either arm of the chair and leaning into GildedFoot's face. "You targeted *my* family." Aydron's voice dropped low, deadly. "Your men *killed* my *wife.*"

Sapphire's heart stopped. Tears pricked her eyes. The memory of her mother's death nearly knocked the wind out of her chest. She cleared her throat lightly, blinking the tears away. Sapphire had tried not to think about it; she had too much to do.

GildedFoot smirked again, looking at the ground. "No, my men didn't do that," he whispered, locking eyes with her father. "*I did.*" His forked tongue flicked menacingly. "And I'd do it again and *again*. Just to piss you off."

Aydron let out a cry, something between anger and grief, and punched the man again. GildedFoot didn't flinch, just smiled a toothy, bloodstained smile. As if he took pleasure from flirting with death.

"Now." Her father's voice caught her attention. She looked over at him; he was extending a gold-handled blade to her and a pair of chains to Tobias. "You've heard his confession. I need you to finish this." He locked eyes with Tobias. "Avenge your mother." Then he said to Sapphire, "Prove how deep your loyalty runs."

Shaking, Sapphire took the blade. She glanced over at Tobias, who seemed shaken as well, for once. *Where's Daddy's perfect prince now?* He took the chains from Aydron and turned to the still-smiling Flamease man.

Sapphire twirled the blade between her fingers, assessing her next move. Part of her wanted to torture him. Make him feel every ounce of hurt that he caused. But the other part of her didn't want to be there at all. She hadn't asked for this.

She met Tobias's eyes, and he nodded, his expression turning cold. She watched as he hooked the chains around GildedFoot's neck and yanked him backwards.

The chair crashed to the floor, breaking under the added weight of the soldier's body. Tobias didn't react, he just looked at Sapphire expectantly, daring her to use the blade in her hands.

She approached, hyperaware of her father's eyes on her. She knelt down beside GildedFoot and raised her blade, calculating her next move.

"You look just like her, Princess," GildedFoot choked out, his eyes hungry. All notions of torturing him dissipated and she jammed the knife into his right eye, directly in the center of the diamond. He gasped, still alive. She yanked the blade out and slid it across his neck, listening to the rest of the life drain from his body with a choked gurgle.

She stood slowly, his blood beading on her shirt. She wished that her skin had the same technology. She was covered in blood up to her elbows, and she could feel the droplets on her face drying already.

She looked at Tobias; his face was grim. He was staring at her in fear. *Good. He should be scared.*

Her father clapped slowly, stepping forward. "Bravo, my dear," he said, pride dripping in every word. "Beautifully executed." He looked over at Tobias. "You could use some training."

Tobias looked shell-shocked, which Sapphire couldn't help but enjoy. Finally, he'd done something her father had deemed unworthy. And she…she was in the spotlight.

***

Sapphire stood in the waterfall shower in her sleeping quarters, her hands still shaking. Surprisingly, it wasn't GildedFoot that she was thinking about. He was a Flamease pig of the worst variety. No, it was the young soldier she had made eye contact with in the main dungeon. His fear-ridden eyes were burned into her brain.

A kid entangled in a war that he didn't start, but he was paying for. That hardly seemed fair. She kept comparing him to Connor—the innocence behind his eyes, the naivety. Flamease or not, there were some things that should never happen.

She scrubbed the captain's blood from her skin absently, her head a mixture of adrenaline and delayed emotion. She hadn't had a chance to tell her father about the meddling of the Olympians. He had spent the climb back to the main floor lecturing Tobias about his convictions, and there had been no way she was going to interrupt that. She knew that she may never see it again.

She stepped out of the cold shower, into a room that felt too warm for her. The mirror in front of her was covered in a thin film of water and she wiped it away, staring into her eyes. She tried not to do that often. Not because she hated her looks, but because she hated the person who stared back. Cold, emotionless; a weapon. She looked tired, but when did she not? She quickly wrapped her hair in a towel. She'd worry about it after she packed.

She opened the door to her bedroom, another towel around her torso, and went to the vanity dresser at the opposite end of the room. She didn't know what to wear, but she didn't have much time. She settled on a black T-shirt and Water Realm tactical jeans, and grabbed her bag from the corner of the room where she had thrown it before her shower. She threw some clothes into it, not really caring if they matched. She undid the towel from her head and quickly threaded her hair into a single braid, holding it in place with a clip embossed with the SwiftStream crest.

She grabbed her knife from the bedside table, pausing as the light caught the hilt. Her father had commissioned the knife as a present when she had finished her assassin training. It seemed like a formality then, but she wondered if perhaps he'd always seen her potential.

Someone cleared their throat from her doorway. She jumped, spinning around to find Tobias standing there, his eyes distant.

"Don't you knock?" she questioned, slightly annoyed.

He shook his head. "You're leaving, aren't you?" His eyes weren't judgmental but resigned.

She paused. How long had he been watching her? "I don't know what…"

"Save it, Sapphire." Tobias said, holding his hand up. "I could tell there was more to your Earth mission than you let on." He inhaled, like the whole world was crashing in on him. "I had logistics run your holodisk comms and other channel pings that occurred while you were there." She held her breath. She hadn't expected anyone, especially not Tobias, to dig that far. "I know the Olympians are moving."

She stared at him, waiting for him to try to stop her from leaving, but he didn't move. "I've reset the portal tether codes." He eyed her like a protective brother. "Father will be too preoccupied making sure I don't falter again to check the portals for a while." His eyes locked with hers. "You'd better be gone before he has time."

Sapphire stiffened, "You're helping me?" She was uneasy. He'd never helped her, not since they were children. He was too afraid to be seen as something other than the golden heir. There had to be a catch.

He shrugged. "Call it what you want. I just don't want to be on the wrong side of the Greek pantheon." His demeanor shifted back to that of a prideful prince. "I've heard the stories of what they do to their enemies, and I don't think they will care about archaic alliances if a war breaks out."

She stared at him, studying him for any hint of a lie. There was none. She didn't blame him. Even the Water Realm's gods stayed far away from Olympus.

Finally, she grabbed her backpack and moved toward the door. As she pushed past him, he grabbed her shoulder. She looked back, sure this was the moment he was going to try to stop her, but he just nodded and said, "Be safe, Sister. Hopefully, we meet again at the end of this."

She nodded solemnly. What was coming next could destroy both of them, and for once, that terrified her.

CHAPTER 36
FINN

Finn paced in the backyard, unable to stop his racing thoughts. Scott was trying to go through realm logistics and other safe house plans for whatever was coming, but Finn had barely heard about any of it.

Fugitives? Of all the titles he thought this mission might bring for him, that was not one of them. All he had wanted was to prove himself again. Maybe get back to the way things used to be before the Outer Coves mission. Now that motivation was gone, and everything was somehow worse.

"Finn?" Scott's voice finally broke through the torrent of thoughts. Finn looked over at him, wordless. Had he asked a question? "Did you get all that?"

Scott had a field guide in one hand and the holodisk in the other. Connor had shown him the best way to access files without being traceable; now he stood in front of the group like a seasoned general. Strategizing, leading. Like Finn should be doing.

Finn stopped pacing and faced the group. He shook his head; there was no use trying to pretend that he wasn't spiraling while the rest of them were being productive.

"I need you and Rainee to check the surrounding area for any signs of portal activity that we weren't aware of," Scott repeated patiently. Finn found himself grateful for his steadiness. He nodded for Scott to continue. "I have a list of known pings, but they don't show precise locations. We need to make sure we're prepared for any attacks."

Finn's eyes flicked to Rainee as he fought to calm his heartbeat. She was looking at him blank-faced. Was she still angry about earlier? Maybe this was his chance to explain. "Understood," he replied, looking back at Scott.

"Good," Scott said, closing the holodisk. "Connor, I'm going to have you monitor the pings in and out of the area." Connor nodded, his excitement visible. Scott turned to Axel, who leaned against the house, arms crossed, and finally wearing a shirt. "And you—" Scott pointed at him with the book in his hand. "—I have some weapons that could use sharpening. I hear you have some knowledge there."

Axel smirked. That was the only expression he possessed, Finn had decided. But something in his eyes said he wasn't pleased with the assignments. He was staring distantly at Rainee. What was his problem?

Scott moved to go back inside, Connor tagging along obliviously. But Axel and Finn didn't move. Not even an inch. Axel watching Rainee, Finn watching Axel. The tension was terrifying, but Finn couldn't place where it came from.

"Finn." Rainee's voice cut through the air like a knife. He finally tore his eyes away from Axel, forcing his expression to be neutral. She was looking at him expectantly as she continued, "Let's go." She was calm, but her eyes added, "Let's get this over with."

He nodded and followed her through the back gate. His pulse was still hammering in his ears, and he could feel Axel's eyes on his back, even after the gate shut behind them. He made a mental note to speak with Axel later.

"Where do we start?" Rainee asked, looking at him. Of course she was asking him. He was the one with the portal experience, he should know what they should be looking for.

He cleared his throat, suddenly feeling nervous. This was war now, after all. A Fire Realm soldier could appear out of nowhere and corner them. The thought of something happening to Rainee made his chest twist in a way he wasn't used to. Maybe it was just the fear of what Scott might do to him if something happened to her.

"Holodisks use a powdered substance called castlight powder to summon portals once a destination is entered," he started to explain. "If there's an active tether or a valid tether code, it acts as a reflecting agent to cast the portal." She was listening intently, soaking in all the new information. He couldn't imagine how crazy all this sounded for someone hearing it for the first time. "If a portal has been cast, or an attempt has been made, there should be castlight powder residue in the area," he finished, looking at her a little too long. But she didn't look away.

"What does castlight powder…" She looked like she was trying to find the right words. "…look like?"

Finn briefly noticed how beautiful she was when she was thinking. Then he shook it off like the thought might bite him if he let it linger for too long. He motioned for her to follow him. He knew exactly where to find an example. "It's easier to show you than describe it. You probably wouldn't notice it if you weren't looking for it."

They both fell silent as he led her toward the clearing near the school. He could feel her eyes on him, but he was having trouble coming up with words. His head was swimming. He had so much that he wanted to share with her, but he had no way of starting a conversation that didn't sound like an excuse. Maybe because they were all excuses. He didn't have a good apology for stalking her, or plotting her death, or even for saving her. She had every right to be mad at him.

"I get what you meant." Rainee said, breaking the silence. Finn stopped and turned toward her.

"I'm sorry?" he asked. He was sure that he had only been ruminating inside his head but wondered if he'd said all of that out loud.

She shrugged. She looked every bit as uncomfortable as he felt, which was weirdly reassuring. "I get it. You meant that the instincts were against your mission—" She met his eyes. "—not that it was wrong to save me."

He froze. Somehow, she had just cracked open everything he had wanted to say without him having to initiate it, and now he had to respond. He cleared his throat, but it did little for the lump that sat there. "Yeah…I wasn't trying to…"

"Hurt me?" she interrupted.

His eyes widened, and he just nodded. That was exactly what he was going to say.

"Well, you did."

His heart dropped to his stomach. Those words hurt more than he expected.

"But not for the reasons you might think."

He opened his mouth to respond, but she kept speaking.

"I put too much weight into you saving me." Her moist eyes latched onto his. "You just did what any sane person would do if someone walked out in front of a car, and I..." She sucked in a breath. "I had no reason to think it was anything more than that."

Finn's breath caught. The thought of him hurting her had stung, but hearing her blame herself for the pain was a feeling he would give anything to change.

"No, it..." *It did mean something.* But he couldn't force the words out of his mouth. Instead, he redirected. "I should have chosen my words better." The admission felt fake. Like that wasn't really what he wanted to apologize for.

She nodded, seeming to accept his apology, even if it was incomplete. They stood in silence for a few moments, Finn trying to muster the courage to say something else—anything —and Rainee still looking at him like he'd just killed her dog.

After what felt like a torturously long time, she gestured behind him. "So, castlight powder?"

He nodded, sighing in relief as he turned back to the tree line. "Yeah, there should be some around here, from my portal tether testing last night." He walked a few paces, stopping at a tree at the far edge of the school parking lot—exactly where he had been standing when Connor had found him the night before. He examined the ground around the tree, looking for... *Aha!* At the base of the tree, just inconspicuous enough to not draw attention, was a powdery blue residue that blended into the grass. He took some between his fingers and rubbed them together. He held his hand out so Rainee could see. "Castlight powder has a special camouflage technology that makes light reflect off it to match the surrounding area. But, if you move it just right—" He moved his hand back and forth, making the powder glisten like glitter. "—it's hard to miss."

She nodded, studying the powder. "How do you find it if it's stationary?"

"You move. Change your visual perspective, let the powder catch the light like it wants to," he said, slipping into his tactical officer training voice. He'd given plenty of demonstrations on castlight powder and portal travel back in the Fire Realm. It was one of his favorite parts of training.

She moved closer to him, searching for more powder around the base of the tree. She grabbed at one of the grass tufts and pulled her hand back, moving it slowly back and forth. It sparkled with the powder residue.

Finn smiled. "Good, that's exactly what we're looking for." His heart swelled with pride, and he paused to look at her. Her hair was pulled into a long ponytail, and her purple sweatshirt hung loosely off her body. Her cheeks were slightly flushed, her eyes still glassy from their talk. She was close enough to him that he could feel her knee brush against his.

"You're staring," she said, raising an eyebrow at him. A small smile tugged at her lips. "Did I get some on my face or something?"

Finn blushed slightly and shook his head. "Nope, just thinking." But he didn't look away. They stared at each other for a while longer. Just long enough that Finn noticed how the sunlight caught her eyes and made them sparkle.

"This stuff isn't dangerous, is it?" Rainee asked softly, holding up her hand.

Finn shook his head, trying not to stutter. "No, it's mainly a reflector, there shouldn't be any health risks…"

Without waiting for him to finish, Rainee lunged forward and swiped the hand that was covered in castlight powder across Finn's cheek, catching him off guard.

She laughed, a soothing sound. She bolted upright, scurrying a few paces away with a grin that was contagious. Recovered from the initial shock, Finn bounded after her, a smile on his lips. It didn't take much for him to catch her, one arm around her waist and the opposite hand still covered in castlight powder, held out like a threat.

"You think this is funny?" he asked, trying to sound upset and failing. "I look like an art project."

She giggled and turned to face him. His arm stayed firmly around her waist. Finn was hyperaware of how close she was at that moment.

"I kind of like it," she said softly, her eyes fluttering a little.

Finn raised an eyebrow, trying to maintain his composure. He slowly reached up with the powder-covered hand and smeared the castlight powder down her cheek as he whispered, "Good, because we match now."

They stayed like that for a few heartbeats. One arm around her waist and a hand on her face. He studied her features, looking between her eyes and her lips. He was all too aware of his heartbeat in his throat and the feeling that he shouldn't be doing this.

He started to lean in, then heard someone speak.

"Hate to break this up, but this hardly seems like the time for whatever was about to happen here."

Finn recognized the voice before his head snapped up to meet her eyes. *Sapphire.*

He cleared his throat and backed away from Rainee. He noticed her cheeks were flushed, and he thought the pink looked good on her.

"Don't you have fish to catch or something?" Finn growled. His tone sounded every bit as annoyed as he felt. But he knew that it was probably for the best that they were interrupted. They didn't need to be distracted.

Sapphire smirked. "No need. *My* realm didn't strand me here to fend for myself." The tone in her voice sounded sure, but her eyes kept shifting like she was hiding something. When wasn't she hiding something?

Rainee was looking at Sapphire, waiting for some sort of explanation. "You're not…"

"No," Sapphire offered, looking at her softly. Like it hurt her to lie to Rainee. She really was a fantastic manipulator. "My name is Sapphire SwiftStream." She took a breath like it might make the words easier to say. "I'm the princess of the Water Realm." Finn noticed her demeanor falter despite the charisma in her voice. She was definitely hiding something.

Rainee stared at her for a while, the castlight powder still smudged across her cheek. Finn could see tears welling in her eyes, confirmed by her shaky breath as she asked, "Is anyone real anymore?"

His heart shattered. Within three days, she had gained some degenerate housemates, learned she was a demigod descendant, and now that a person she thought was genuinely her friend was another spy. He couldn't imagine the betrayal she felt, but he could read it on her face. He hated himself for contributing to it.

"Rainee…" Sapphire started, stepping forward. Her mask was gone. Was that…*remorse?* From the queen of manipulation herself?

Rainee shook her head and turned back toward the house. She looked up at Finn with a look that said, "Don't follow me." It ate him alive with guilt. But he felt paralyzed as she walked away, unsure of what to say, or if anything he could say would actually fix this. If it could even be fixed.

CHAPTER 37
AXEL

Clang. Axel hit ran the sword in his hands against the whetstone, willing the noise to drown out his stewing thoughts. He knew that he shouldn't be as angry as he was, but watching Scott pair Rainee with Finn made him painfully uncomfortable, which made no sense. It wasn't like Axel owned her. He was actively trying to keep her away from him, even.

There was something in the way she spoke to him, though. Like she wasn't scared of him. Like he wasn't some ticking time bomb waiting to explode. It had been a while since anyone had treated him like more than a warning of what not to become.

Clang. He couldn't blame Scott. Finn was the safe choice, a natural protector. He'd let his own guilt destroy him before Rainee got hurt, and that was more appealing than sending her off with an ex-criminal who had a vendetta against shirts. Axel got it, but it still angered him.

Shhhk. Screeeet. Shhhk.

He took the blade in his hand, testing the edge on his thumb. Blood pooled around the edge of the blade, and a sharp pain shot through his fingertips, reminding him that he was alive. *Lucky fucking me.*

He stood and propped the blade against the wall. Scott had a lot of swords and battle axes and not enough knives, if you asked Axel. But it wasn't *his* armory, so he couldn't complain. He also owned a lot less firearms than he had imagined a human would. Most realms didn't use guns, but Axel had expected at least one here.

"You're quiet today." Connor's voice snapped him out of his thoughts. Of course, Connor was the first to notice. The kid always noticed when he had something on his mind.

Axel looked up, his face calm while his heart tried to beat out of his chest. "What's it to you?" he asked, his voice low. He didn't mean it as harshly as it sounded, but it was the only way he could keep his voice from shaking.

Connor shrugged, but he seemed to brush Axel's irritability away for a moment. "I just wanted to make sure you were okay." He raised a hand to the back of his neck, his nerves surfacing as he added. "Almost dying would take a toll on someone, I'm sure."

He was right. It *should* be weighing on him more than it was, but instead, all he could think about was Rainee and how it made sense for her to get close to Finn. And it also made sense for her to run far far away from Axel. Forget him altogether, if she could.

"I'm fine, kid," he said. He forced a small smile. "Thanks for asking." He walked over and slung his arm over Connor's shoulder with all the swagger of an older brother-mentor. "How's the ping monitoring going?"

Connor's face lit up. "It's interesting!" He gestured to the room that had been locked the day before. "Scott has a huge beacon tracker that catches any pings—in or out, divine or mortal. It's insane!" His excitement was contagious, and Axel couldn't help but listen to every word he said. At least Scott had made one of them happy with their assignments.

His excitement was cut short by a sound from the monitoring room. An alarm. Axel hadn't heard that one yet. Connor's expression shifted to one of concern, and he hurried back to the room to investigate.

Axel followed him, curious, although he tried not to show it. A new line flickered across the screen as he walked into the room.

[Ping 234360. 05082025. Origin: Water Realm.]

Axel's eyes widened. They hadn't heard from Sapphire in a while, he realized. Just long enough for her to call in reinforcements.

"Get Scott," Connor whispered, typing on the keyboard.

Axel didn't wait another second. He bounded up the stairs, skipping a few steps, and nearly broke down the door to get it open. His thoughts were wild. Rainee was out there; the Water Realm was coming for them. He couldn't move quickly enough.

He tore through the hallway into the kitchen, nearly colliding with Rainee. She looked upset. He felt a wave of anger. Who upset her?

"Rainee? Are…" he started, reaching for her.

"I'm fine," she threw out coldly as she pushed past him. He knew she wasn't. He almost forgot about the ping for a moment, but he knew he needed to find Scott.

Scott was standing in the backyard, talking to Finn…and Sapphire. Axel flung open the screen door, his blood boiling.

"What the *hell* is she doing here?" he growled. He was seeing red, moments away from losing his cool completely.

Scott held up his hands in a calming gesture. "Axel, let's just talk…"

"Talk?" Axel chuckled lightly, offended. "Sure, let's talk while her backup from the Water Realm gets here." He glared at all three of them.

Sapphire eyed him, a confused look on her face. "What backup?" That was it—her playing dumb. That was the icing on the cake.

Axel flew forward, pulling his knife from his pocket. He was going to end this like he should have earlier. Leaving her breathing after everything that had happened was just tempting fate.

Scott and Finn each caught one of his arms and held Axel back as he fought against them. "Don't lie to me," Axel spat, his eyes wild. "I saw the ping. You called them." His heart felt like it was about to beat out of his chest as he resisted the other two men.

"Try again, hot shot." Sapphire snarled, stepping closer to him. "I came alone."

Finn finally gained a grip that was strong enough to push Axel backwards as he confirmed Sapphire's statement. "It's true." He looked Axel up and down. "It's just her."

Axel was still seething. "Why?" He wasn't buying whatever trickery this was, not from the only person who was possibly a better manipulator than him.

She sighed and pulled out her holodisk. "I assume you all have seen the unknown pings in the area already?" She held up the holodisk, hitting a button to bring up the tracking screen. Axel had noticed the two pings she was referring to on Scott's mainframe, but had figured they were malfunctions.

He looked over at Scott, who was nodding his head. Finn was studying the holodisk screen like it might hold all the answers, but he looked just as clueless as Axel felt.

"The pings that are labeled with unknown origins, I checked into them," she continued, pulling up a few surveillance photos: hidden beacons in the depths of wooded areas that all look untouched. "These are the beacons that picked up the pings. I searched their radius areas for castlight powder or other signs of disturbance."

Axel's mind was racing now, why would pings be going off if no signs of activity were present? And why were there no origins attached to the pings?

"As you can see—" Sapphire zoomed in on the photos. It looked like nothing except wildlife had touched the areas in the last century. "There are no footprints, no disturbances to the local flora, and no traces of portal science." She closed the holodisk. "Which means…"

"Something divine is tampering with the signals," Scott finished. Sapphire looked at him, nodding her acknowledgment. There seemed to be more she wasn't saying, but she stayed silent.

"Couldn't it be a malfunction?" Finn chimed in, his eyebrows knit together as he processed the information.

Scott shook his head. "Based on the other pings coming through and no known malfunctions to date, it is highly unlikely that these are simple technical problems." He paused for a second, locking eyes with Sapphire. "Something is trying to keep the balance of the realm, but I don't think it—or they—are succeeding."

"How long have you known about the unknown pings?" Axel asked, staring at Scott. He wasn't mad anymore, just trying to process onslaught of information.

Scott cleared his throat and made eye contact with Axel. "Since early this morning. I hadn't had a chance to check the beacons in a few days." He looked from one soldier to the other. "I've been a little busy."

"Did you know that they were potentially divine interferences? Or were you just going to keep that to yourself?" Axel shot back, slightly annoyed at being kept out of the loop, especially when it could cost him his life.

Scott nodded. "I knew there was a chance, but I didn't want to say anything until I had a chance to investigate."

"And when were you planning to investigate?" Axel growled, his anger starting to consume him again. "Before or after we all died?"

"Axel..." Finn started, putting his hand on Axel's shoulder.

Axel shrugged him off. He pointed a finger at Scott's chest. "Even after this morning? After *knowing* that we're targets now." Axel's voice shook. "You still didn't think this was information we needed?"

"You'll lower your tone when you talk to me, son." Scott's voice deepened, his eyes glaring daggers at Axel. But Axel didn't retreat. "This is still my house," Scott said, taking a step closer.

Axel's eyes intensified. "I'll change my tone when you stop withholding information." He looked Scott up and down, and the worst words he could think of flew from his mouth. "Or maybe you want your daughter dead, is that it?"

In one swift motion, Scott grabbed Axel by the collar of his shirt and lifted him into the air. Axel's knife dropped to the ground as he fought against him. He was strong for a human.

"Axel," Scott snarled, his face inches from Axel's. "You can mouth off about almost anything, and I won't bat an eye; but my desire to protect my daughter is not one of them." He searched Axel's eyes like he was thinking about which one to rip from its socket first. For once, Axel was scared into silence. Scott dropped him to the ground before hissing, "I saved you from death, but I'll gladly dig your grave if I have to."

He turned and stormed back inside, leaving Axel in the mud and Finn and Sapphire staring at his back in shock. Axel looked after him, only just realizing that Rainee had been standing in the kitchen doorway watching the entire thing. *Dammit.* Strike two for the bad boy image.

He jumped to his feet quickly, dusted himself off, and retrieved his knife from where it had dropped.

"Axel…" Finn started to say.

"Don't start," he growled back. "Not now."

He moved over to the fire pit in the backyard and fumbled with a few of the logs nearby. He needed to keep his hands busy, or he might actually feel the strike to his pride.

After a while, he heard Finn and Sapphire shift inside. The sky was starting to get dark, but he could still feel Rainee's eyes on him. She watched him start the fire, wordless. He could feel her thinking. Feel her judgment. At least, that's what he thought he felt.

Once the fire was lit, he sat in one of the folding chairs with his back to her. She could stare at him all she wanted, but he didn't have to stare back.

It wasn't long before he felt her slip into the chair beside him. He looked at her and was going to tell her to leave him alone, but was surprised by the look on her face. She looked sympathetic? His heart rose to his throat. *What the hell?*

"He didn't mean that, you know," she said, making him jump.

He watched her, trying to read her expression for negative sentiment. Judgment, hate, fear, anything he was used to. But there was none. Just calm understanding, and that terrified him even more than Scott's threats. "About which part?" he asked, still searching her eyes. "About protecting you or killing me? Because both seemed pretty authentic." He let out a forced chuckle, still reeling from the altercation.

She smiled. "The threats might have been genuine, but only because you hit a sore spot." She paused, the fire lighting up one side of her face. "All of this is a lot for him, whether he admits it or not." She looked up into Axel's eyes, and his breath caught in his throat. The firelight highlighted the intensity of her features. Or maybe he was just noticing them for the first time.

"He doesn't have a lot left to lose, so…" She trailed off, thinking. "Any allusion to losing me is his last straw."

He was somewhat comforted that he wasn't the only person that she could read like a book, and he wondered how Scott had hidden anything from her for the past eighteen years.

He smiled back at her, a real smile, one that only she could elicit from him. "I can't blame him for that," he murmured.

She placed her hand on his knee, and the touch alone threatened to give him a heart attack. He stiffened, trying to keep his composure, but his heart was pounding too loudly for him to think.

She looked at him a while longer, then got up and started back toward the house. "Don't stay out here for too long; it's supposed to rain," she offered.

He nodded, but he had hardly heard her. He was focused on trying to breathe again after her hand had been on his knee and the way her eyes looked at him like he was worth something more than his criminal skills. He inhaled deeply to calm himself down. *Damn.*

CHAPTER 38
RAINEE

Rainee shut the sliding door behind her as she entered the air-conditioned kitchen. She wasn't sure what it was about Axel, but the way he always picked himself back up—sometimes literally—was admirable. At the same time, she could see some of his walls coming down, and she wondered how long it had been since he had let that happen.

Her dad was standing in the kitchen, a glass of water in his hand, his eyes fixed out the window toward the spot where Axel still sat by the fire.

"You didn't have to threaten him like that, you know," she said, catching him off guard. She wasn't upset with him, but had been surprised by his reaction. She'd never seen him so reactive.

He sat the glass down on the counter and looked back out at Axel. "He needed an attitude check," he murmured. "I don't do the tough guy act." He looked back at Rainee. "Especially when it comes to you."

She rolled her eyes. "I don't need protecting," she said, crossing her arms.

He stared gravely at her for a moment, as if a piece of him had been stolen. "Yes," he said quietly. "But you're my daughter. And I'll be damned if I let something happen to you."

She stopped, gaping at him, speechless. She hadn't expected him to admit what she already knew, but she was glad that he did. "Thanks, Dad," she whispered. "But I promise I'll be okay." It wasn't defiance. It was a boundary, one that she knew was necessary if she ever wanted to be someone more than just his daughter.

She turned to go upstairs, but his voice stopped her. "Just—" he said, clearly battling something in his head. "—stay away from Axel." He looked back out the window. "He's already too deep into all of this, and I don't need him pulling you in, too."

She cleared her throat and replied, "I don't think that's your call to make." Then she retreated to her room, not waiting for his response. She didn't need to see his face to know that it broke him, the fact that he couldn't stop her from growing up, and that he couldn't keep her away from people, either. But still, her chest was tight. She had always been his perfect angel. Had always done what he asked. However, if she was going to be the symbol for a realm-altering war, she needed to learn how to make decisions for herself. The necklace hummed softly, almost like an affirmation.

She looked at herself in the mirror, the castlight powder from earlier that day glistening like glitter under the warm lights of her room. She thought back to that moment in the forest clearing. She had no idea why she had smudged Finn's face with the powder to begin with, but it had lightened the mood, even if it was only for a second.

She smiled. He had almost kissed her. And she knew that she would have kissed him back in that moment. Even if he was a lying, tongue-tied idiot.

Then, there was Axel. Something about him intrigued her. He was mysterious, but he always seemed less guarded when it was just the two of them. And the way he had stiffened when she touched his knee. He probably hoped she didn't notice, but she had. She couldn't ignore that he made her feel something. Different from Finn, but still very much there.

The necklace's humming grew a bit louder. Rainee found herself wishing it would just be quiet for once. She didn't need to be reminded that she wasn't normal with every thought and movement.

She shook the thought away and climbed into bed, not even bothering to change her clothes. The ones she had on smelled like fire and leather, which was the most comforting and conflicting thing she could think of.

CHAPTER 39
FINN

Finn lay on the couch in the basement. He'd given Sapphire his room, figuring she needed the privacy more than he did, in a house full of guys. He was following the swirl patterns on the ceiling with his eyes, trying to stop replaying the almost-kiss in his mind.

He couldn't help but wonder if she would have kissed him back, if this night would have been completely different. If, maybe, he wouldn't be staring at the ceiling alone right now.

His thoughts were interrupted by the sound of the basement door opening. Axel trudged down the stairs, his clothes wet from the rain. Always so dramatic. They made eye contact, but neither of them said anything at first. There was nothing to talk about, anyway. Axel had needed someone to put him in his place, and Scott was the perfect one to do it. Hell, Finn wished he had that kind of power over Axel.

Finally, Finn sat up, a smile already tugging at his lips. "You know there's a shower in here; you don't have to sit in the rain."

Axel glared at him, peeling his rain-soaked shirt off and tossing it to the side. "Wasn't sitting in the rain for cleanliness," he said, running his hands through his wet hair, which made it stand up in uneven spikes.

"So, it was just to be dramatic?" Finn asked. He finally appreciated the thrill Axel got from poking the bear, and he was enjoying flipping the script on him.

Axel smiled and exhaled through his nose, obviously irritated, but he responded, "Just needed a reset, I guess."

Finn was going to throw out something about him needing a whole system wipe, but the look on Axel's face stopped him. He looked seriously fazed, an expression Finn had never seen on him before.

"Something on your mind?" Finn asked before he could think better of it.

Axel looked up, surprised, but he shook his head. "Nah, don't do that, *Cap.*" He let out a small laugh. "Don't make this more than what it needs to be."

He started to shuffle toward the bathroom, but Finn interjected. "We don't have to."

Axel paused and turned to look at him.

"But if you ever had something to say," Finn added, sighing. "Just know that I am here to listen. As your captain." Finn looked at him seriously. "Or as a friend."

Axel let a small smile slip, but his eyes were distant. "Yeah." He turned back toward the bathroom. "That's why you're the safe one."

Finn nearly choked. What was that supposed to mean? Was that a compliment or a dig? Or was it both? Whatever it was, Axel meant it, and it seemed to hurt him.

Axel shut the bathroom door behind him before Finn could say anything else, but the tension in the air was palpable. Surely this wasn't just about Scott threatening him? Finn had never seen Axel shaken by authority. This felt different. It felt like more than just a hit to his rebellious pride. It was deeper, and Finn's chest tightened at the thought of it.

CHAPTER 40
AXEL

The bathroom door clicked shut behind him. His chest hurt, his body was soaked to the bone, and the words that he had said echoed in his head.

That's why you're the safe one.

It was true. Finn *was* the safe one. The obvious choice for pretty much everything. He was strategic, he listened, and he was intensely loyal. Axel was barely loyal to himself, and had a temper that made the Fire Realm's gods look soft.

This wasn't even about Rainee. Not really. This was about *life*. About being the wrong choice for almost any scenario, unless it involved killing or stealing.

He pressed his head against the door and slid down to a sitting position. He was freezing from the rain, but he hardly noticed. He was serious when he had told Rainee he wasn't a good person to get close to, and he still fully believed that. But the way she looked at him like *she* didn't believe it, that's what made this all harder.

He knew he was chaos. Destruction. Everything bad about the world. But she didn't see that, and he realized that he didn't want her to anymore.

CHAPTER 41
SCOTT

Scott stood in the kitchen. The rain had been thrumming against the house for a few hours. Axel had come inside soaked, but Scott hadn't said anything to him. He figured he'd already made his point earlier. But he had noticed that the rain did little to wash away that...look. The one that insinuated that he was trying not to unravel. A look that Scott knew all too well. He'd felt it a few times himself, even. It was dangerous if left unchecked, especially for someone like Axel.

Scott set his coffee mug on the counter and opened the cabinet above the refrigerator, where he kept the only type of liquor he'd ever allowed himself to partake in. A Fire Realm special brew that had notes of lavawood and charberries. It was ironic, really. Using the Fire Realm to drown out his problems that the Fire Realm had created for him.

Kai had gifted him the bottle as a wedding present; he knew it was his favorite. He'd only broken it open once before—the night after his wife was taken, as Rainee slept in a crib across the room, oblivious to the world crashing around them. He hadn't touched it since. He didn't drink anymore; he had never cared for how it made him feel. But tonight. Tonight felt like a problem that only this brew could fix.

He poured two fingers into his empty coffee mug, without adding ice first. Ice was a crime in the Fire Realm, and he'd probably offended that culture sufficiently for one night.

He grabbed a chair and sat down facing the sliding door, watching the rain as he sipped the liquor. It burned down his throat in a familiar way, taking him back to his realm travel days.

He had just turned eighteen the first time he stepped foot in the Fire Realm. Kai was still the crown prince then. His father, Soren, was ruling the realm with an iron fist. Kai had been the one to greet Scott's team when they arrived, showing them the sleeping quarters and giving a brief history of the Fire Realm and its major exports.

Kai was young, but he was smart, charming, and held himself like he was already the king. Scott was immediately drawn to him. Somewhere between Scott's diplomatic mission as a Realm Guardian and Kai's princely duties, they found time to laugh over a bottle of Char Brew. They were friends from that point on, and Scott had visited on friendly pretenses several times in those early years. He'd even attended Kai's coronation as a guest, not a guard, and celebrated with him afterward. And Kai had been a groomsman in Scott's wedding.

That was all before the prospect of the Line Severance Decree arose. Kai supported the decree under the pretense that Greek demigods and their descendants posed an unequivocal threat to the Eastern Division if there were ever another Divisional War. Scott had argued with him countless times, citing his wife as an example of who could be hurt by the decree. But Kai's loyalties had always resided with the realm first. A fact that hurt Scott more than he had cared to admit. And now, his shithead little brother wanted his daughter dead, even more than Kai had.

He took a sip of the liquor, savoring it in his mouth for a minute. Suddenly, he felt someone's eyes on him. Figuring it was one of the boys, but not recalling basement door clicking or the alarm buzzing, he turned around slowly and was startled to find Hermes leaning on the far wall of the kitchen, gold cuffs shining in the LED lights.

"Hermes. I thought I was clear..."

"Oh yes, yes, god-binding chains and whatnot," Hermes interrupted, completely unbothered by Scott's dad act. "I have a message you might actually want to listen to before you kick me out...again." Hermes eyes were mischievous, but sincere. Well, as sincere as Scott had ever seen them. Scott gestured for him to sit down.

"You've got five minutes before I get the chains out." Scott sighed, his head spinning slightly from the alcohol.

Hermes didn't sit. Instead, he paced in front of Scott like he was verbalizing an epic tale. "As you may have noticed, the gods are growing restless." He paused, eyed Scott, then continued pacing. "Some of them, mainly Zeus and Athena, want to protect your daughter, to train her as a warrior. Others—" He stopped, locking eyes with Scott. "—a lot of others. Want. Her. Dead."

Scott's heart pounded. Rainee wasn't even safe from the gods now?

"What?" It was all he could manage to say. His mouth felt dry.

"Nearly half of the pantheon sees your daughter as the catalyst for a Divisional War…A war they want no part of."

Since when did the Olympians not want war? They must have gone soft in their old age.

"There is, however, one caveat that could end this…predicament," Hermes offered, feeding off the panic in Scott's expression.

Scott leaped from his chair a little too eagerly; he knew better than to show interest in front of the gods. But this was his daughter's life he was bargaining with. "What do I need to do?"

Hermes smirked and gestured vaguely to the rest of the house. "The assassins you're harboring." His eyes became cold. "You bring them to us. *All* of them."

Scott's heart pounded. He didn't like this option either.

"We make examples out of them, and shut the door on this Divisional conflict." He took a step toward Scott, the toes of their shoes nearly touching. "Then you and your precious daughter can forget all of this ever happened."

Scott swallowed hard. These boys, who had started to trust him, that he had patched wounds for and provided emotional support for, were the only way to keep a full divine war from breaking out. To keep his daughter safe. How was he going to sleep at night?

"I'll let you think about it," Hermes said flippantly. "But don't take too long, the gods don't like waiting," he added, then he was gone. Scott was alone in his kitchen with his heart in his stomach and his mind racing.

CHAPTER 42
RAINEE

Rainee stepped into the kitchen, freshly showered and no longer smelling like a fire pit. Everyone else was already at the table except her father, who was cooking a piece of fish. That was new.

The kitchen was eerily quiet; only the clink of dishes could be heard. No one looked up when she entered except Connor, who gave her a small wave as he shoved bacon in his mouth.

She grabbed a plate without a word and took the last empty seat beside Sapphire, who offered her a small smile that said, "I don't know if you're still mad, so I'm just going to smile and hope not."

Rainee smiled back. She wasn't mad anymore, but she *was* feeling out of the loop.

She noticed Axel chewing slowly, like the bacon tasted foul, with his eyes fixed on an imaginary point on the table. Finn hadn't touched his food at all by the looks of it; he was just sitting in spacey silence. Had she missed something?

Scott brought the fish over to Sapphire, who thanked him. He didn't look at Rainee. Had what she said hurt him that badly?

Rainee let the silence continue for another few minutes, then she dropped her fork onto her plate. Everyone looked up at her. "Okay, what's going on?" She was annoyed and not trying to hide it. "Did you all decide that ignoring me is how we stop the war?"

Everyone froze. Axel looked away from her; it was weird that he had nothing to say. Him of all people.

"I think—" Finn finally broke the silence. His voice was rough and scratchy, like he'd spent all night screaming. "—we're all just tired." He glanced at her, which was the first interaction she'd gotten from him all morning. It did little to console her, though. "A lot has happened since yesterday and..." He paused, trying to find the words. "It's a lot to process."

It didn't sound like he was talking about the mission anymore. His eyes were softer, but haunted. Her heart twisted a little and she wondered what he was thinking about so intensely.

Connor sipped his orange juice with a nod, like that explanation was all he needed. But Rainee wasn't satisfied. She opened her mouth to say something else, but the sound of a chair scraping against the floor intervened, as Axel stood up abruptly and left the table. *What the hell?*

The last she knew, they were on good terms, after the moment by the fire. Had her dad threatened him again? Told him to stay away from her? The thought made her blood boil. She pushed her chair back and stormed after him.

"Rainee..." her dad called. *Nice of him to care now.* She ignored him and followed Axel down the basement steps.

Her skin was buzzing, and the necklace had started humming somewhere between the kitchen and the basement. "Axel," she growled after him. He kept walking.

She charged after him, grabbing him by the shoulder. "Axel, what the hell?" He stiffened at her touch but didn't turn. Rainee's entire body was buzzing at this point. She could take a lot, but the silent treatment and complete disengagement was too much to handle. The lights flickered around them. "What did I do to be treated like this?" she whispered, her voice catching. The lights stopped flickering as her anger melted to hurt. The necklace still hummed softly.

"Rainee..." came his grumbled reply. "Don't do this."

That sent her over the edge. The necklace pulsed against her as she retorted, "Do what?" Tears welled in her eyes. He glanced at her over his shoulder, then quickly looked away. "Ask not to be treated like I'm some taboo topic, in my own house?" A small sob escaped her throat. "Or want the full truth for once in my life?"

Her eyes stung, and her throat felt like it was closing. The humming from the necklace had taken over all of her senses. The lights in the house were dimming as if she were drawing all their power.

"The truth?" Axel asked, turning to look at her, his eyes wild. "If you want the truth, you're asking the wrong assassin." The pain in his voice was clear. Rainee's heart pounded. He looked at her for a moment, his face inches from hers, then he turned and started for his room again.

Rainee's pulse thudded in her ears. The lights flashed around her, and before she could stop it, a flash of light arced out of a nearby outlet and hit the door to Axel's room just as he was about to open it. "Stop walking away from me," she felt herself hiss.

The next few moments were a blur. The humming from the necklace got louder, her head spun, and she thought she heard Axel call out her name, right before her face hit the carpet and everything went dark.

***

Rainee's head throbbed. She had no idea where she was, or even *who* she was. Her mind was spinning, trying to grasp the last memory she had before the blackout. "Axel," she felt herself murmur before she could stop the name from rolling off her lips.

She opened her eyes slowly and her bedroom ceiling came into view. Her dad was beside her, his eyes afflicted by worry and guilt. She forgot for a minute that she was supposed to be mad at him.

"Hey, Rae," he whispered. The relief in his voice was evident. "How's your head?" He was searching her like he was checking for any other wounds he may have missed.

She sat up slightly, scanning her room. No one was there besides her dad, which stung a little more than it probably should have.

Her dad sighed. "I'm sorry." She looked at him, and he continued. "I had a lot on my mind this morning, but I shouldn't have shut you out. None of this…" He took a deep breath. "None of this is your fault and I shouldn't have taken it out on you." He sat down on the edge of her bed, his head down, looking at the floor.

It was obvious he was still torn up about everything. Rainee unwrapped herself from her blankets and hugged him. "I'm sorry, too. I shouldn't have acted like I don't need you." He placed a hand on her back and leaned into her.

After a few minutes, he patted her back and stood up, a small smile on his face. "If you're feeling up to it, I know the strike squad downstairs is dying to check in on you." He cupped his hand to one side of his mouth like he was telling a secret and whispered loudly, "It's mostly Connor, he's a mess."

Rainee laughed and nodded, almost relieved to hear that they were worried. After this morning, she wasn't sure they'd care. Her dad smiled and left the room, leaving her to her thoughts.

She slowly slid out of bed, taking a deep breath to steady herself, then made her way to the mirror. She looked absolutely drained. Her eyes had dark circles under them and seemed more sunken-in than usual. The necklace rested against her collarbone, unassuming. The amount of power she had felt course through her earlier that day was terrifying, and she half-wondered if she had accidentally shocked herself. She didn't even know if that was possible.

She slipped downstairs to where everyone was waiting in the living room.

Connor was sitting on the couch, staring at the stairs expectantly. He was the first to notice her, and stood to greet her. "Are you okay?" he blurted out.

She nodded, a small smile on her lips as she looked at everyone else. Finn had dozed off in the armchair, his hair messy and his eyes blinking, trying to refocus. Sapphire was curled up on the other end of the couch, a mug in her hands. Rainee searched the room. Axel wasn't there. A sharp pain hit her chest. Really, after all of that, he didn't even wait to make sure she was okay?

CHAPTER 43
AXEL

Axel paced across the length of the backyard, wondering if he should go back inside to check on Rainee. He hadn't meant to leave; the living room had started to feel suffocating.

He ran his hands through his hair. *Fuck.* He felt like he was going insane. She's just a girl. There was no reason for him to feel like his heart was trying to escape from his chest. He tried to tell himself that this was a normal amount of concern for someone you had just watched drain all the electricity in the room and then collapse, but it didn't feel normal. None of this was normal. *She* wasn't normal.

The house was dark by the time he slipped back inside. Everyone had retreated to their respective corners of the house and the home felt empty. He moved toward the basement, to hole up and forget about this whole thing, but he heard movement from upstairs.

Without thinking, he quietly snuck up the staircase and found himself outside a white door with Rainee's name painted on it in purple lettering. Then his brain had caught up to his body, and he was about to walk away when the door opened.

"Axel?" Rainee asked, shocked. The sound of her voice was enough to send his heart into a frenzy again. She sounded tired, but she was okay, and that's all he had wanted.

He turned to face her, taking in her messy hair and pajamas. She looked incredible. He cleared his throat, trying to maintain his composure, or what little of it was left. "I-I wanted to make sure you were okay."

She smiled slightly and raised an eyebrow. "You could have knocked, instead of standing out there like a stalker."

The tone in her voice sent his heart into overdrive, and he chuckled, maybe a bit too nervously.

"Yeah, I guess so. I just—" He paused. He wasn't sure what would come out of his mouth, but he took a chance and kept talking. "—just didn't know what to say…after everything."

Her eyes softened a little, and she opened the door a little wider. "How about you come inside?" She stepped aside, motioning for him to enter. His breath caught. "Maybe we can finish the conversation we started earlier." She looked up at him. "Minus the electric shock, hopefully."

He laughed, but it already felt like electricity was running through him. He should have said no and gone back to his room, but his feet moved before he could think, and all of a sudden he was standing in her bedroom. Scott would kill him if he knew.

She shut the door quietly and motioned for him to take a seat on the bed. He sat down, somewhat awkwardly, and watched her as she sat beside him, close enough for their arms to brush. His breath caught at the contact. It felt like he was going to burn alive every time she touched him. He hated himself for letting someone affect him like this. But she wasn't just *someone*. Not really. She was a demigod, and who knows how much that counted for in these situations.

"You know you don't have to lie to me, right?" Rainee broke the silence, her gray eyes staring up at him. "In fact, I'd prefer if you didn't."

His mind swirled. She'd called him out in fewer words than the military had used to break his spirit. What was she trying to do to him?

He cleared his throat. "What?" His mouth felt like cotton, and he was trying his best to focus on the conversation, but the way she was looking at him made it difficult.

"Axel, you've been pushing me away like I'll burn you if I get too close." She paused. But Axel knew he was pushing her away because of what he might do, not the other way around. "But listen," she continued, "I don't make a habit of hurting the people I care about."

But I do.

Axel was pretty sure his heart stopped. Had he heard her right? "You shouldn't care about me," he said, his heart climbing to his throat. It was the only thought echoing in his head.

"So you keep saying," she retorted, her eyebrow raising again. "But you've failed to give me any good reasons."

He stood up, anxious to break their eye contact so he could breathe again. "I have a million good reasons, trust me." He took a deep breath.

He paced from wall to wall of the bedroom, raking his hands through his hair. She watched him for a second, like she was memorizing him. "Then start with the first one," she said quietly. "I want to know."

Axel paused mid-stride, staring at her. No one had ever said that to him before. No one had ever *wanted* to know. That's how he knew it was dangerous.

"I'm not safe…"

"I didn't ask you to be," she interrupted.

He sucked in a breath. It was getting harder and harder to stay calm. "Rainee, you don't understand." He locked eyes with her. "I'm a criminal. Or at least…I was."

She was silent, willing him to continue. He searched her face for judgment and found none. There was never any judgment from her, only acceptance.

He sat back down on the bed with his hands in his hair. "I've hurt—" He tried to count, but any attempt at rational thought was diminished. "—a lot of Flamease. And most of them didn't deserve it." He looked at her, her eyes were still soft, listening. "I was born into that lifestyle. It's all I knew…until recently."

"How did you get out?" she asked. Her voice was quiet. Not accusatory, just curious.

He took a deep breath, forcing away the tears that had started to prick his eyes. "I wish I could say it was by choice." He stared at the ground, his mind in a different place. "But the military gave me an ultimatum, and I took the path that ensured my own survival." He smiled bitterly. "Not exactly a hero origin story." His voice was shaking. He knew the words were true, but they still stung. "Even if I wanted to be good, I don't think I would know how to be, at this point."

She moved closer to him, her hand resting on his shoulder, sending small pulses of electricity through him. He didn't know if that was her or her powers, but either way it was making it hard to breathe.

"You're already doing it," she offered. His head snapped up to look at her, his heart pounding. "A bad guy would have killed me, ended it all before it could start." She searched his eyes, hers longing and soft. "But you didn't. You're still here, talking to me about being the villain when all you've done is spare people and risk your own life." She leaned in a little closer. "Doesn't seem like something the bad guy would do, does it?"

He didn't think. The second the last word left her mouth, his lips were on hers. He kissed her like he'd been dying of thirst for ages and she was the only thing that could quench it. And she kissed back. Not as desperately as him; soft, timid, and full of something he had never felt. Care?

As soon as his thoughts caught up, he pulled away.

No. No. No. He couldn't let this happen. He couldn't let her care. Or let himself care. Every person in his past who had ever cared about him died. He couldn't let the same happen to her. And it would happen if he stayed, because that was his curse. He broke things. Hurt people he never meant to. He didn't know any other way.

He flew off the bed. Rainee was still leaned in, stunned from the kiss. "I have to go. Sorry!" he blurted as he barreled toward the door.

"Axel! Wait, you can't just..." Rainee tried to persuade him, but he couldn't hear her. The blood in his ears was too loud.

He was out of her room and down the stairs before she could follow him. His chest hurt in a way that made him prefer the sword wound. She cared about him. She wanted to know his darkness, and she didn't shy away. She kissed him back, even. And he'd let himself believe for a moment that maybe, this time, he could care without it breaking something. But reality was cruel, and it crept back in before the elation wore off. How was he supposed to look at her now? How was he supposed to keep his distance when all he could think about was the way her lips felt on his? The way she seemed to stick his broken pieces back together, without even trying?

Walking away was the right choice, he told himself as he sank down against the door of his bedroom. He knew he shouldn't be bothered like this. He had been through so much worse, but still. Anything or anyone that he had ever let himself want or love was dead, and he couldn't let her get close enough to suffer the same fate. Everything felt numb except for his lips, which were a gentle reminder that he had blown everything. But it still felt good. And that would be his undoing.

CHAPTER 44
SYREN

Syren had managed to claw his way back to the surface of his own mind, a feat that was getting increasingly difficult to accomplish. Kai had been with him for years, acting as advisor. There had never been any issues until recently. Kai was getting darker, more twisted. In fact, he didn't feel like Kai at all, rather a shell with his brother's voice attached to it. But Syren didn't know how to get rid of him. There was no safe place to plan, not when the enemy lived inside him.

    He had kept Kai a secret from the entire realm, letting them think he was really dead. It had seemed to be the safest option at the time. Now he had no one to help him. No one to recognize when his actions weren't his own. What actions *were* his anymore? He wasn't even sure of that himself.

    He had tried a handful of times to reverse the strike orders on the men, but each time Kai had forced his way in and smothered Syren in a cloud of black fog. Syren had figured out how to fight his way out, but Kai was getting stronger. Or maybe Syren's will was getting weaker.

    He had managed to make a small stride, in a trade deal with the Water Realm. They had agreed to return a quarter of the Fire Realm soldiers they had imprisoned in exchange for any information Syren had obtained about the demigod. It wasn't the *best* deal, but it meant that some of their soldiers would come home. And he doubted that their intel on Rainee was anything substantial compared to the details held in the Western Division's Archives. They were supposed to be allies to the Olympians, after all.

He sat on the edge of his bed with his head in his hands. The headaches had dulled for now, and Kai had been oddly quiet this morning, which seemed like a victory in a swarm of losses. He forced himself to stand and walk to the mirror. He was starting to look more like himself, but older. So much older. Eighteen years of fighting for control of your own mind and body would do that to an individual.

As he stared in the mirror, the image started to shift. He blinked, hoping it was just an illusion due to weeks-long sleep deprivation. Even in his void state, there was no rest, only a struggle for control. But the reflection continued twisting and distorting until it was Kai staring back at him. It was Kai, yet he looked different. More fractured.

Syren didn't move; he just stared at his brother. The man that he once would have trusted with anything, the one he would have died for just to get an ounce of his approval. Now he looked like a corruption of that version of Kai. His eyes were even a subtle red color, like he was something else entirely.

<Brother,> Kai greeted, a smile on his lips.

Syren sighed. The quiet had been nice while it had lasted. "Kai. What now?" His head throbbed as Kai pushed against his consciousness.

<Are you going to cooperate today, Little Brother?> Kai's voice reverberated through his skull. <Or do I need to be in charge again?> Syren felt the fog starting to close in on him.

He clawed mentally to stay afloat, gasping as he momentarily broke free. "I-I'll do what you want, Kai," he stumbled. "Just please, let me have one day as myself."

The fog vanished as quickly as it had come, and it was replaced by the fading sound of Kai's laughter. Syren looked into the mirror again, and this time his own face stared back, sweat beading on his forehead. He had learned that resisting Kai's will was futile and would only end up with them at the brink of war…just how they were right now.

CHAPTER 45
SAPPHIRE

Sapphire lay in the bed that Finn had offered to her, her holodisk blinking beside her. Her father had been trying to trace her for hours, but she had thought ahead and had Connor put a tracer block on her device. She could still get messages and track other people, but she was officially off-grid to the Water Realm. It was bittersweet, really.

Her holodisk rang, causing her to sit straight up. She prayed it wasn't her father, but her heart jumped to her throat when she saw the caller tag: Tobias SwiftStream. Her head swam with ideas of what he might have to say, and she almost didn't answer. Remembering that he had helped her leave, she sighed and hit Accept.

Her brother's face appeared in holograph form, but she could tell he was hiding somewhere.

"Sapphire…" His voice crackled. The signal must be weak in this realm. "You need to…Father…He's coming…" The signal died there. Her brother's face flashed and then disappeared. But she had heard enough to comprehend.

Her father was coming to get her. And, by the tone of Tobias's voice, it didn't sound like he was happy. She knew her father. He'd tear through this realm like a hurricane and drag her back home by her hair. She'd never be allowed to leave her room…if he even let her keep it. He may even string her up in the courtyard, just to show people that no one crosses Aydron SwiftStream. Not even his own daughter.

CHAPTER 46
SCOTT

Scott had been sitting in the comm room for an hour, waiting for the rest of the house to fall asleep. He'd heard Axel finally storm in sometime around eleven, slam his bedroom door, and not re-emerge. He didn't want to know what that was about.

He had typed and deleted the same message three times. A simple coordinate string. A pickup location. He hadn't worked up the nerve to press Send yet. He hesitated every time he got close. He thought about how much he'd given up already, and how much these boys challenged him, but he couldn't force himself to turn them in. Being given to the gods was a fate worse than death. They never *just* killed someone. There were always trials and games and just enough hope to convince the victim that they might survive. They never did.

He took a swig of Char Brew from the bottle. It was too late for cups. Every decision he had ever made, every mistake, had led him here. And he was paying for it. The liquor tasted bitter, the only sign that he'd probably had too much, but he didn't care. He took another drink for good measure.

He'd never admit it to their faces, but those Fire Realm brats had started to feel like more than harbored fugitives, even felt dangerously close to his sons. They each had their quirks—Finn's quiet loyalty, even when he was clearly terrified; Axel's sarcastic deflection because he couldn't handle his own emotions; and Connor's hopeful innocence that hadn't yet been destroyed by the world. Each of them was different, but each of them had given Scott a reason to fight for them. And he didn't know what to do, knowing he had to give that up.

Fuck you, Hermes. He slammed his bottle down on the comm.

He deleted the line again. Just in time to hear a small knock behind him. He jumped, pulling his feet off the comm table and spinning around.

There stood Connor, wide-awake, looking like he'd spent the last hour running his hands through his hair because he didn't know what else to do with them. "Is that…Char Brew?" he asked, motioning to the bottle.

Scott raised the bottle and nodded, his pulse hammering in his ears. He'd nearly been caught betraying the boy in front of him. "Last bottle I ever got from the Fire Realm. Must be…eighteen years old, at least." He paused, searching Connor. He looked so young standing there in Scott's old clothes that swallowed him up. Scott's heart ached. "What are you doing awake?" His tone was soft and concerned.

Connor shrugged. "I thought I heard the beacon ping go off; I wanted to check just in case." He looked between Scott and the bottle of liquor. "What about you?"

Scott sighed, trying to decide how to answer without sounding like the worst person imaginable. "Just some loud thoughts, I guess." He gestured for Connor to sit down.

Connor took a seat, staring at Scott like he could see right through him. And, maybe he could. "I've been thinking…" Connor started. Scott's heart fell. This kid was going to break him without trying. Again. "About the holodisk files…about the fact that we're fugitives now." He looked into Scott's eyes, fear shining in his emerald pools. Scott could tell he was having trouble putting his emotions into words, so he leaned forward and put a hand on Connor's shoulder. Connor smiled gratefully, his eyes still haunted. "It just feels like…" He took a deep breath. "I never got a chance to be…good."

Scott's breath caught. Connor didn't know that he was calling Scott out, but he was. In the most innocent way possible. Because Scott had been given the chance to be good, to make the right choices, and he was actively choosing his villain story.

"Not a lot of people do, kid," he choked out, trying to sound neutral. Like a parent giving advice instead of a traitor.

Connor nodded, leaning back in his chair. He stared at the floor for a moment before looking back at Scott. "But, *you* did." Scott nearly collapsed in on himself. "You helped us when you could have killed us." Connor's eyes shone with admiration, and it set Scott's chest on fire. "Thank you for that, by the way," he added sincerely.

The kid thought so highly of him, but he didn't really deserve it. He was a fraud. A moral complex hidden behind dad guilt and god-binding chains. He was worse than Syren at this point.

He nodded slowly. "Anytime, kid." He was trying to smother the ache in his chest, but Connor's words, and the way he was looking at him with heroic wonder, wouldn't allow him to shut the ache down.

He stood, gesturing for the door. "I think it's time we both got some sleep." Connor stood and followed him. Scott turned, placing a hand on his shoulder. Then, before he could think better of it, he pulled the kid into a hug. Connor fumbled for a second, surprised, but then hugged him back awkwardly.

Scott pulled away, clapped him on the shoulder, and whispered with a smile, "And for the record, you *are* the good guy. I don't care what some glitchy holodisk file says." He winked at Connor, who looked like he might cry.

Connor smiled, a silent thank you, then retreated to his room. Scott stood in the doorway of the comm room, still reeling.

He nodded to himself. He knew what his decision was without a doubt. And it started with the fact that the gods could go fuck themselves. How dare those smug assholes give *him* an ultimatum. But now he needed to figure out how to keep them all safe. From a foe that was much older and meaner than he could ever be.

He turned the lights off, shut the door, and made his way to the stairs. But not before checking on the other soldiers. Finn was passed out on the basement couch, one arm slung over his face and a blanket draped across his legs. Then Scott peeked in on Axel, who was sleeping restlessly on the floor, still in the clothes he had worn that morning.

He could hear Sapphire stirring in her room, but opted not to bother her. He hadn't gotten to know her much yet, but she didn't seem like the type for late night check-ins from her host. She might stab him by accident.

    He snuck upstairs and made sure Rainee was asleep, then went to his bedroom. He felt at peace, despite the coming storm. History was about to be made, and he'd be damned if he was going to be on the wrong side of it.

CHAPTER 46
AXEL

The morning came too quickly for Axel. He pushed himself up off the floor where he had practically collapsed the night before and wiped the drool from his cheek. His mouth still tingled slightly, and he wished briefly that he had just died in his sleep. Just so that he didn't have to face Rainee after what had happened in her bedroom.

He opened the door to his room slowly, checking for anyone who might question his outburst last night, even though he was pretty sure everyone was asleep when he had flown downstairs. He marched over to Connor's room, barely knocked, and pulled Connor, still half asleep, over to the weapons he had sharpened yesterday.

"Rise and shine, kid. It's training day," he said gruffly.

Connor rubbed his eyes and looked down at his plaid pajama pants. "Can I at least put on actual clothes?"

"You have five minutes or I'm dragging you back out here, clothed or not," Axel threatened, waving his knife at Connor.

Connor groaned and trudged back to his room. He knew Axel would make good on his threat. Finn stirred slightly from the couch, sitting up and blinking away sleep.

"Axel?" he asked, a yawn in his throat. "Isn't it a little early for sparring?"

Axel shook his head, overly eager to move. To get his mind off everything for a little while. "Never too early when the world is ending, Captain." And boy, was Axel's world ending.

He picked out a dagger from Scott's collection, one with a gold hilt. It was one of the only knives in his collection, but it had a good grip on it—perfect to teach Connor the basics.

Finn lay back down on the couch with a groan, then forced himself into a sitting position. Perfect, he could join them for knife practice.

"Where were you last night?" Finn asked, making Axel jump slightly. His heart pounded in his chest. "We all stayed around to make sure Rainee was okay, but you disappeared." Axel let out a sigh of relief. *Oh, just that part. Not the...*

He shrugged, swinging the knife in absentminded strokes. "I needed some air." He paused and looked at Finn. "When a girl shoots electricity at you—" He sighed. "—it makes it a little hard to breathe."

It wasn't a lie, not really. It *had* been hard to breathe, but not from shock. He didn't have a name for the feeling he had when she collapsed. But he knew he'd do anything to never have to feel it again.

Finn nodded, unconvinced, eyeing the wrinkled clothes that Axel had worn yesterday, still clinging to his body. He knew he looked like a wreck. He *felt* like a wreck, too. But he would never admit that. He couldn't.

Connor emerged from his room then, breaking the awkward silence. He'd thrown on a new T-shirt and shorts, but had left his hair an unruly mess. Axel respected that.

"Ready?" he asked, already heading for the stairs. Knife combat was best practiced outdoors, where there was more space for errors and less chance of damaged drywall.

Connor nodded reluctantly, but he didn't argue. The boys all knew that Axel was going to drag them into this whether they really wanted to or not.

No one else was awake when they emerged from the basement; the first light of dawn had just started to creep through the kitchen window, which made it a perfect time for stealth melee training. This was Axel's prime time.

He was also glad that Scott wasn't in the kitchen yet. Axel had briefly made eye contact with him as he returned to his room last night, and he wanted to avoid as many questions as possible. He was hoping that if he was locked in a training session when the rest of the house woke up, he would be able to avoid answering any questions for a few hours longer.

But he knew he couldn't avoid Rainee forever. She wouldn't allow it, first of all, not after he'd kissed her. He'd practically sealed his own fate. He just hoped they could talk about it away from prying eyes. The last thing he needed was for Finn to find out. Not when Axel had teased him so relentlessly at the start of this mission.

Maybe Connor would accidentally slit his throat during training, and he could just die in peace. Was that too much to ask?

They stepped into the backyard, the morning air cool and thick with mist. *Even better.* Axel turned to Connor and offered him the gold-hilted dagger, holding it gently by the blade. He had sharpened it perfectly, something that had taken him years to master.

He pulled out his own knife and held it up, getting into a ready position. "Okay, the first rule of any melee combat is to be faster than your opponent." He crouched, bouncing on the balls of his feet. "You keep moving, making sure your footsteps are light, and you move just unpredictably enough that you're one step ahead."

Finn chuckled lightly. "And then you get run through by a sword."

"That…" Axel said, trying not to laugh. It was true, he was one to talk about agility and maintaining unpredictability, when he'd nearly died in melee combat. "That was a one-off. Too many external factors." He brushed it off. In a way, he was happy that Finn could joke about the sword incident. He was worried that he would always feel guilty about it. Then Axel would have to bully him until he felt better, and that sounded exhausting.

Finn held his hands up in fake innocence, but Axel could see the smile on both his and Connor's faces. It hit him at that moment that he was grateful that he was on this mission with them. That somehow, the most unlikely team had been chosen to do this. Despite them both being annoying.

He lined up with Connor, motioning for him to take a few practice swipes. "Axel…I don't…" He hesitated, looking between Axel and the knife.

"Trust me, just try to hit me," Axel reassured, toe to toe with Connor.

Connor sighed, getting into a ready position and taking a few weak swings at Axel with the knife. Axel easily dodged them.

"You're not even trying," Axel accused, waving his knife at Connor. "I can't teach you anything if you're not going to put effort in." He motioned for him to get back into the ready position. "Try again. This time, pretend you want to kill me."

"Who's pretending?" Finn murmured.

Axel let the jab slide with nothing more than a glare in Finn's direction. Connor got ready and took his first swing. Axel dodged, grabbed Connor's arm, and flipped him onto his back in the grass before anyone could blink.

"That was too predictable," Axel said gently.

Axel helped Connor, who looked slightly embarrassed, to his feet. Axel couldn't help but smile. The amount of times he'd ended up in similar situations while learning how to fight was more than he would ever admit, but it was refreshing to be able to share his skillset.

"If you three are going to spar at six a.m., at least wear helmets." Scott's voice startled Axel. Scott was standing in the doorway, coffee in hand, still in pajamas. "Last thing I need is a bunch of Divisional Council members showing up and executing one of you for breaking common form." He sipped his coffee. "We're in enough trouble already." He turned to go back inside, gesturing vaguely to the house. "I have helmets in the attic."

Of course he does.

***

The clinking of dishes sounded too loud to Axel that morning. It was deafly quiet, save for Connor, who was talking about their training session with Rainee. She was smiling politely while stealing glances at Axel across the table. He was so screwed.

Scott had finally cooked the last of the bacon and had left the house with a promise of getting more groceries after work, while mumbling, "Cleaning out the butcher, at this rate." He was still trying to maintain some mask of normalcy for the outside world, which Axel could respect.

Finn was up in the attic, digging around for the helmets Scott had mentioned. Sapphire hadn't made her way to the table yet, which was fine by Axel. Less witnesses for his inevitable breakdown.

"So, you know a lot about melee combat?" Rainee asked, staring at him. His heart hammered in his chest. He briefly thought about walking away, but he knew she'd follow him. And he knew how that scenario ended. He nodded slowly, not trusting himself to speak without his voice cracking. Her eyes lit up, and he about died.

"You should let me join the next training session." She leaned in closer. "I spent eight years doing martial arts and self-defense classes because my dad insisted." She eyed him. "I think we'd be a good match."

He didn't think she was just talking about fighting.

Axel cleared his throat, trying to swallow his heart back into his chest. "Yeah…"

"That is, unless you're scared." She smiled slyly, leaning back in her chair. "Which I get, honestly."

He stiffened. Kiss aside, that was a challenge, and Axel never backed down from a challenge. He stood, placing his hands on the table. "If you really think you stand a chance, let's go. Right now."

She stood to meet him. "Challenge accepted, blondie." She walked to the sliding door and opened it. "Don't forget your helmet." She gestured to Finn, who was standing in the kitchen doorway, with the helmets in his hands. He looked dumbfounded.

Connor looked between Axel and Rainee like he wasn't sure what just happened, but he was all for it. Rainee led the way outside, grabbing the gold-hilted blade from where Connor had left it in the grass. Axel ignored her comment about a helmet. She wouldn't be getting a move in, let alone hurting him.

She was twirling the dagger in her hand, watching him closely, reading him. He didn't like that. She got into a crouched position, staring at him as he slowly did the same.

"On three?" he questioned. She nodded, her eyes never leaving his. His pulse was already thumping in his ears as he started counting. "One….two…"

"Three!" she shouted, lunging at him. She swiped her knife, and he caught it with his own, just before it nicked his chin. She didn't wait, ducking under him, circling like a wolf. Axel was impressed. She was quick. Almost as quick as him.

He followed her movements with ease, at first. Then she smiled, and he lost his concentration for a split second. That was all it took; her foot hooked under his leg and yanked him to the ground. She kneeled beside him, her knee on his chest, and smirked. "Looks like you need more practice, blondie."

He couldn't breathe. His heart was drumming in his ears, and all he could feel was her knee on his chest. His senses were overwhelmed by her touch, her smell. *Her.*

He could hear Finn and Connor clapping distantly as she helped him up. He wasn't embarrassed, but he was impressed. He couldn't remember the last time someone had actually beaten him in a spar.

Her hand lingered in his a bit too long, so he pulled her closer and whispered, "I'd like to see you do it again, static."

He was trying to control his breathing, but she smirked, locked eyes with him, and said, "Anytime."

She broke away and went back to the house, handing the knife to Connor as she passed. Axel was aware of Finn's gaze on him. There was no way he hadn't noticed that tension. Axel was practically unraveled in a single sparring match. And he'd do it again just to feel her close to him. *What was happening to him?*

"Are you okay?" Finn asked. Axel knew he didn't mean physically.

Axel shrugged. "Fine. Just a little tired." He started back toward the house.

"Tired?" Finn questioned. "Axel, I've never seen you lose a spar..."

Axel gritted his teeth and kept walking. "Just lost my concentration," he murmured. "Won't happen again." He didn't know why the words sounded like an apology.

He went inside, shutting the door and leaving Finn and Connor to their own devices. Rainee was standing by the island, sipping a glass of water. Obviously waiting for him.

She set it down on the counter. "So," she said, looking him up and down. "Are we going to talk about last night, or are you still pretending it didn't happen?"

Axel froze. He knew this would play out eventually, but he had hoped it wouldn't be so soon. He was still recovering from the feeling of her knee on his chest. "Look, I didn't…"

"You didn't mean to?" Rainee chuckled. She sounded angry.

Axel didn't blame her; a hit-and-run kiss doesn't leave the best feeling.

"You *kissed* me." She looked up at him, the kitchen lights flickering slightly. "Then you ran away like I repulsed you." She looked away. "How am I supposed to take that, Axel?"

Axel sucked in a breath. His heart was pounding relentlessly. It was a miracle he hadn't had a heart attack from the events of the last 24 hours. His mouth went dry. There was nothing he could say to talk himself out of this one.

"You did what?" Finn's voice sent another chill down his spine. *Dammit.* Axel looked at him, the guilt plain on his face. Axel was never going to live this down.

"Don't act so innocent, Mr. almost-kiss" Rainee said, shooting a glare at him. Finn looked like he had been hit by a truck. Axel knew it. He *did* have feelings for her.

Axel perked up a little. "I'm sorry, what was that?"

He was both relieved and angry that Finn had tried to kiss her, but he was ignoring the anger for the sake of his own sanity. Connor was standing behind Finn, fidgeting relentlessly as he watched the scene unfold.

Rainee stepped closer to Axel, her skin radiating electricity. "You two—" She motioned toward him and Finn. "—need to figure this out." She pushed past Axel on her way to the living room. "My emotions aren't something you can just play with and fight over," she threw over her shoulder. Then she was gone.

Finn and Axel stood there staring at each other, neither one of them sure whether they should fight each other or forget the whole situation. Connor nudged his way around Finn and held the knife out to Finn. "Here, you may want this."

Axel smirked. It wouldn't help him if Axel ever got hold of him.

CHAPTER 47
FINN

Finn was standing in the basement common room, his mind spinning. He knew he should have kissed her. Now Axel—*Axel*—had beaten him to the punch. He didn't know why he was so angry, it wasn't like they had committed to anything. He just thought that maybe there was some sort of mutual attraction after the castlight powder and the almost-kiss.

He shook his head and tugged a clean shirt over his chest. Rainee had gone to school, while the boys had opted to stay behind today. There was no need for surveillance when the target already knew you were there…and lived in the same house.

Finn sat down on the couch, his mind drifting to home. It was weird how much he missed about his old life, despite it taking a downward spiral recently. He had finally reconnected with his parents, whom he hadn't seen since he had joined the military at thirteen. Now they had probably been told he was dead…or a criminal. Finn wasn't sure which story was worse.

He had given his entire life to the military, save for a few years of childhood bliss. He had put everything he had into climbing the ranks, being the best anyone had ever seen. Only to be unraveled by one decision. Not even a decision he regretted, either. He'd make the same call again, if given the chance.

He always dreamed of retiring from the military after his service was over and settling down. He hadn't paid much attention to emotions or love until this mission; he had always been too busy. Now, if he lived long enough to settle down, he wouldn't hesitate. He thought maybe that new life could start with Rainee. He thought about the way she had looked at him after she had smudged castlight powder on his face. She was happy, but there was more there. She looked at Finn like he was safe, and he took pride in that. But he knew all of that was about to go up in smoke. He shook his head. What was he saying? He barely knew her.

Now Axel was in her sight. And you didn't win against a man like him. He would fight you without trying and still win. He dripped charm, and obviously Rainee had noticed. Finn couldn't compete with a man who looked like Axel, either. He'd seen goddesses swoon for less.

He'd been trained to wait for the right moment and read the openings, but Axel had never cared about technique. Now, Finn had to deal with the knowledge that his hesitation might have opened the door for Axel. At least, she was angry at both of them now. That could be his only saving grace. He didn't want to overwhelm her; she had too much to think about without a couple of degenerates fighting over her.

That's why you're the safe one. Axel's voice echoed in his head. It made sense now. That night was Axel's first undoing. When he was still trying to convince her—and himself—that he wasn't a good choice. He'd said those words with longing. Like he'd *never* be the safe one.

But Finn didn't know if being safe was what got the girl. It sure didn't seem like it.

"You okay?" Connor asked from the hallway. Finn hadn't seen him standing there. He was drying his hair with a towel, wearing fresh clothes. His other outfit was dirt- and grass-stained from Axel's sparring lesson.

Finn sighed and pushed himself to his feet. "Yeah, fine…"

He started to pace. Connor didn't say anything, just stared at him. Why was he so good at that? The kid could be an interrogation expert, but all he'd have to do was stand there.

"Do you know where Axel is?" Connor asked. It was an innocent enough question, but it tore a hole in Finn's mask.

His face twitched. "No. Probably ripping his own heart out in the backyard." *Or he's kissing her again.*

Connor nodded, sensing that he had hit a nerve. Finn sighed and sat down on the couch with his head in his hands. "How did we get here?" he mumbled, not expecting an answer.

Connor took a seat across from him, looking a little uncomfortable.

Finn studied him. "This was supposed to be a simple mission," Finn said, his voice tight. "Kill the girl, go home. Nothing more." He exhaled, trying to keep his voice even. "Why couldn't I do it?"

Connor tilted his head slightly, then spoke up. "I don't think we ever had a choice."

"What?" Finn was floored. Of course they had a choice, and Finn had made the *wrong* one at the time. He knew that, even if he could go back, he would save her again and again. The spiral would have started no matter what. This was the same dilemma—with a different overlay—as the one that had resulted in his demotion.

Connor continued, "We were chosen based on our skillsets." He met Finn's eyes. "Even with limited resources, there were other soldiers on the list that IceHeart could have sent." He straightened his torso, as if this thought was new to him, too. "So why did he pick the soldier with a history of insubordination, the ex-criminal, and the rookie?" He shook his head. "I don't think we were ever meant to succeed. And maybe...IceHeart knew that from the beginning."

Finn was shaking, the thought had crossed his mind and he hadn't given it much merit, but the more Connor talked, the more it made sense to him. "I think you've talked to Axel too much," he said simply, but he couldn't hide the quiver in his voice.

"Have you ever listened to him?" Connor asked. "Sometimes he makes too much sense to ignore."

Those words were enough to turn Finn's blood to ice. If Connor, the hopeful one, the one holding everyone together with his optimism, had fully slipped into Axel's cynical hellscape, Finn didn't think this world would be worth saving.

"It's not all bad, you know," Finn tried to insert, but even he knew it was a lie.

"It's not all good, either," Connor murmured, looking up at him again. For the first time, his green eyes didn't shine, and that was enough to nearly break Finn.

He was right. Gods, he was right. But Finn wished like hell that he wasn't. That he'd say something stupid and naive to break the tension. They'd been there five days, and they'd already killed two men, Finn's stoicism, Axel's sanity, and now Connor's innocence. He had a feeling the next thing to die would be a lot more tangible, but he didn't know how to say that without sounding like a pessimist. He just had a feeling. Dread. Like something was looming over them, and there was no way they all were getting out unscathed.

CHAPTER 48
SCOTT

Scott should have taken the day off. He thought that immersing himself in the normal world would help him forget the hell that was waiting for him back home. However, there was no such reprieve. He pulled into the driveway, his car silent. There was no radio station loud enough to drown his thoughts that night. He'd been thinking about how he was going to keep all these realm rejects safe, and how the war that was coming had a chance to destroy this realm completely. There was no way to cope with that.

He got out and pulled the grocery bags from the butcher shop out of the backseat. The look on the butcher's face when he'd asked for hundreds of pounds of meat and fish was priceless.

"Feeding an army?" the butcher had quipped. But he didn't know how close that was to the truth.

Scott had laughed and said he was just stocking up for the next few months. He knew they'd run through it in a month or less. He'd seen how those boys ate. He'd purchased bacon and a few different fish varieties. He didn't know what was closest to Spritan fish, but he hoped that salmon was okay.

He unlocked the door to a quiet house. *Weird.* Rainee usually greeted him when he walked in, and the boys had been getting more comfortable just milling about. He expected to see or hear at least one of them. He was about to panic and check all the rooms when Axel ducked in from the backyard. With the amount of time he spent outside, Scott wondered if he should just build him a doghouse.

Scott nodded at him, setting the groceries on the counter. "You didn't kill the others while I was gone, did you?" he joked.

He saw Axel's expression lighten a little, but his eyes remained distant. He shook his head. "Nah, but none of them want to spar with me anymore." Axel coughed and looked away, "Except maybe Rainee…"

Scott raised an eyebrow. "You sparred with Rainee?"

Axel nodded slowly.

Scott knew Rainee could hold her own; he'd made sure of it. But he was curious. "And how did that go?" He started unpacking the grocery bags, putting most of it in the freezer to thaw later.

Axel coughed and let out a small laugh. "She kicked my ass."

Scott smiled. He expected nothing less from her, and someone needed to be able to put Axel in his place when Scott wasn't around. Axel was quiet, but not in the normal way that made him Axel. It was more in a thinking way, which seemed new for him. He was usually a "stab first, ask later" type of person.

Scott continued putting the groceries away, but threw out, "You doing okay?" It was a simple question, yet Scott wasn't sure he wanted to hear the answer.

Axel sighed and shook his head. "Yeah, I guess."

Scott didn't reply, just nodded, and went back to cleaning up the kitchen after all the groceries were put away. He waited. He knew there was more; he could feel it, but he wouldn't pry into business that wasn't his, even if it involved his daughter.

Axel ran his hands through his hair and exhaled slowly. "You ever have someone look at you like maybe—" He spoke as he paced around the kitchen. "—you weren't all bad?"

Scott paused before answering. It was obvious that he was talking about Rainee, but he didn't think either one of them was ready to admit that out loud. "Yes," he said quietly. He thought back to Rainee's mom, the way she had looked at him like he hung the stars. Tears pricked his eyes. "That's how they get you," he whispered, mostly to himself. He'd been nothing more than a rowdy young Realm Guardian when they'd met. He had been more trouble than he was worth; he knew that for a fact. But she didn't care. She made him feel like much more.

He busied himself with wiping down the island counter. It was already spotless, yet he kept scrubbing.

"What was her name?" Axel asked, catching Scott off guard. "Your wife, I mean." The question was innocent enough, but coming from Axel it felt out of place.

"Liora," he choked, but he was able to bite back a sob. He scrubbed the counter harder, moving from one end to the other, not meeting Axel's eyes.

Axel watched him for a few beats longer, like he had more questions but didn't know how to ask them. After what seemed like an agonizingly long time, he sighed and said, "Thank you."

Scott looked up, a little dumbfounded. "For what?"

"Not letting me die." He turned to leave the kitchen, throwing the last bit over his shoulder. "And for this. Whatever this was." Then he was gone.

Scott froze. For a moment, it almost felt like he and Axel were the same person, separated only by age, and that terrified him more than any war threat.

He tucked the cleaning products into the cupboard, then went to do his nightly rounds. Finn wasn't in his normal spot on the couch, but Scott could hear the shower running.

He knocked on Connor's door, poked his head in, and asked if he needed anything. Connor was sitting cross-legged on the bed with multiple field guides spread out in front of him. The kid was always learning.

Scott moved to knock on Sapphire's door and got no response. He knocked again. Nothing. He opened the door slowly, trying not to disturb her if she was asleep. But the room was empty.

Panic hit him. He stepped inside, looking around. The bed was neatly made, and on it was a folded letter with Rainee's name scrawled on it in neat calligraphy handwriting.

He opened it, his blood turning to ice. All it said was, *I had to leave, or he'd take you too. I'm sorry.* —*S*

Who was *he*? And what would he possibly want with Rainee? Was Sapphire working with IceHeart? Or someone worse? He realized that he hadn't asked her enough questions. He knew she was from the Water Realm, but his knowledge stopped there. *Stupid.*

He turned to walk out of the room, the letter still in his hand, and nearly collided with Finn.

"Did you talk to Sapphire today?" he asked, holding up the letter.

Finn shook his head. "No, she's been in her room all day." He was wearing a pair of gym shorts and had a towel slung over his shoulders. Do any of these boys wear shirts? Scott wondered briefly.

"And no one thought to check on her?" Scott asked, panicking. How long had she been gone? He knew she was still there when he went to bed, but he hadn't seen her before he left for work. *Fuck*. What was that? Twelve hours? Was there a way to file a missing person's report on a Spritan?

Finn grabbed the letter from Scott's hand and read it slowly, his eyes widening. "Who's *he*?" he asked, echoing Scott's own thoughts.

"Hell if I know. But he doesn't seem like someone we want to take chances with," Scott declared.

Hearing the commotion, Connor emerged from his room, a field guide open in his hands. "What's going on?" he asked, looking from Scott to Finn.

"Sapphire's gone," Finn answered without looking at Connor. He was studying the note like it might give him more answers if he stared at it hard enough.

Connor shut the book and peeked over Finn's shoulder at the letter. "She told me this morning that she was going for a walk," he said casually. "Is she not back yet?" Scott and Finn looked at him simultaneously.

"You saw her?" Scott asked.

Connor nodded, still not worried. "Yeah, before I showered. She was coming out of her room. She seemed…fine, just like maybe she hadn't slept much."

Scott pushed past him, nearly sprinting to the comm room. He typed the serial number he had pulled off Sapphire's holodisk into the computer. Nothing popped up.

Connor sucked in a breath. "She had me put a tracker block on her holodisk yesterday. I didn't really think anything of it. Tracker blocks are probably a good thing for all of us right now."

Not when she might be in danger and we can't find her.

"Did you pack her bag for her, too?" Finn snapped. It sounded harsh. Panicked.

Scott looked over at Connor, who seemed like he was about to cry. "Finn, that's enough. Connor couldn't have known this was her plan."

Finn backed off, realizing that he had taken it too far. He stood with his arms crossed in the doorway of the comm room.

"What now?" Connor asked quietly.

Scott sighed. "There's not much we can do. She's been gone for at least a few hours." He looked at the boys. "We'll wait for a beacon ping if there is one, but until then, there's not much more that I can do." It killed him to admit that. Sapphire hadn't been there long, but he still felt responsible for her.

Whatever this was, he needed to make sure they were ready for an attack at any time. This was getting real too fast for his liking, and none of them were ready.

CHAPTER 49
SAPPHIRE

Sapphire had decided it was best if she left. There was no sense in her father destroying the human realm, looking for her when she wasn't even sure what her actual business was there. It wasn't like she could stop the divine undoing that was about to happen.

She could, however, protect Rainee from the king. If there was any chance of stopping this war, Rainee didn't need any other odds against her.

Sapphire stood in the clearing, her heart pounding in her ears. She held the holodisk out in front of her and pressed the button combinations that would undo the tracking block. She knew that Aydron would find her with or without the tracker, but she didn't want him tearing up the wrong side of Earth when she could make it easier for everyone. She also wasn't going to go to him. He was already on a rampage; let him find her. Let his holodisk ping the beacons.

It's not like turning herself in would lessen his wrath, anyway. He was already angry, and he didn't play nice when he was angry. She'd learned that when she was far too young.

The sun had already set by the time a portal opened across the clearing. Aydron SwiftStream stepped into the clearing like a storm front. The wind picked up speed around them and the sky seemed to darken like the stars had been snuffed out. The portal closed behind him. No guards. No portal light. Just them. And somehow, that was scarier.

Sapphire stood, and he was on her like a lion. "You dare to make a fool out of me, *Daughter*?" He spat the word at her like an insult. Like it was a disgrace for her to be associated with him at all.

The feeling was mutual. He drew his sword and tilted her chin up with the end of it.

"I was completing my mission..." she started to explain. She was calm, too calm for someone with a sword to their throat. This song and dance routine was nothing new to her.

"You were mingling with known enemies of the realm," Aydron growled. "What do you take me for?" His eyes were shining with anger and bloodlust. It was a look she'd seen on him many times in her life. The king's hands were far from clean. She had just never pushed him far enough for it to be a personal concern.

She stared at him calmly, forcing her heartbeat to stay steady. "I was keeping her safe," she said simply. It wasn't a lie. She *had* been trying to keep her safe, but she had realized that that task was beyond her skill set. Nothing could keep her safe if the realms *and* the gods were both fighting over her.

"And the Fire Realm soldiers?" he asked, pressing his blade deep enough for her to feel it, but not deep enough to break skin. Yet. "Why are they still alive?"

She didn't answer.

Aydron smiled coldly. "Just as I thought." He removed his sword from her chin but didn't sheath it. "If you were really protecting her, you would have killed them already."

How could she explain that they weren't enemies? That their own realm had forsaken them and put a hit on their heads? They were as helpless as Rainee.

She knew that her father wouldn't listen. Anyone from the Fire Realm was an enemy, even if the circumstances told a different story. They disagreed on that often. He ruled with a diplomatic ruthlessness that looked elegant on the outside but stripped those closest to him down to nothing. Just like he was trying to do now.

Little did he know that Sapphire had already surrendered to her fate. Whatever he could do to her, she refused to fear him— refused to bow down to someone who used fear as a power structure and committed war crimes to assert dominance, all while playing the part of the peaceful king. Maybe some part of her, the young child who wanted her father's approval, would have cowered and begged for forgiveness. But she'd seen his dungeons, and she'd rather be thrown in one than for him to continue to torture and kill soldiers just for their realm of origin. She would sooner die than believe that all Flamease were bad. They couldn't be any worse than the man standing in front of her, threatening his own daughter for the act of sparing lives.

"Nothing else to say, Daughter?" he questioned, stepping closer to her. She locked eyes with him and shook her head. He didn't deserve her words.

The hilt of his sword hit her face before she could think. She crumpled to the ground, staring up at him, still unbreaking, but with a throbbing jaw. "You will speak when spoken to," he hissed, his eyes gleaming.

"Aydron SwiftStream," a familiar voice called from the trees. Sapphire's head was reeling from the blow, but she would recognize that voice anywhere. *Scott.*

No! It was too dangerous for him to be there. Her father would...But her father's demeanor shifted immediately, like he also recognized the voice. He was back to his diplomatic mask. The peaceful king.

"Scott!" he replied, stepping forward. "I wasn't expecting you here. How long has it been?"

Sapphire watched Scott step from the trees and offer his hand to Aydron. They shook hands like old friends. What the hell was going on here?

"Aydron, I saw a Water Realm portal ping hit the beacons I monitor. I wanted to make sure there was no danger." Scott eyed Sapphire, just enough for her to realize he was bluffing. The ping was probably true, but he came for her.

Aydron shook his head, the fake smile still on his face. "No danger here, brother. Just came to retrieve my daughter."

"Daughter?" Scott looked genuinely shocked. Sapphire realized that she hadn't had a chance to fully introduce herself to him, but she figured the boys would have filled him in. The smile never left Scott's face. "If I had known she was yours, I would have prepared a better living arrangement," he said. It was subtle. Scott didn't know how much her father knew about the Fire Realm soldiers living in his house, but he was fishing.

Her father faltered, like he was about to say something about the boys—that he knew they were here, that Scott was helping them—but he quickly regained composure. "No need to worry there, I should have sent you a notice." He cleared his throat. "I was unaware that you still served the pantheon."

"I don't," Scott said, his voice even. He eyed Aydron before continuing, "I monitor beacon pings as part of my inter-realm duties. I'm one of the last humans who knows how." He paused. "I have long since broken my ties to Zeus and his court." He talked like a practiced diplomat; someone who knew the right things to say, the correct names to drop, and how to de-escalate a rampaging king.

Aydron's mask dropped, his smile cold and calculated. He drew his sword. "If you have no alliance, then I can assume you have no backing."

"You could assume that." Scott nodded, still not breaking the diplomatic character he had on. "But you'd be wrong."

Faster than Sapphire could blink, Scott had pulled god-binding chains from his belt and had one cuffed around her father's sword arm. She was shocked. Her father had always been fast, and to see a human outwit and outmaneuver him was unheard of.

She heard a rustle from the trees, and Finn, Axel, and Connor stepped into the clearing. Aydron looked at Scott, dumbfounded. "This is treason against the Western Division. The council…"

"I'm sure the council would love to hear what I know about you, Aydron." Scott interjected, glaring at him. "The torture, the genocide. If it's anything like it was when I was still Realm Delegate, I could have you executed," He tightened the chain around his hand, forcing Aydron to drop his sword. "Now, you're on my turf. You play by my rules." He yanked the chain hard, sending Aydron to the ground. "*I'm* the king here. You don't get to bring your sloppy realm politics here and expect me not to react."

Aydron scowled at him from the ground, all pretense of diplomacy gone. "Mighty words for a man who broke the Line Severance Decree *and* let his wife be executed for it."

Scott yanked the chains harder, retrieved Aydron's sword from the ground, and pointed it at his throat. "I'd watch what you say, fish king. I'm not afraid to break more pacts."

Sapphire was stunned. She'd read about the Line Severance Decree, but figured it had long since become obsolete with the gods no longer having a lineage. Everything started to fall into place. Scott had broken the pact for love, and he'd lost Rainee's mom in the process. She read his face; there was no bluff in his eyes this time. He had broken laws before, and he wasn't afraid to do it again.

She'd never seen her father frightened, but the way Scott stood over him, one hand wrapped around the chain bound to Aydron's wrist, and the other pointing the king's own sword at him, made him look pitiful.

"What do you seek to gain from this?" Aydron spat, still trying to remain defiant. "What use is my mistake of a daughter to you?"

Sapphire flinched slightly. She knew how he felt, she always had, but it didn't make it hurt any less. Any trace of the little girl who wanted his approval was gone. He'd burned that bridge once and for all. Aydron smiled at her knowingly. *Evil bastard.*

Scott pressed the knife deeper into his chin, blood beading on the blade. "She's obviously more to me than she is to you," he whispered. "I'd be ashamed if I were you."

Aydron stayed silent, staring daggers at Scott. Scott pulled the chains slightly and pressed the sword into his chin, forcing him to stand. "Now," Scott growled. "I can incite a Water Realm revolution tonight, or—" He got closer to him until his face was right by Aydron's. "—I can call you a portal."

"You'd let me go?" Aydron choked. "You're dumber than you look, Bennett."

Scott laughed and shook his head. "Not letting you. Telling you. Leave this realm and don't come back." He pushed him away but kept the chain on his wrist. "If I see you here again without a formal invitation, the Water Realm will have a funeral and a coronation on the same day."

He unhooked the chain and dropped it to the ground, keeping the king's sword aimed at him. He grabbed a holodisk from his pocket, holding it up before summoning the portal.

Aydron backed up, moving toward the portal, but never took his eyes off Scott.

"You'll regret this one day, Scott," he hissed.

Scott shrugged and moved with him, the sword still on him, ensuring he retreated. "I'll be dead before then," Scott stated, barely loud enough for Sapphire to hear.

The portal closed around Aydron, then blinked out of sight. Scott was still holding the sword and the holodisk. He fell to his knees as the light dimmed and the residual blue castlight powder rained down around him in the darkness.

Sapphire hurried to her feet, her jaw still aching from her father's blow, but she didn't care right now. She knelt down beside Scott, touching his shoulder gently.

"You didn't have to rescue me," she said quietly. She wouldn't have rescued herself, had she been in his shoes.

He looked up at her and smiled softly. "I didn't have to. But I wouldn't have been able to sleep for the rest of my life if I had walked away." He moved to stand up. "Besides, I've been dying to put Aydron in his place since I was your age. I finally had my chance."

Sapphire smiled at him, but something inside her felt amiss, as though a part of her had been severed.

Scott noticed and clapped her on the shoulder. "Your father was evil long before you were conceived. His actions today are just another scar." Sapphire searched his eyes and only found sincerity. "But you aren't. Your actions and your legacy belong to you. SwiftStream means nothing here."

She blinked away tears. No one had ever talked to her like that before, as if she were her own person with thoughts and desires outside of her father. She opened her mouth to thank him, but nothing came out. He smiled like he understood anyway.

The boys had made their way over with Connor leading the pack, checking to see if Sapphire was okay, followed by Finn. But Axel hung back, twirling that stupid knife of his between his fingers. She saw it, anyways: the relief in his expression. He didn't like her, but he was happy her father hadn't killed her. Maybe that was enough for now. She didn't need any of them to love her, just to be there. That night, they had proven they were capable of that.

CHAPTER 50
RAINEE

They'd left her behind. Rainee had been gazing out her bedroom window, thinking about the altercation with Finn and Axel that morning, when she saw her dad and all three boys rush out the back gate and move like a gang toward the school. She hadn't even heard her dad come home. Why had no one come to get her? Surely, she could be of some help with whatever situation was happening.

    She had followed them but soon wished she hadn't. She'd watched her father nearly kill a man—the king of the Water Realm, she had gathered—and now she had to act like she knew nothing?

    She stood in the kitchen, still shaking slightly. She had snuck back while they were all regrouping, so they wouldn't know that she had been gone. Was this how it was going to be from now on? Lies and sneaking off without her? She understood that it was probably her father's way of protecting her, but he could have at least told her they were leaving. She tried to justify that it was just the heat of the moment, that they forgot her out of panic, not out of malice. But it didn't help.

    The sliding door abruptly opened.

    "Oh, you're awake," Scott said, surprised. He placed the chains that were attached to his belt on the kitchen table and crossed the room to the fridge. He smelled like castlight powder and blood, Rainee noted.

    The others funneled in after him. Connor and Finn were chatting about seemingly nothing, Sapphire was listening, but not contributing much, and Axel was trailing behind, his eyes distant.

"Where were you guys?" she asked softly, locking eyes with Axel first. "I would have started dinner had I known when you'd be back." They all froze, like it was just dawning on them that she hadn't been there.

No one spoke. No one had words for what just happened, she guessed. She looked between Sapphire and her dad, hoping one of them would have more to say than this. She set her cup down on the island with a thud, the sound rattling through the otherwise silent kitchen. Everyone jumped.

Sapphire sighed, stepping forward. "They came to get me." She looked at her apologetically. "I got myself into a bit of a mess."

Rainee nodded; she knew at least that much was the truth. She looked around the room, waiting for one of the guys to explain why they had left without her. When no one did, she broke the silence. "I could have helped, too, you know," she said.

Scott shut the fridge and turned to her, four packs of steak in his hands. "It wasn't like that. We got the ping and ran."

He's brushing it off.

"I thought you were asleep." Connor shrugged.

She smiled sourly. "And no one checked?" She looked at Finn. He looked guilty. That was usually something he would catch. He still didn't answer.

"Forget it," she murmured, tears in her eyes. "I'm glad you're safe, Sapphire," she added before storming upstairs.

CHAPTER 51
FINN

They should have checked, Finn thought, as he watched Rainee march out of the kitchen. He hadn't thought anything of it, and no one had mentioned her absence. How could they have overlooked that? He looked over at Scott, who was cooking steaks in a lined pan on the stove, pretending that none of this was happening.

"Did you leave her here on purpose?" Finn asked, staring at Scott.

Scott looked up slightly, but he shook his head. "No, why would I do that?" There was something in his voice that didn't sound so sure.

Finn took a step toward him. "Then why didn't you remind one of us to grab her?"

Scott shrugged, seemingly unfazed. "Why did none of *you* remember?" He continued cooking the steaks, but Finn couldn't shake the feeling that something in his responses was wrong.

"You were protecting her, weren't you?" Axel's voice cut through Finn's thoughts. That's exactly what he was hearing in Scott's tone. He wasn't nonchalant because he didn't care. He was nonchalant because he left her on purpose to keep her safe.

Scott froze briefly, then nodded before returning to the steaks. He was silent, but the answer was clear.

Without giving it much thought, Finn bounded up the stairs after Rainee. No one followed him. He thought momentarily that maybe this wasn't his mess to clean up, but he was knocking on her door before he could stop himself.

The door opened slightly, and Rainee poked her head out. She had tears in her eyes, and her face was red from crying. Finn's chest ached. "Rainee…" he said. He was ready to explain everything and apologize right there.

"Don't, Finn….just…" She took a deep, shaky breath then continued, "Whatever you're about to say, save it." She looked up at him, her eyes shining with tears. "I shouldn't even be this upset. It's not like you meant to."

Except Scott. Scott meant to.

He sighed and ran a hand through his hair. "Just because we didn't mean to, doesn't mean—" He cleared his throat. "—that it was the right call."

She smiled bitterly and nodded. "So just another wrong instinct, then."

His stomach dropped. He hadn't expected her to throw that back in his face again. But he deserved it, and he'd take it as many times as she needed him to for her to feel better about it.

"I deserved that," he said, placing a hand softly on the door. "But I'm telling you that it won't happen again." He locked eyes with her, making sure she heard him. "I won't let it."

The door opened all the way, and she moved forward, wrapping her arms around his torso. Finn was slightly stunned, but he hugged her back, one hand in her hair, the other on her back. He rested his chin on her head and thought that this outcome had made the entire thing worth it.

"Thank you," she whispered softly against his chest. She looked up at him again, tears running down her cheeks.

He brushed them away with his fingers, a smile on his face as he whispered back, "Of course." He couldn't help but notice that her eyes were gorgeous, even if they were wet with tears. He knew now wasn't the right time to make any moves. She was still slightly upset, and he didn't need to make it worse. So, he settled for the hug, and the look in her eye told him she felt safe, even for the moment. That was enough.

She pulled away after a few moments and gestured toward the stairs. "We better get down there before my dad overcooks all those steaks."

Finn laughed slightly, and she smiled at him. His heart skipped a beat, but he quickly forced it back into rhythm. He followed her down the stairs, thanking the gods that he had made the effort to comfort her.

"Salmon and Swordswalin are nowhere near the same, for the record," he heard Sapphire quipping from the kitchen. Her tone was light and teasing. The atmosphere felt a lot less heavy as he and Rainee entered the smoky room.

Scott was desperately trying to open the window over the sink as the smoke thickened. He finally succeeded and turned to her. "I'll let the fishmonger know that his Water Realm selections are scarce."

Sapphire smiled at that and took her plate to the table where Connor was already devouring a steak.

Finn felt Axel watching him and Rainee suspiciously from across the room. *Let him watch.* Finn felt like, for once, he had beaten Axel to the punch, and he was riding that high.

CHAPTER 52
AXEL

If Finn had kissed her, Axel was going to kill him. He sat at the table, arms crossed, seething silently. He watched Finn and Rainee share a few smiles, chat quietly, and occasionally laugh. All great things. But not for him. *He* should have been the one to comfort her. But what was he going to say? He understood why Scott had done what he had, and Axel didn't blame him. He probably would have done the same, if he really thought about it. Rainee was in enough danger sitting at the house; she didn't need to be thrown into a realm skirmish with *Aydron SwiftStream*, unless it was an absolute last resort.

He took a bite of his steak, still watching them. The meat was atrociously overcooked, but he was glad they had actual food. Rainee glanced over at him a couple times, locking eyes with him briefly before returning her attention to Finn. Was she playing with him?

He smirked, and for the first time that night, she smiled at him. He thought his heart might stop. That smile was enough to turn every ounce of jealousy into caring, and he still hated that she did that to him.

"So, how did the rest of your sparring practice go?" Rainee asked, looking directly at him.

He faltered for a moment, then smirked again. "Perfect. Connor might actually be able to hold his own now."

"The grass stains imprinted on my skin beg to differ," Connor added, rubbing one of his elbows.

She smiled sweetly, too sweetly. "And who's teaching you?" She offered a mischievous smile, throwing his own energy back at him.

He paused mid-bite, still holding his fork in the air. Gods, she was trying to kill him. One jab at a time. He smiled. "Very funny." He pointed his steak-loaded fork at her and continued, "Your little stunt today was impressive, but it won't be happening again."

Her eyes narrowed at the dare, and she said, "Was that another challenge, blondie?"

He leaned back in his chair, eying her. He was extremely aware of Scott scrutinizing him from the head of the table. His next words mattered. "I guess we'll find out tomorrow, won't we, static?"

It was all he could do to keep his heart in his chest. The way she stared him down with no fear, called his bluff like she utterly understood him, and the way she smiled at him.

Just kill me now.

Scott continued eating silently, so Axel must have passed his test. One of many, if he ever wanted to be with Rainee. Good thing he had always been good at breaking things, especially barriers, and nothing was going to stand in his way now. That smile she had thrown his way, paired with the challenge, was all the encouragement he needed. He was going to earn her attention, whether he thought he deserved it or not. He was pure destruction, but he wanted her to be the only thing he didn't destroy.

CHAPTER 53
SYREN

The portal room was eerily quiet when Syren stepped into it. He wasn't sure how he'd gotten here, but he knew what Kai was trying to do. The boys had failed, and now he wanted to finish the job himself.

"This isn't going to go the way you think, Kai," Syren tried to reason under his breath.

<What do you know, Brother? They were supposed to kill the demigod, and they failed. Now I must take matters into my own hands.>

The fog was starting to close in again, and Syren's brain swirled. "The gods won't let you," he managed to choke out.

The fog retreated slightly, giving Syren room to breathe and think.

<The gods will be powerless if I destroy the demigod bloodline,> Kai threw back.

"And how do you plan to get close to her? You're going to start the war you were trying to stop." Syren pushed forward, forcing his consciousness to the front of his brain. He was exhausted. This fight had been never-ending for far too long, but he couldn't let Kai through the portal. There was an innocent realm and *their* men on the other side. This had to end here.

<I have my ways, Little Brother. Stop doubting me.>

The fog tried to surge again, but Syren was ready for it. He forced it back, pushing his entire conscious being against Kai's power. The smoke suddenly dissipated, like Kai was surprised by the resistance.

Syren took in a shaky breath, leaning his forehead against the stone wall of the portal room. He was sweating, though he had barely moved. "Please," he begged. "Just wait until Aydron sends the men we bargained for back to us." He exhaled. "They are set to arrive tonight. We can take backup."

It was a long shot, and Syren knew that. Kai wasn't a wait-and-see-type person, and his patience had only thinned as he got older. Or rather, as Syren got older.

<Very well,> Kai hissed, retreating to one corner of Syren's mind. <We wait for more soldiers, but we hesitate no longer.>

"Understood." Syren gulped with a small nod. He may not have completely spared Earth, but he had given himself enough time to come up with a plan to stop Kai. He just had to be sneaky about it.

Gods help him if he was caught; Kai would take Syren down with the realm. He knew that for certain. He hoped that his team on Earth would be ready for when Kai *did* manage to cross the barrier, because Syren was getting tired and didn't know how much longer he could fight.

CHAPTER 54
SCOTT

There was something wrong. Something that Scott could feel but not place. There was a shift in the atmosphere, yet everything remained calm, at least for the time being. The kids were all talking and eating, save for Axel who looked like he was glaring daggers at Finn. The problem with Aydron was settled for now, but there was still this issue of the gods…and Syren, whatever he was up to.

Scott found it odd that he hadn't heard from Hermes again. No nudge toward making his decision, no threats. It was very unlike the gods to stay this silent when an ultimatum was hanging. He excused himself from the table casually, cleaned his plate off, then retreated to the basement. He needed to investigate a matter beyond the routine beacon pings.

He typed a few lines of code into the comm—a simple query to pull up the inter-realm beacon logs. Something he should have done two days earlier. As he scanned the logs, he noticed exactly what he had feared. A little over a week prior, there was a forced portal tether created between the Fire Realm and the Water Realm. It looked like the tether code was hacked and used as an attack to open the portal.

Scott couldn't quite remember all the logistics of each realm, but he knew that you had to have a specific tether open to travel to or from the Fire Realm, due to them severing their tethers after each use. The Water Realm had more of an "open to our friends, closed to all others" policy. You had to be invited in and given a tether code for access.

Earth had some trade channels that stayed open, but those mostly led to government-run facilities to keep them out of view of the public. Other portals, like the one the boys had used, were a form of attack that was only used during war. That's how he knew that IceHeart wasn't trying to stop the war; he had purposefully started it, whether the boys knew it or not.

Earth was a no-travel zone for most of the realms, unless there was an ongoing trade, or a diplomat had been invited in. It had been that way for centuries. Scott had never heard of any cases where that travel ban had been broken. There was no reason to break it unless there was a war. That was why he'd kept Rainee in the human realm and not somewhere else.

He thought about his words to Aydron: *I'm the king here.* Technically, it wasn't true, but it had gotten the point across. Beings from the other realms had stayed off Earth's territory for centuries, and they weren't going to start invading if Scott had anything to say about it. The government had worked too hard to erase the realms from civilian memories for their own safety. Making the realms publicly known would do immeasurable damage to everyday life. Some information was better off staying secret. He knew that too well.

Still, he wondered at what point he needed to alert the higher ups. It was part of his responsibility as a beacon monitor to report instances like this.

He should have reported the first portal, the Fire Realm tether. But something had stopped him. Those boys would have been wiped from existence before they had a chance to set up camp had Scott been doing his job correctly.

Even when it had first appeared, he knew that it was a bad sign. But part of him had hoped that *maybe* it was an act of peace. That was wishful thinking, considering the Fire Realm's history. If he reported things now, he'd go up for investigation. Not just to Earth's government, but to the Divisional Council.

He had no plausible explanation for not having reported it, other than he had seen the boys, decided that he could handle the threat, and left it at that. But he wasn't handling it. Not in the way that he had thought he would, and definitely not in the way the council would agree with.

So, maybe Syren had started the war. But Scott had fueled it, and now it was at his doorstep. It was painfully karmic. As he was staring at the logs, another tether opened. This time from the

Water Realm to the Fire Realm. Not forced, but intentionally tethered. The tether codes and establishment were all coded green. This was a planned meeting. He thought for a second that him spiting Aydron had flipped the hand so absurdly that Aydron might be teaming up with Syren; but that was unlikely, even in this world. They brutally hated each other. Their families hated each other. Their fathers had tried to kill each other during a peace banquet, when Scott was first realm traveling. No act in this world would make Aydron side with the Fire Realm. So, what was he doing? And why did Scott have such a bad feeling about it all?

CHAPTER 55
RAINEE

Rainee's chest had finally lost its heaviness by the time she left the dinner table. Finn had successfully convinced her that this was a one-off mistake, and it wouldn't happen again, which made the whole situation seem silly.

She was still a little upset with her dad, but mostly because he wouldn't acknowledge that anything had happened or that she had been hurt by it, even if it had been done unintentionally. He'd always been avoidant when it came to conflict with her, but it had been getting extreme lately. She wasn't sure what she could do to fix it, or even if it was hers to fix.

She was standing in her bedroom, looking in the mirror hung on her door. The pendant shone brightly against her skin, casting that eerie fairy light magic that she almost resented. Why couldn't anything just be normal? No power, no weird pendant, no emotionally-distant father who kept secrets from her.

The lights were humming lightly around her, a feeling she was getting used to. It was like they all flickered a bit brighter when she entered the room.

She had been thinking about her powers a lot over the past few hours. She hadn't fully figured out how to channel them without extracting all of her energy in the process. That probably wouldn't be too helpful in battle, unless they were looking for a single-use weapon.

She didn't really know where she would train to control her powers, or even if she could. Was there even anyone who knew *how* to train her? She looked into the mirror again, noticing a slight movement in the corner of the reflection, behind her. She spun around, the lights flickering like they were reacting to her fear.

No one was there, but a note lay on her pillow, folded and sealed in gold wax. She crossed the room and grabbed it, her fingers tingling slightly. As she undid the seal, it felt like a wind current swept through her bedroom. She looked around, bewildered. The room was still empty. Had her father left this note earlier, and she was just noticing it now?

She looked back at the letter, her hands trembling. It was a simple message, scrawled in script letters.

If you want this war to end here, come to the clearing at sunset tomorrow.

There was a space, then in slightly sloppier handwriting, *You'd be wise to come alone.*

***

She would have ignored the note, under most circumstances. Or, she would have told her dad about it. But he still hadn't spoken to her since they returned from the Sapphire mission. He'd been tucked away in the basement doing who knows what.

So here she was, packing a small bag of odds and ends like she was leaving forever, because her intuition told her that might be the case. She waited until the house was preoccupied; the boys and Sapphire were downstairs discussing a logistics plan, and her father was still not home from his day job. Accounting must seem mundane when he had this chaos to come home to. But if anyone understood trying to hold 'normal' together, it was her.

She slipped out the back door as quietly as the sliding door would allow, then she snuck out the back gate and into the dimming light of dusk.

As she stepped into the clearing near the school, her nerves nearly got the best of her. She was about to turn around and go home, but the wind suddenly picked up.

"Have to admit, I didn't think you'd show." A man's voice stopped her. The voice wasn't familiar, but it was ethereal.

She turned. *Too late now.* Standing a few feet from her, in the remnants of what looked like a fire pit, was a man in a white tunic and gold bracers. She felt like she should know him, but his appearance wasn't ringing a bell.

He smiled at her. "The name's Hermes...." His eyes darkened slightly. "It's nice to finally meet you, little spark."

H-Hermes? Her stomach dropped. She'd studied a bit of Greek mythology in school and knew that Hermes was the messenger of the gods. Gods that she had thought lived only in stories, up until that week.

She stared at him, dumbfounded. "W-why are you here?" she stumbled, unable to take her eyes from him.

Hermes clicked his tongue. "Did your father not tell you?" He smirked. "You belong to the gods now."

"What? My dad?" She was reeling. Had he really sold her out to the gods and not even mentioned it? Is that why he had been so quiet? He knew that Hermes would be coming, and he was making it easier on himself to let her go.

Hermes's smirk widened slightly. "I'll take that as a 'no'." He stepped forward and wrapped an arm around her shoulders in a comforting manner. But it felt anything *but* comforting. "Your father was given the choice to turn in those Fire Realm degenerates to the gods, or—" He scanned her up and down. "—to hand you over."

Her heart thudded in her chest. "You're lying," she murmured, trying to convince herself. Her father was a lot of things, but there was no way he would have picked the boys over her. *Right?*

"Lie? Me?" Hermes put his hand to his chest in feigned offense. "I would *never*." Her necklace hummed slightly, and she hardly noticed it. But Hermes did. "I see you found my gift." He tapped the necklace with a perfectly manicured finger. "You know your father wasn't going to give it to you." He put his lips to her ear and whispered, "He's scared of your power. Scared of what you might do. But I—" She could hear the smile in his voice. "—I'm not scared, and neither are the other gods."

She wanted to believe him, wanted to believe that there was a place where she belonged, but the pit in her stomach was making his words sound deadly. Then she thought about her dad and the boys. She had left without even saying goodbye. She hadn't given them a choice to save her from this, and she doubted that Hermes would let her leave, unless it was with him.

"So, what do you say?" He moved behind her, hands on her shoulders, framing the necklace around her neck. "Let us show you your true potential."

She looked toward the trees. She could try to run, but she assumed that Hermes would simply appear anywhere he wanted to. Running away would just mean playing into his sick game. He wanted her to fight, she realized. He wanted her to beg, squirm, and struggle against him. But she refused to give him that satisfaction, even if that was the only power she held.

Her necklace hummed more deafeningly, matching the thumping of her heart. She nodded slowly. Hermes laughed. His lips were at her ear again. "Perfect." He sneered and grabbed her hair, yanking her head backwards. "You'll be the greatest weapon…" He cleared his throat. "I mean *guest* that Olympus has ever seen." He ran a finger up her neck, sending chills down her spine. She hated him, she decided.

She inhaled forcefully and closed her eyes, half-expecting to be warped elsewhere, but everything seemed unchanged. She opened her eyes, confused. Her necklace was the only sound in the clearing.

Then suddenly, *crack*. Hermes screamed and pushed her away from him.

He was holding his left hand, which now looked charred and distorted. The necklace kept humming, and the hair on the back of her neck stood on end. Then, a bolt of lightning—thin, precise, and white-hot—struck the ground near Hermes a second time. He stumbled backwards.

Rainee felt her body vibrating. Was she doing this? Usually, when her powers surfaced, her body felt immediately drained afterwards, but she felt charged. Two more strikes hit the ground between them and the wind picked up, swirling her hair around her face.

"What's your plan, little spark?" Hermes called, clearly seething. "You can't kill a god. You should know that." He looked smug, and that was enough to send Rainee's rage through the roof.

Another crack of lightning struck right at his feet, sending him toppling backwards.

"I don't need to kill you, Hermes," she threw back at him, her voice echoing. It didn't sound like hers, not fully. "But I will show you what lightning tastes like."

Two more cracks of lightning, one on each side of the god. He raised one hand, as if to warp himself away, but a chain hooked around his wrist as he raised it. He screamed like the chains were burning him.

Scott stepped around the tree on the other side and slapped the other cuff on Hermes's free wrist. Hermes pulled against the chains, his eyes wild.

"No. *No.*" He looked around frantically, like there might be something that could save him. "You can't do this to me."

Scott leaned down and growled at him, "I warned you what was coming if you didn't leave my family alone, Hermes." He tightened the chains behind the tree. "I don't make false promises."

Seeing him made Rainee falter. *How did he know where to find me?* The humming quieted slightly, and the wind died down. *He came for me.* She fell to the ground, finally feeling the effects of the lightning coursing through her. But she wasn't instantly unconscious this time, and she would take that as a win.

She felt someone run to her, but it wasn't her dad. She could tell by the footsteps. They were too fast, too light. She looked up, and Axel nearly bowled her over by grabbing her so hard. "Are you okay?" he whispered gruffly. She nodded, too tired to speak. He sighed. "Thank gods."

Or maybe don't thank the gods just yet, she thought.

Before she could regain her strength in any capacity, Axel was scooping her up and running toward the trees. "Axel…" she murmured, her head foggy. He paused in the cover of the trees and pulled her tighter to his chest.

"I got you, don't worry, static," he whispered back. Her heart steadied. She could hear Finn shouting at him from somewhere close by, but her strength was already spent, and it wasn't long before her brain went blank.

CHAPTER 56
AXEL

Axel's heart was beating out of his chest. He was still holding Rainee, his body shaking.

"What were you thinking?" Finn growled. "Hermes could have killed you."

Axel looked at him, tired. He didn't need a safety check right now. He also didn't have a good reason for running into the line of fire, other than it was better him than Rainee.

"Scott had him," Axel said simply. "Rainee was crashing, and I wasn't going to leave her out there."

Scott emerged from the trees, meeting them in the parking lot. He looked between Rainee and Axel, obviously deciding to let it slide for the moment.

"You guys head back to the house," he said, gesturing toward the back alley. It wasn't a choice; it was an order. "Sapphire and I have a smug messenger boy to interrogate."

While Axel vaguely wished he was involved in the interrogating, he was perfectly fine making sure Rainee got home safely.

"You sure you don't need us?" Finn asked, looking toward the clearing.

Scott shook his head and turned toward the trees. "Not right now. I'll come get you if something changes." His voice was stern, like he wasn't going to take an argument from either of them. "Just…make sure she's safe," he said, glancing at Rainee before disappearing into the trees.

They stood there for a moment, watching, until Finn pushed past Axel and started toward the house. "You heard him. Let's go."

Axel could tell that Finn was upset about something, and it went beyond being told to stand down or Axel rushing into battle without thinking. There was something he wasn't saying, but Axel could tell it was eating away at him.

"You okay, Cap?" he asked. The nickname had started as a dig, but it was slowly sticking.

Finn looked at Rainee, then back at Axel, but didn't stop walking. "Fine," he said. But he didn't sound fine.

"Bullshit. Try again." Axel said, stepping in front of him. He didn't care if he was carrying Rainee, he'd still kick Finn's ass if he needed to.

Finn glared at him. "Don't do this, Axel. It's not worth it," he ordered as he pushed around him again.

"It's her, isn't it?" Axel yelled after him. Finn paused and looked back at him. That was all the answer that Axel needed. "You know I'm not trying to take her from you, right?"

Finn turned around, his hands in fists. "Then what the hell is all this?" He gestured vaguely to Rainee. "You say you don't care, then you kiss her, then you risk your life to save her." He turned his back to Axel. "Doesn't sound like someone who doesn't care. Not to me."

"I never wanted to care," Axel said before he thought better about it.

Finn stopped walking. "What the hell does that even mean, Axel?"

He had exposed himself, so he might as well own it. "It means—" He sighed. "—that I didn't *choose* this. I tried to keep her at arm's length." He stared at the back of Finn's head. "She kept coming to me. Kept looking at me like I meant something, other than corruption and destruction." His voice darkened a little as he choked back a sob. "So, no, I didn't *want* this. And I still hope every day that she comes to her senses and chooses you." He looked down. "It would be a lot safer for her that way."

Finn didn't speak. He just kept walking. Axel waited a bit before following, not wanting to make this situation any worse. His arms were finally getting tired as he caught the gate with his foot behind Finn. Thanks for holding the gate, Axel thought bitterly.

He'd meant every word, whether Finn believed him or not. He didn't *want* to care this much about Rainee, but she had made it impossible not to. She looked at him like he was something good, even though he knew he wasn't. He wasn't trying to take her. He had known that Finn had a thing for her since the beginning of the mission, despite him denying it. He might not like Finn all the time, but he wouldn't go out of his way to hurt him, either.

He slipped into the house, leaving the sliding door open, vowing to come back and close it after Rainee was tucked in and safe. He took her upstairs, opening her bedroom door quietly, and laid her in the bed.

He was about to turn to walk out when she stirred slightly.

Just keep walking, Axel. You did your part.

He tried to leave the room, he really did. But he wanted nothing more than to hear her voice again, just to make sure she was okay. He stayed where he was, between the door and the bed, and turned to look at her.

"Axel…" He jumped a little. She was still waking up, her eyes closed. There was no way she knew he was here yet. He could still leave, and she would never know.

He found himself kneeling beside the bed, waiting patiently. He took her hand in his, softly. Probably the softest he'd ever touched anything. "I'm still here," he whispered. Her eyes fluttered open and locked in with his. "Hey," he whispered softly. "You were pretty badass out there, I have to say." He was joking around, but his heart was in his throat.

She smiled through her sleepy fog and muttered, "Did you carry me all the way here?"

He shrugged. "Wasn't a big deal." His eyes stayed locked with hers, like she might disappear if he blinked.

"You didn't have to do that," she murmured. Her eyes shone. Gods, he hated when they did that. It made his legs weak.

"The alternative was to leave you unconscious in a field, for who knows how long." He smirked. "I'm not that big of a jerk."

She pushed herself up on her elbows, looking at him. "You know," she smiled. "This just proves my point."

He raised an eyebrow. "What point?"

"That you, Axel Taylor, are good." His breath left him. "And I refuse to believe anything else." His chest hurt. Had she stabbed him when he wasn't looking? Part of it still felt like a lie, she didn't even know his real name. Still, she was sincere. He didn't think he would recover.

"Rainee…" He took a shaky breath and pushed himself away from the bed. He was starting to feel cornered again. He should have left when he'd had the chance. Every time he was in her bedroom, every time they were alone, she found a new way to tear down his defenses. It had taken him years to build those up, and she was wrecking them like they were made of cardboard.

She moved to sit on the edge of the bed, watching him. "You're about to run again," she observed.

That stopped him in his tracks. The look in her eye was like she knew how this ended, the running that never got him anywhere. He shook his head. Something in his chest shifted. He didn't want to run anymore. "Not…" He took a deep breath. Did he really want to do this? "Not if you want me to stay."

She nodded slowly, her face neutral. She patted the bed beside her. He took the spot timidly, as if she might take her kindness back without warning. He wouldn't blame her.

"Will you…" she started, looking a bit unsure. "Tell me more about your realm?" Her voice got a little softer as she added, "About you?"

He didn't know what to say. No one had ever wanted to hear that sort of stuff from him, and no one ever stayed around long after hearing it. "I can try…but there are a lot more bad parts of me than there are good, trust me."

She nodded like she understood. "Again, no proof until you show me, blondie." She smiled at him, and his heart skipped a beat. She was going to pry his past out of him no matter how hard he fought.

"Firstly, Taylor is an alias name. The Fire Realm and a lot of the other realms have a two-object naming system for surnames, based on class and faction. My realm surname is AxeClaw."

"And what does that mean? Like class structure-wise?" she asked, her eyes full of curiosity.

He feared her reaction to the answer, but he provided it anyway. "My family is from the slums. AxeClaw is a surname only given in a specific crime syndicate in the Fire Realm." He broke eye contact. "My parents were the leaders."

"Were?" she questioned softly.

He looked back at her, expecting judgment, but she just sat there with her legs crossed, waiting for him to continue. He nodded. "The military destroyed my sector in a surprise raid." He coughed, clearing his throat and trying not to let the memories sting his eyes. "My parents, my siblings, my *friends*...all gone." He bit back tears. *Dammit.* This is exactly what he didn't want to happen.

Rainee moved a little closer but didn't touch him. "How did you escape?"

He shook his head. "I didn't." He looked at her, his eyes glassy. "The military kidnapped me and gave me the choice of either enlisting or being executed." The words hurt like a knife wound and tasted bitter in his mouth. No matter how many times he spoke that truth, it still didn't sit right. If it happened now, he would have told them to get the guillotine.

"How old were you?" she asked, slightly shocked.

The question was simple enough. And he'd answered it before—with Connor—but this felt different. The talk with Connor was a cynical briefing. This was a memoir.

"Seventeen," he offered. She placed her hand on his, and he didn't pull back. He let himself feel the comfort she was extending, even though it stung a little. "I was old for a new recruit, by Fire Realm standards. Finn and Connor both enlisted at thirteen, which is typical." He looked at her. "But I never wanted to be in the military. It just sounded better than dying at the time."

She moved to lay her head on his shoulder. He relaxed a little, wrapping one arm around her. "Did you want to stay with the syndicate?"

He smiled weakly. "If they were still around, I wouldn't have a choice. I was being groomed to take it over once my parents stepped down."

She turned, resting her chin on his shoulder and peering up at him. "But is that what you would have been happy doing?"

He blinked. No one had ever asked him that before; it wasn't a valid concern in the Fire Realm. You did what made sense, what your class structure dictated. You played your role; nothing more, and nothing less. "I never really thought about it," he said finally, looking back at her.

The way she gazed at him sent chills down his back. She didn't flinch, didn't move. She looked at him like he was her favorite book, being read aloud. And he felt that in his soul. "Thank you for telling me," she whispered.

He braced himself for the next part. The part where she kicked him out, told him to leave her alone. But she didn't. She stayed there, her head on his shoulder, her hand resting on his, for what seemed like an eternity. And Axel wished it really had been that long.

She yawned, breaking the silence. He looked at her, noting that she still looked exhausted. "You should sleep. You just summoned an entire lightning storm without any training or preparation."

Her eyes searched his. "Will you stay?"

His breath caught. Did she mean that, or was this some sort of bait? He nodded. "If that's what you want..." He looked around the room. "I don't mind sleeping in the chair."

She laughed a little and shook her head. "You don't have to sleep in the chair." She grabbed his hand before he could ask and pulled him down beside her.

He was stunned. "Are you sure? The chair really isn't a problem."

She settled down beside him and laid her head on his chest, burrowing in closer. His arms naturally wrapped around her, but his body was still stiff and tense.

"Is this okay?" she asked, looking up at him.

He played with her hair lightly and smiled. "Yeah, this is okay."

Truthfully, this was the most complete he'd felt in years, and he didn't think he'd be able to give that up if she chose Finn. That was when he decided that he wanted her to choose him, for longer than just tonight. Because he'd sooner die than watch her look at Finn the way she had just looked at him. So, whether he deserved it or not, he was keeping this. He was earning it. For her sake.

She fell asleep within minutes; her breathing became even. Axel watched her, feeling his chest crack open. He'd known before this moment that he wouldn't be able to conceal his feelings forever, but now he didn't even want to. He wanted her to know. He wanted more nights like this. Before the world ended, if it ever did.

He kissed her head softly and tightened his arms around her. She didn't even stir. He let himself sleep. Not in the chair, not on the floor, collapsed from exhaustion, but next to her. He had never felt more relaxed.

CHAPTER 57
SAPPHIRE

Sapphire wasn't sure why Scott had picked her, specifically, to stay behind and interrogate Hermes, but she wasn't complaining. She'd had a bad taste in her mouth since their first meeting. Now, he was godbound to a tree, sweat streaming down his face, with his eyes staring daggers at Scott.

And Scott. She thought his confrontation with *her* father was scary, but this? This was pure, unhinged protective father-meets-former Realm Guardian mode. He was *done* talking, especially to the gods. He had drawn a sword from his belt—the Spritan sword he had taken from her father. Sapphire would recognize that custom-carved hilt anywhere.

"Now Scott." Hermes breathed like he was on fire. It probably felt like it. God-binding chains used on mortals did little more to hold a captive than a regular iron chain; but to a god, they were like an eternal chemical burn. "We can talk about this. You and I…"

Scott didn't move, but he wasn't listening either. He was planning.

"We've always been friends?" Hermes asked, clearly as a question rather than a statement, hoping Scott would affirm it.

Scott held the sword up, letting it catch the moonlight briefly. "Is that what you've been calling us? *Friends?*" He slid the tip of the sword down Hermes's left arm, leaving a trail of blood in its wake. "Because I've been calling you a winged *bastard*." Hermes squirmed under the chill of the knife, but he didn't cry out.

"You came after me," Scott reminded him, as he swung the sword in a precise motion, slicing into the left arm. The cut was deep. "You came after my soldiers." Another swing. Still no reaction from Hermes, aside from a smirk. "And worst of all, you came after *my* daughter."

Slice.

The blade pierced straight through Hermes's right forearm. Finally, he let out a cry, cut short by Scott taking the blade out and smacking him with the hilt. "I served Zeus's temple faithfully for *years*. And this is how I'm repaid?" He stepped back, seething.

All Sapphire could do was watch. She'd never seen anyone stand so firmly against a divine being. Scott wasn't just an ex-Guardian. He was a dad. And a pissed-off one at that. She felt a dull ache, a longing to know a father's love like that. Instead of utter emotional neglect. She was sure you couldn't even call what Aydron doled out "love".

Scott looked back at her and pulled a flask out of his pocket. "Here." He tossed it to her. "Get ready to pour this down his throat *when* he doesn't answer the questions the way I want him to."

She opened the flask, a little confused, but she didn't dare disobey. The smell of bone meal and sulfur filled her nostrils. It was godbane. She'd know that smell anywhere. It was used as a medicinal cure for nearly everything mortal, but if a god ingested it, they'd be in agony for weeks. It had been outlawed by the Divisional Council over a decade ago, except for very specific circumstances. *Where did he get this?*

"W-wait…What is that?" Hermes cried, kicking his feet, trying to get away from her.

Scott held the sword out again, ready to strike. "Consider it a truth serum," he spat. "Tell me what I want to know, and you'll never taste it. But lie or withhold information—" He waved the sword toward Sapphire. "—and you'll have an idea what death tastes like." Scott smirked. "Too bad you can't die."

Hermes's expression turned from realization to panic. He struggled against the chains, to no avail. "Fine," he growled as he dropped his arms, letting the chain fall to the ground. He was still secured to the tree. "I'll tell you what I know, but I assure you it's not as much as you think."

Scott used the sword to tilt the god's head up. "Tell me what side you're really on," he snarled.

"Come again?" Hermes asked, looking dazed.

Scott pressed the sword harder against his chin. Sapphire noticed that the wounds on his arms had already started to heal. "You said the gods were divided. Some want to train her, and some want her *dead.*" He narrowed his eyes slightly. "Which one are you?"

Hermes blinked, pondering the question. "I don't pick sides, Scott," he said matter-of-factly. "I play the field, and I clean up after everything is over." He smiled thinly. "They don't trust me with much else."

Scott slid the sword up his chin and raked it down his cheek. Sapphire watched the god's face contort in pain. "One more chance, messenger boy," Scott growled. "Who keeps sending you?"

Sapphire stepped forward, the flask ready. She could play this part. In fact, she'd been born to play it. The cold, torturous assassin? Sign her right up.

Hermes struggled against the chains again, blood running down his face. "No... Please..." He tried in vain to push himself away from Sapphire. "It's Zeus," he panted finally. "Zeus sends me."

"Zeus?" Scott confirmed. He didn't sound shocked; he sounded hurt. He pulled the sword away from Hermes's face, wiping the blood on his shirt.

Hermes nodded. "He wants to get to her before the others do." He looked up at Scott. "He has managed to convince over half the pantheon to side with him. Everyone has chosen their side. *Except* Hades." He smiled slightly. "He remains neutral. Says his duty is to the dead, not the living."

"And the others? Who wants to kill her?" Scott rushed him, waving his sword.

Hermes chuckled slightly. The cut on his face was nearly gone. "Hera leads the opposition. You know how she is when she starts on a tangent about balance and the order of things."

Sapphire knew enough about the Olympians to know that Hera was supposedly married to Zeus, but Zeus rarely acted like it. It was no surprise to her that they were on opposite sides of this skirmish.

"What the *hell* does my daughter have to do with the order of things?" Scott spat, nearly ramming the sword through Hermes's chest.

Hermes coughed and choked out, "Really? You don't get it?" He smiled wickedly. "The demigod descendant who slipped around the Line Severance Decree, defied fate, and holds the key to a pantheon that should be dead?" His eyes shone. "Come on, I took you for smarter than this."

Scott drove the sword further into Hermes' chest, making him sputter. "I could say the same about you."

Scott motioned for Sapphire to come closer. He grabbed Hermes's face by the chin and squeezed, forcing his mouth open. Hermes fought, but the god-binding chains made it impossible to break away from Scott's grasp.

"Tell the gods I'm on my way," Scott commanded, then grabbed the flask from Sapphire with his free hand and forced the whole thing down Hermes's throat. The reaction was instant. Visceral. Hermes writhed in pain, his mouth foaming. Scott removed the sword from his chest and slowly unlocked the god-binding chains. Hermes collapsed, his body convulsing.

"They'll... be... here... first..." He gurgled before warping away.

Scott let out a sigh and dropped the chains. He looked older than he had at the start of the conversation. Sapphire couldn't blame him, though. He'd just tortured one god and threatened the rest of them. He was either taking them down or he was going to die trying. After everything she had witnessed, her money was on him.

CHAPTER 58
SYREN

The men stumbled through the portal, all of them beaten and on the brink of collapse. Not a captain in sight, Syren thought. He hadn't expected Aydron to give him his top soldiers back, but he had expected some mixture of talent.

The men before him were all second- or third-year soldiers. They were children still, definitely not the battalion he had hoped to take with him to Earth.

<We waited for this?> Kai hissed in his head.

Syren couldn't blame him. Kai could do more damage by himself than all these men combined. Worse yet, Aydron had done everything short of killing them before sending them back. They all had healing wounds, bruised faces, and their eyes looked like they had lived far beyond their years.

Still, they all stood at attention when they saw him, ready for their next orders. There might be hope yet.

"Men," he addressed, scanning the crowd. There were about a hundred of them, if he had to guess. At least they had manpower on their side. "Welcome home."

<Get to the point, Brother.> Kai seethed.

Syren faltered for a second, but the smile never left his face. "We have run into dire circumstances in the human realm. I regret to inform you that your services are required."

Murmurs erupted in the portal room. The human realm? Wasn't that still off-limits?

"Silence!" Syren growled, his voice echoing off the walls. They all fell silent, their eyes like saucers as they stared at him. "We've had a case of treason and must take matters into our own hands." He pulled a holodisk from his pocket and displayed the files of the men. The tension in the room was suffocating. They all recognized the men pictured and had probably worked with all of them in some capacity.

Syren could feel Kai pushing against his consciousness, threatening to force him into the void again.

<You're stalling,> Kai hissed.

"Our mission—" Syren continued, trying to keep his visible composure. "—is to find these men and eliminate them." He looked over the soldiers in front of him. "No questions asked."

Syren's chest hurt from pretending to be ruthless. He still couldn't fathom killing his own men over a mission that had been doomed to fail from the start, but he would never tell that to Kai. He was already angry, but that may be the only emotion Kai was capable of these days. The soldiers saluted, waiting for their next orders. IceHeart pulled the portal tether codes up on his holodisk and directed it toward the portal wall.

The holodisk beeped a warning: NO TRAVEL ZONE. CONTINUE? Syren smiled. It wasn't the first time he'd bypassed the same message that week, but hopefully it was the last.

A portal whirled to life, initially blue, then giving way to a picturesque clearing. He'd changed the coordinates slightly from where the men had been set, to ensure some element of surprise. No need to come in right on top of them.

He stepped through the portal, the air tousling his hair as the atmosphere changed. His mind went dark then, consumed by a fog that he couldn't pull himself out of again. Kai was in charge, and he wouldn't be going easy on this realm. He'd tear it apart to get what he wanted, that Syren was sure of.

CHAPTER 59
CONNOR

Connor had stayed back to monitor the pings, while the others went to investigate the unusual beacon signal they had received about twenty minutes after dusk. That was right after Scott had noticed Rainee was gone and stormed downstairs, ready to kill all of them.

Part of Connor was relieved that they didn't ask him to go with them, the other part was starting to wonder if he was even an asset to this team. He couldn't fight, he hesitated too much, and he still believed in good, which he was sure Axel and Finn had given up on at this point. He heard Finn come downstairs, each step sounding like a brick hitting the floor as he descended. He sounded angry. Probably because of something Axel had done.

Connor walked out slowly, poking his head around the corner. Finn sat down on the couch, his head in his hands. Connor could see him shaking. Did something happen to Rainee?

He stepped around the corner and inched closer. "Finn?" Connor whispered, his heart pounding. If something happened, did he really want to know? He wasn't sure he could handle it.

Finn looked up, tried to smile, but Connor could see it was broken. Alarms sounded in Connor's brain. This had to be something bad. Finn never looked this broken up about anything. Emotions weren't his thing. Connor had seen him worried, stressed, tactical, but never broken. And it scared the hell out him.

"Is Rainee…" he started.

Finn exhaled, looking at the ground. "She's fine." His voice was shaking, like he was trying not to break, but Connor noticed. "Axel has her." His voice cracked slightly when he said Axel's name.

Connor nodded. He understood now. He'd noticed the tension between them when it came to Rainee, and he had secretly hoped they would just drop it. "Neither one gets the girl" sounded better than whatever this was turning into. Maybe Sapphire should get the girl at this rate. It would cause a lot less conflict.

Finn didn't speak again, but Connor moved to sit beside him. "Did she choose him?" he asked. It was an honest question. He didn't know much about relationships, but he knew that both parties had to agree in most cases.

Finn shook his head, slowly, defeated. "No. But he chose her." He breathed. "He rushed into a battle without thinking because he could tell she was crashing." He looked at Connor, his eyes glassy. "I would have, too. But I was thinking about the outcomes."

Connor inhaled sharply. He was not equipped for this. "But if she didn't choose…it doesn't matter what Axel wants…right?" he added, processing aloud.

Finn let out a pained laugh. "Maybe. But I know Axel. He won't stop until she chooses him." He covered his face with both hands. "I lost the minute he kissed her."

Connor was having a hard time following that logic. He furrowed his brow. "If you want a shot with her, why don't you just tell her?" The room fell silent. Connor wondered if that was the wrong thing to say. His hand went to the back of his neck as his nerves went awry. "She can't make an actual choice if she doesn't know the options."

Finn looked up from his hands like the realization had just hit him. "You…" he started, his brows knit together. "You're right. I never gave her the choice. Not really." He stood up and started for the stairs. "I need to tell her. I don't care anymore. Even if she still chooses him—" He let out a breath. "—at least she would know how I felt."

Connor smiled as Finn disappeared. He didn't really mean it like that. But he was glad he made Finn feel better. He probably would have sat there a little longer, reflecting, but the beacon alarm sounded. He jumped up. Everything had been quiet since the others got back to the house, so he was hopeful this was just a residual ping.

He entered the comm room and froze, his face pale. There, in block letters that sent chills down his spine:

[Ping 234363. 05102025. Origin: Fire Realm.]

CHAPTER 60
FINN

Finn bounded up the basement steps. Connor's words had lit something in him, and he refused to go another second without Rainee knowing. He opened the door, stepping into the dark living room. He looked toward the kitchen and noticed the door was still open. He figured that Axel was probably outside and would close it when he came in. He practically lived in the backyard these days.

Finn treaded quietly up the stairs. He didn't want to wake her if she was still recovering. When he reached her room, her door was slightly cracked. He knocked lightly, pushing the door open. He normally would have waited for a response, but he was tired of waiting. It had never worked out in his favor.

His heart dropped the minute he entered the room. Rainee was curled up in bed, pressed into Axel's chest like he was her anchor to this life. Finn gasped, but not because he was surprised, because he couldn't breathe. He was too late…again.

Axel's eyes flew open. He saw Finn and immediately tried to talk his way out of it. "No. No. It's not like that," he stuttered in a hushed tone. Finn couldn't hear him, he'd already turned to leave, his chest twisting.

"Sorry to interrupt," he whispered over his shoulder. He could hear Axel wrestling to get up without waking Rainee, but Finn didn't want to hear his explanations. Not anymore. It would most likely be something like "I didn't want this" or "I didn't mean to" and Finn couldn't handle any of his cryptic self-loathing right now.

He hurried down the stairs, desperate to get away from them. Scott marched into the house at that moment, and Finn hoped he wouldn't ask.

Scott didn't even look up, he just muttered, "Can't even shut doors. If they made any money, I'd make them pay the utility bill."

Then he caught Finn's eye. He opened his mouth to speak, but was interrupted by Connor nearly knocking the basement door down. He flew into the room, looking between Finn and Scott, frantic.

"IceHeart's here," he said, nearly hyperventilating.

Finn's pain turned to fear. *Fuck.* They were all dead.

"What? No." He hadn't noticed Axel behind him until he spoke. The devastation in his voice was evident. Finn felt for him, even now. He had gone straight from happiness and bliss, to suddenly fearing for his life, in less than an hour.

CHAPTER 61
SCOTT

Fuck. Could they not go ten minutes without a crisis? Scott's mind reeled. They had to fight, but Scott already knew that they didn't stand a chance. Especially not if Syren had teamed up with Aydron, as Scott had expected.

He couldn't protect them. But he'd rather die with them than surrender and let them be executed. He raced to the basement. They had one last card to play.

He frantically typed something into the comm and hit Send. Alarms sounded throughout the room. A message appeared on the screen in big red letters: GOVERNMENT ALERTED, THREAT DETECTED.

He hadn't wanted to involve them, but Syren was about to destroy the human realm and any sense of safety held by the civilians.

Scott grabbed as many weapons as he could carry and rushed upstairs, taking the steps two at a time. Sapphire was just slipping into the house as he tossed the weapons down on the rug and pointed at each of them. "You four, grab your weapons and your helmets." Axel looked like he was about to argue about the helmet part, but Scott stopped him. "If you don't wear a helmet, *I'll* be the one knocking the common form out of you." The threat was mostly hollow. There were lines Scott wouldn't cross. But it shut Axel up for the moment.

They grabbed their weapons. Finn opted for the crossbow and quiver that Scott had seen him haul in their first night there. The way Finn held the bow told Scott everything he needed to know: The man could take out a fleet from a rooftop and be home in time for dinner. Axel had a knife in each hand, both sharpened precisely. One swipe and anyone in range was missing a limb. Sapphire picked up a sword, but kept her knife strapped to her hip. Connor stood, gawking at the pile of weapons. He slowly picked up a helmet and slipped it on. Scott couldn't help but notice how much younger he looked with it on. He grabbed a shield from the pile and a Windward Staff that Scott had picked up while visiting the Realm of a Thousand Winds. It was said to be unbreakable. He hoped that was true.

Scott looked around the room. "Sapphire, go get Rainee," he ordered. No way was he sending one of the boys. She nodded and charged up the stairs. He knew Rainee was probably exhausted, but he wasn't going to make the mistake of leaving her behind again. He was already feeling like "Dad of the Year" with his current track record.

Finn stiffened at her name, but his attention was focused on his bow, surveying it for any weaknesses before taking it into battle. Axel wouldn't meet Scott's eye, he was twirling one of the knives between his fingers, his gaze pointed at his feet. Connor was staring sheepishly at the staff in his hand, and Scott wondered whether that had been a choice made in confidence or panic.

Sapphire returned with Rainee in tow, a few moments later. Her hair was pulled back lazily, and she still had grass stains and burn marks on her T-shirt from her encounter with Hermes.

"Now," Scott said, his voice deep and commanding. "We knew this day would come eventually." *I just really hoped it would be later.* "Whatever we face out there, whatever Syren has brought with him, we're going into it together." He looked between Axel and Finn. "Is that understood?"

Both boys nodded. Finn didn't look too pleased, but Scott hoped that the war speech had tapped into whatever soldier wiring he had left in him. He was trained to protect his own, even when his own were assholes.

Scott picked up a helmet and handed it to Rainee, who still looked like she was half asleep. "You may not have a common form to destroy, but you still need to be safe." It came out sappier than he really meant it, but no one said anything. It was just another dad thing.

She nodded and took the helmet, slipping it over her head. She picked up the remaining dagger from the pile and tucked it into her boot. It made him nervous for her to choose a melee weapon, but he knew she was capable. She'd managed to knock Axel off his pedestal in one sparring match, which Scott wished he'd been around to see.

Scott picked up Aydron's sword. He had to admit, for a man with few redeemable qualities, he had good taste in swords. He studied it for a moment, then moved toward the sliding door, deciding where they needed to check first. He was pretty sure that the clearing near the school had been empty when they left, so that left the larger glade near the park or the quarry grounds. Those were the only areas flat and secluded enough to portal into without drawing attention.

Against his better judgment, he knew that he had to split up the group, for the sake of efficiency. The pairings needed to be even in both number and relative power, which meant that Connor and Rainee should be separated. Not because Rainee couldn't fight, but because she was exhausted and needed a team that would have her back.

He pointed a finger at Finn and Sapphire and gave his order. "You two. Take Rainee and check the quarry. Axel, Connor, and I will check the park glade." He looked around at the group before adding, "I have the holodisk the boys brought, and it is synced to Sapphire's comm channel. Send an SOS if you find something." He paused and locked eyes with Finn. "And don't do anything reckless without backup."

Scott wasn't sure who needed to hear that message more, him or the boys. He'd been reckless himself lately, and reminded himself to remain calm when he saw Syren. He knew some past wounds were about to be torn open, whether he liked it or not.

Finn nodded, his eyes fixed in a glare. He was shutting down everything but his instincts, Scott could tell. Say what you want about the Fire Realm, but they knew how to train soldiers.

They exited through the back gate. Scott took a second to pull Rainee into a hug and whisper, "Be safe, Rae." He pulled away and looked at Sapphire and Finn. "We'll see you on the other side of this mess." He said it confidently, even though he wasn't sure any of them would make it out alive.

CHAPTER 62
FINN

Finn followed a few feet behind Rainee and Sapphire, watching for any sign of an ambush. As much as he tried to turn his brain off for the sake of the mission, his eyes kept flicking to Rainee. She still had no idea how he felt, save for the one almost-kiss they had in the woods. That didn't equate to anything if Axel had already earned a spot in her bed. So, he decided not to tell her at all. Let her choose Axel like she was already planning to do. He could accept that eventually, especially if she was happy.

Everyone was silent; the weight of the mission was too crushing to speak. IceHeart was there. They all thought the gods would be their final boss, but they'd have to go through Syren to get to them. The thought seemed absurd.

They approached the quarry, which was dark except for the streetlights at the perimeter. Finn waited for a moment, listening, waiting for any indication that they may not be alone. They skirted the rock wall, verifying that it was nothing but limestone and dirt.

"Now what?" Rainee asked. Her weariness was showing even more than before. It was late, and she had just assaulted a god with her own divine power. Finn couldn't imagine how exhausting that must be. Unfortunately, none of them would be getting much sleep that night.

Sapphire pulled her holodisk out just in time for it to beep. A video call rang through, showing Axel's caller ID. Sapphire answered it, but the screen was too dark to make out the face of the caller

"Axel?" Finn asked, moving to where the disk could locate him.

"Ahh, *Captain* FangSword," a familiar voice taunted. Finn's blood ran cold. *IceHeart*. But if he had the holodisk…that meant…*No*.

"Don't look so excited to hear from me now," he continued. "You had to know I was coming." He paused for a second, letting Finn process his words. Finn's heart thumped in his ears. "Bring me the demigod, FangSword. We're ending this now."

Finn's eyes widened. "Where are the others?" he asked, trying to keep his voice from shaking.

IceHeart chuckled. "Oh, they're here. I'm keeping them safe with me. For now." The holodisk clicked as the signal went dead.

Finn fought against the urge to panic. If IceHeart had managed to capture Scott and Axel, he feared their group wouldn't stand much of a chance either.

"Finn, we should go." Sapphire nudged softly, already hurrying past him. Finn nodded, following her. He looked at Rainee. He had to keep her away from IceHeart. Even if she never knew how he felt, he would never forgive himself if something happened to her.

He looked at Sapphire, who was still clutching the holodisk at her side, hard enough that he thought she might break it. They could portal somewhere else, beg for help from someone, anyone who would listen. But that would mean leaving the others behind with IceHeart, and Finn wasn't sure they'd still be alive when they returned. He wasn't sure they were even alive at that moment. IceHeart was known to bluff, especially if it gave him the upper hand. He was scared for the other team, but he also had no desire to hand Rainee off to IceHeart. Finn stopped walking mid-stride, his mind racing.

Rainee nearly collided with him. "Finn? What are you doing? We have to…"

"We can't go to the glade," Finn answered, his tactical brain in overdrive. "He wins too easily that way." He spun around and headed for the other clearing, the one near the school.

Sapphire jogged to catch up to him. "If we don't show up, he's going to tear this entire town to shreds, looking for Rainee," she reasoned.

He shook his head. "We draw him out and strike first. It's the only way to win against a man like IceHeart. We don't stand a chance head-on. Not if he's strong enough to capture Axel *and* Scott." He glanced at Rainee. "We need a diversion. Something he can't ignore."

"How are we going to accomplish that?" Rainee asked. She was wide-awake now; the adrenaline had finally kicked in.

Finn sighed, his eyes flickering to her necklace. "We give him a show he can't stand to miss."

CHAPTER 63
AXEL

Axel continuously glanced over his shoulder as the other group disappeared. Finn had better pray to whatever gods he believed in that Rainee came back alive. Or, if not, that he didn't come back either.

Axel wasn't stupid. He knew Scott had deliberately split them up. The worst part was that Axel didn't blame him. From Scott's standpoint, he was a bomb with the potential to detonate at any time. Axel wouldn't want himself around his daughter either, if he had one.

He turned back around, keeping his eyes on Connor. He wasn't going to let what happened in the last fight happen again. Connor had to be protected at all costs. Axel's conscience couldn't take that type of loss.

As they approached the glade, the incoherent commotion of a group of people could be heard. *Dammit. IceHeart brought backup.*

Scott motioned for them to stay quiet and out of sight, as he moved between the bushes and trees with expert stealth. Connor followed, his timidness showing in the way his hands shook. Axel stayed a few paces behind, checking their surroundings. He'd become good at sensing danger, a skill that his days in the syndicate had taught him.

Through the trees to his right, he caught glimpses of familiarity. Fire Realm soldiers, dressed in full armor emblazoned with the Fire Realm insignia. His gut twisted. These weren't supposed to be enemies. These were soldiers just like him, with orders they probably didn't fully understand and no way to break free.

"Where are all the captains?" Scott asked in a hushed whisper.

Axel had been wondering the same thing. He saw roughly a hundred low-ranking soldiers, but he couldn't see any red-feathered captains anywhere. There was no leadership, except for IceHeart, who stood on the opposite edge of the glade, smiling sadistically as his troops swarmed in from the portal. These weren't just soldiers. They were kids. Fourteen- to sixteen-year-olds at most, and some of them looked even younger. All had terrified looks on their faces, despite their obvious strength in numbers.

Axel looked over at Connor, who had paused to gawk at the gathering battalion. They were all just Connors. And that pissed Axel off even more. The kids shouldn't be there, let alone sent on a mission to kill men who were their comrades.

"Hey," Scott hissed, forcing Axel's attention. He motioned with two fingers to keep an eye on the soldiers. Then he held up the holodisk.

Axel nodded, but when he refocused on the glade, IceHeart was gone. Panic set in. How could he have lost him? He was the only one dressed in royal armor, which would stand out no matter where he was.

He scanned the area frantically, urgently seeking a glimpse of him. Connor let out a small yelp from beside him. Axel was about to turn to shush him when he felt the unmistakable weight of a blade on his throat.

"AxeClaw. FalconTail." IceHeart's voice sent chills down his spine. "So nice of you boys to join us willingly." Axel scanned the area for Scott, finding him a few paces away, surrounded by five soldiers. *We are so screwed.* "I thought I was going to have to come find you."

Axel smirked. This recon mission was going to hell, but at least Rainee was on the opposite side of town. She was safe, for now. He was starting to appreciate the way Scott split the teams a little more.

IceHeart forced them to their feet, and he and several soldiers crowded around Axel and Connor. Axel's hands were in the air; there was no point in fighting. They were severely outnumbered and had fallen right into IceHeart's trap.

IceHeart moved the blade to Axel's back and prodded him toward the open glade. He wasn't just going to kill them. He was going to make examples of them to all these young soldiers. This. This is what you get when you think you're doing the right thing. Gods, he sounded like Finn, and he almost wished Finn were here so he could fight with him one last time.

They were standing in front of the soldiers now, all eyes on them. Axel looked at Connor, mouthing a silent apology. Connor's eyes were filled with fear and unshed tears. All hope that they would get out of this alive was gone. In any other world, Axel would have protected that hope, but a war was no place for optimism. Just like it was no place for children.

He looked up in time to see IceHeart swipe the holodisk from Scott's palm and dial up Sapphire's comm channel. Axel's worst fear came to life. He was using them as bait for the others. Finn was smart enough not to take it, though. At least, Axel hoped he was. For Rainee's sake. If he couldn't get out of this, at least they had a chance to. He could die with that truth if needed. As long as she was safe.

IceHeart laughed evilly as he switched the holodisk off and chucked it against a nearby tree. It shattered into pieces. He paced over to Axel and placed his sword against his chest.

"I gave you a second chance once before, AxeClaw." He smiled coldly, but his eyes flashed, like his mind was elsewhere. "You won't get that luxury again."

Axel spat in his face. "I don't need pity chances from a king who would sacrifice his own men to prove a point." He didn't know where the words came from, just that they were true and, if was going to die, he was going to die with venom on his tongue.

IceHeart chuckled, wiping the saliva from his face. "Such anger." He clicked his tongue. "If only we were able to channel that into something more useful."

He turned and looked at Connor, but didn't say anything. Instead, he crossed to Scott who was staring at him with eyes like ice.

"Syren," Scott greeted coldly. "You've grown." Even with his life in danger, Scott was still able to joke. Axel respected that.

Syren lifted the tip of his sword to Scott's chin. Scott was much taller than the king, but that didn't make IceHeart any less threatening. "Scott Bennett. It's been a few years." Syren nodded, his face twisting into a sneer.

"I stopped realm traveling," Scott said simply. "Nice of you to notice." He searched Syren's eyes, keeping his posture calm and collected. "Congratulations on the crown. Sorry, I missed the coronation."

IceHeart smirked and kept his blade pressed to Scott's chin. His eyes flickered again, Axel was sure of it this time. It was like he was battling his own mind before he spoke. "Yes, I heard. Pity." He looked Scott up and down. "I suppose that's the traitor's price, old friend."

Scott stiffened a little. "I wasn't a traitor until your brother made me out to be one." He hissed. "I never wanted this," he added quietly.

IceHeart swung the sword, slicing into Scott's chest through his shirt. Scott let out a grunt, but otherwise didn't break his mask. "I did n-..." He paused, like he was regaining some sense of himself. "*Kai* did nothing of the sort. You became a traitor the minute you married that demigod." His tone was sinister, but Axel had caught the slip. *I*. It might have been nothing more than a slip of the tongue, but Axel couldn't shake the feeling that the cause was more substantial.

Scott opened his mouth to fire another insult at Syren, but he was interrupted by a large boom in the distance. Axel turned, and his heart leaped to his throat. A lightning storm crashed in the direction of the school.

Finn was baiting back. Trying to distract IceHeart while they escaped. But he was putting Rainee at risk, and that was unforgivable. If they all made it out of this alive, Axel was going to kill him.

CHAPTER 64
RAINEE

Rainee hadn't known what Finn meant when he said they were going to cause a diversion, but she should have. Now, she stood in the middle of the clearing, trying to focus enough to channel her powers. It was easier said than done; she had never used them on purpose before.

"Just take a breath and focus on striking the firepit," Finn coached, watching her intently. He seemed different, but she couldn't quite place why. He was more pointed with her, definitely not the timid guy who had almost kissed her a few days ago. Maybe this was his captain persona. Whatever it was, she found herself missing the old him.

She tried to concentrate, and the necklace hummed lightly, but nothing else happened. She sighed. "I-I don't know how…"

Finn took a small step forward, but Sapphire shoved him out the way. She grabbed Rainee's shoulder and stared at her face intently. "Listen. I know you can do this. Think about your dad." She searched Rainee's eyes. "Think about Connor. Poor, innocent Connor, who is currently trapped by the only man who might be more evil than my father."

Rainee felt her heart pounding, and the necklace started to buzz more intensely.

Sapphire backed away slowly and added. "Think about Axel. How angry he is that he got caught. How he's never going to see you again."

That did it. Something inside Rainee snapped. Her heart felt like it was being ripped in half. The necklace whirred like an engine coming to life, and, without much warning, a bolt of lightning crashed into the fire pit, singeing the grass around it.

Finn motioned for Sapphire to keep going, even though his face looked pained.

Sapphire nodded and continued, "He'll never see you again and he's probably telling himself some bullshit lie about how it's better this way, because that's how he is."

She was right, and that made Rainee's pulse race. Two more bolts of lightning hit the clearing.

"He'd rather die here than tell you how he really feels."

Crash. Pop. Crash.

It was no longer just single bolts of lightning. It was multiple hits, followed by claps of thunder that shook the surrounding neighborhood. The wind swirled around Rainee as her chest heaved.

Why him? Why was it him? And why couldn't she stop thinking about him or wanting him close to her? What gave him the right to make her feel like this, while he was the most painfully self-loathing person ever? What gave him the right to kiss her and then run away?

The wind speed surged, but Rainee couldn't feel it. She felt like she was floating. She couldn't see much of anything anymore; the clearing was lit up with constant lightning strikes. And all she could feel was the sob in her throat climbing. He had to be okay.

She felt the rage and the fear dissipate, along with the lightning around her, and she collapsed on the ground, nothing more than a pile of sobs and regret. Exhausted, barely hanging on, she looked up just in time to see Finn dive toward her.

He grabbed her and pulled her into the tree line, talking to her softly. "You did it. You can rest now. We'll take care of the rest." He was gentle, but she vaguely felt like he was holding back, like there was more behind his words that he didn't dare say out loud.

Her vision blurred slightly, but she tried to smile. She wasn't sure if she succeeded before her mind went blank. The last memory she had was Finn kneeling over her, cradling her softly, like she might break. *So gentle.*

CHAPTER 65
SCOTT

Scott hoped Finn knew what he was doing. The minute Syren had seen that lightning storm, he'd taken all but the five soldiers surrounding them with him to investigate. That was fine with Scott, he could deal with five kid soldiers, and by the look on Axel's face, he was thinking the same.

Scott looked at the one closest to him, dark skin and eyes, and a cut healing under his eye. He couldn't have been older than sixteen. He beckoned him over and said, "What's your name, kid?"

The soldier looked at him, startled by the question. "I, uh…Julius." His voice cracked.

The kid beside Julius elbowed him in the chest, "We're not supposed to talk to them, just hold them here," he growled.

Scott turned his attention to him. "What about you? You got a name?" He said it like a curious father, not like a hostage. *Fake it till you make it.*

The second kid grunted. "Shut up. I know what you're doing."

Smart kid.

"I'm not doing anything. Just chatting," Scott replied, smiling.

"His name's Kiran," Connor murmured. Scott's heart twisted slightly. Connor knew these boys. These were his peers, and had likely been his friends at one point.

Kiran pointed his sword at Connor, who just looked back at him, defeated. "Just because you're a traitor doesn't mean I'm interested in joining you," Kiran snapped. There was fear in his voice.

"You'd understand if you'd seen what I have," Connor retorted. Scott wondered where this version of Connor had been hiding, and if this skirmish had been his last straw.

Kiran looked between Scott and Connor. It was obvious he had more questions, but his fear was keeping him silent. Scott took the moment to step in.

"Sometimes, the way we believe things are isn't how they actually are." Scott glanced over at Connor, recalling their conversation in the kitchen the first night he had stayed with him. "And that's terrifying," he admitted. "But it's more terrifying to be on the wrong side of the battle when you have a choice not to be."

Scott looked over to the other three soldiers. They were watching him, wide-eyed. It was obvious that Kiran was their makeshift leader, and they didn't know how to handle watching him stumble.

"I said, *stop* it," Kiran said weakly, poking at Scott with his sword. "You're the ones on the wrong side." He looked at Axel and Connor. "They betrayed their own realm for a *girl*." He glanced back at Scott. "And you helped. Doesn't seem like the right side to me."

"That girl," Scott whispered, "is my daughter, and she didn't ask to be in the middle of this war." He locked eyes with Kiran, letting him see his pain for a moment. The weight of a father just trying to keep his daughter safe, but not sure that he could anymore.

Kiran's eyes widened further. "But she's dangerous. She would *start* a war."

"No," Connor interrupted. "IceHeart had already started the war. He was trying to weaken the Western Division before they had a chance to retaliate against him."

He looked like he was staring at Kiran, but Scott could tell his mind was somewhere else. To hear the truth come out of Connor's mouth, even if Scott had known it already, was a gut punch. Even the purest of them had figured it out, and there was no going back from that.

Kiran shook his head in disbelief. "No. Why would he do that?"

Axel chuckled slightly. "I don't know, kid. You were in the Water Realm before this, right? Did it look like they were ready for our attack?"

Scott thought back to the ping from the Water Realm to the Fire Realm, and the fact that no captains had come with this battalion. It finally dawned on him. These weren't soldiers who were waiting to go to battle in the Fire Realm. These were the scraps of a failed mission that Aydron hadn't completely shut down.

Kiran let his sword fall, the tip hitting the ground with a dull *thud*. Scott could see the realization in his eyes as he viewed his fellow soldiers. He started to raise his sword again, but not with the same confidence as before.

Julius took off his Fire Realm helmet and tossed it aside, catching Scott off guard. "I'm not going to be a bad guy," Julius declared as he stripped the Fire Realm armor off to his red tunic.

"Julius, you don't really believe him, do you?" Kiran asked, but his voice was shaky.

Julius nodded. "I do. I saw the chaos in the Water Realm. We weren't there to keep the peace."

The other soldiers looked at him in awe; then, one by one, they each stripped off their own armor and tossed it onto the ground.

Kiran looked up at Scott and said, "What now, Captain?"

Scott's heart twisted. While Captain Bennett had a nice ring to it, the implication of these kids putting their trust in him wasn't insignificant. He had to stop accidentally adopting kid soldiers. He didn't have any more bedrooms.

"Here's the plan…" he started, gesturing for everyone to form a circle around him. He shot a look at Axel, who nodded approvingly. Scott was starting his own battalion made completely of Fire Realm rejects.

Suck it, Syren, he thought, as he briefed the soldiers around him. He would convert Syren's entire military, five soldiers at a time.

CHAPTER 66
FINN

Finn could hear IceHeart's men coming before he saw them. Their armor was a noticeably foreign sound, punctuating the quiet of the night air. The footsteps sounded like fewer men than he expected, but still enough to outnumber them substantially. IceHeart entered the dusk-fallen clearing first, his cloak flowing behind him. He looked just like Finn remembered, but slightly more sinister.

He smirked when we saw Finn, standing beside Sapphire with his crossbow loaded. "FangSword. I see you've sided with yet another enemy. Not the best track record."

Finn didn't move. Didn't speak. He wasn't going to give IceHeart the satisfaction of getting to him.

"Where's the demigod?" he asked bluntly.

Finn shrugged and lifted his crossbow. "She's safe."

Sapphire twirled her dagger, her sword strapped firmly on her back. If Finn had to face a group of enemies with only one other person, Sapphire was among those he would choose.

IceHeart stepped forward, drawing his sword. "You can't be trying to protect her still." He looked Finn up and down. "She's a danger to the survival of the Fire Realm."

"Then maybe it's time that the Fire Realm dies," Finn threw back, his face neutral. He wasn't sure if he meant it, but it felt right.

He noticed the soldiers waiting in the tree line. All of them young, all of them visibly frightened. Where were the captains? He recognized a few boys from his old battalion—all privates, no more than sixteen. What game was IceHeart playing? Where were the adults?

"Spoken like a traitor," IceHeart hissed.

Finn noticed him hesitate before taking another step toward him, which was unlike him.

"I should have had you executed for the first act of insubordination," IceHeart growled, waving his sword at Finn. "Would have saved us all some time."

Finn remained silent, his crossbow trained on IceHeart. He knew what the king was trying to do, and he refused to let it happen. Since leaving the Fire Realm, he had learned a lot about himself. Enough to know that he was comfortable in his morality, and dying for it wasn't the worst thing that could happen.

IceHeart laughed. "Always so stoic and noble." His eyes flashed. "If only that was enough."

Those words stung more than the attack on his morals. They were the same words he'd been repeating to himself since he caught Axel with Rainee. *If only.*

Finn tightened the grip on his crossbow, his finger grazing the trigger. He knew the minute he let an arrow fly, the soldiers in the tree line would rush them. He looked over at Sapphire, who was crouched down, ready to pounce. He bet she could take on at least ten of the men by herself and not even mess up her hair. If Finn could get to higher ground, they'd be at an advantage, but there was no escaping the army, as things stood.

Sensing their hesitation, IceHeart grinned. "You are more than outnumbered, FangSword." He spun his sword lazily in one hand. "Give me the girl and turn yourself in. There's no use in fighting a war you can't win."

"I'd rather die with my morals than bow to a coward," Finn growled back, his temper flaring.

"That can be arranged," IceHeart hissed, lunging at him with the sword.

Finn was centimeters away from loosing the arrow he had nocked, but a knife flew from behind him, lodging itself in the tree beside Syren's head. Finn looked at Sapphire, who seemed to be just as confused as he was. He glanced behind him to find Axel there, twirling his second knife.

IceHeart backed up, slightly taken aback. "Who let the prisoners escape?" he bellowed. His eyes glowed with anger as his head moved in every direction.

Axel took the opportunity to move to Finn's left. "Where's Rainee?" he asked, looking around.

"She's safe, I promise." Finn answered sincerely, but Axel didn't seem convinced. Finn scanned the clearing in front of him, "Scott and Connor?"

Axel nodded toward the tree line, where all the soldiers were waiting. Finn could see Connor and a handful of other soldiers moving through the ranks, whispering. They all seemed to shift uncomfortably, but none of them moved to strike Connor.

Scott was crouched near the edge of the trees with his sword drawn, speaking to a soldier behind him. Finn raised an eyebrow at Axel curiously. Axel smirked knowingly, and for once, Finn was happy to see that smirk.

No one answered the king, and he turned back to face Finn with a growl. "No matter. Even with AxeClaw, you still hardly stand a chance."

"I wouldn't be so sure about that," Scott called as he leaped from the shadows.

The king turned, his eyes wide.

Finn used the moment of distraction to retreat to the other side of the clearing where a lone tree stood. He scaled it easily and squatted on one of the middle branches. He had a much better view from there. Axel and Sapphire had moved to flank the king, while Scott had his full attention.

Finn glanced toward the far side of the clearing, where the stream ran through the trees. He'd tucked Rainee away near there, away from anyone entering the clearing. He hoped she'd be okay until he could get back to her.

"You all think you're so smart." IceHeart laughed. "My men will dismantle you piece by piece." Finn's heart pounded in his ears as he readied his crossbow. He had nineteen arrows in total, and he knew how to make his shots count if needed. He hoped that the others would be able to handle the rest of the soldiers from the ground.

Finn thought he saw Scott smirk as he lunged forward, crying, "Then, let them try."

IceHeart's sword met Scott's with a loud clang as IceHeart yelled, "Destroy them!" to the soldiers in the tree line.

Only a few of the soldiers obeyed, rushing forward to attack Axel and Sapphire. The rest stayed back in the trees. Confused, Finn shot an arrow at one of the soldiers nearing Sapphire, taking him down instantly. He took down two more, but none of the other soldiers moved. What were they waiting on?

"What are you all doing?" IceHeart shouted at the soldiers. "Attack them!"

The remaining soldiers still didn't heed his command. Sapphire and Axel had managed to cut through the forces from the first wave easily.

The second wave remained at the tree line. Then Finn remembered the way Connor had moved through the battalion...how they had all stiffened yet didn't strike him. Connor was staging a coup.

CHAPTER 67
CONNOR

Connor slipped through the trees as stealthily as he could manage, Kiran and Julius tagging along behind him. Every now and again, they'd stop, whisper a few words of doubt into a circle of soldiers, then slip off again. Things like, "These men were our friends, why are we killing them?" and "IceHeart sent us to the Water Realm out of spite. What makes you think this isn't the same scenario?"

Just enough information to stir up uncertainty in their minds. The murmur rose around them, especially toward the back of the group. Some of the soldiers had even joined them in spreading the doubt. Connor smiled mischievously. He might not be able to fight, but by the gods, he could question the status quo. And he could make other people question it, too.

He could hear the commotion in the clearing as the first wave of soldiers, the ones they hadn't been able to reach, stormed to their deaths. Even if this tactical morale-breaking didn't work, it at least gave the team time between waves, to stand a fighting chance.

Connor paused and looked into the clearing. Finn was gone, from what he could tell. Then he saw it: the flash of metal from the large tree near the other edge of the clearing, and a sharp *ping* as one of his arrows pierced through the air, hitting its mark without so much as a *thump*. Connor had heard stories about Finn's sharpshooting skills, and this moment made him relieved to know that Finn was on his side. He'd hate to be on the opposite side of his sight right now.

"What are you all doing?" Connor heard IceHeart call out. "Attack them!"

Connor looked around, waiting for the next wave of loyalists to sprint into battle. But none of them did. Of the hundred men in the tree line, at least eighty of them were hesitating.

"You know he can't kill us all for insubordination," Connor whispered in the soldier's ear that was closest to him. The boy stiffened, glanced at Connor, and nodded, turning to whisper a similar message to those around him. This is how rebellions were made. And Connor was the leader. He may not have Finn's precision, nor Axel's battle-hardened knife skills, but he could talk. And sometimes, that's all you needed.

CHAPTER 68
RAINEE

Rainee had regained consciousness sometime between the first wave of soldiers charging and Axel arriving. She was still too weak to move much, but she could view most of the battle from where she was sitting beside the river. She hoped they couldn't see her.

Her body felt like oatmeal—mushy and unstable—but she was slowly recovering. Plus, it comforted her to see Axel. He was alive, and his knife skills were incredible when it wasn't *her* that he was fighting. She would definitely be mentioning that to him later.

The first wave of soldiers had been no match for the hodge-podge group of mercenaries in the clearing. Finn's archery skills shone through, as several of the soldiers had dropped before they even reached Axel and Sapphire. If the boys had been at battle when she had first met them, she would have been terrified. These were the kind of skills she would expect from assassins. Having known them as she now did, she was impressed and grateful that she was no longer their target.

Her dad had IceHeart locked in an intense sword fight, and she wondered how long he'd known how to use a sword. By the looks of it, probably longer than she'd been alive. He was poised, calculated, and kept IceHeart's full attention, even as the army around him noticeably faltered.

She watched for a while and saw IceHeart call for another charge, but the army didn't move. Her heart pounded in her ears. Why were none of the soldiers attacking?

That's when something caught her eye—a flicker of movement in the trees. Connor moved through the crowd of soldiers like he belonged there. She could tell he was speaking, but wasn't close enough to read his lips. Each soldier who heard him became rigid, like they had seen a ghost. She understood—he was instilling unrest, in the way only Connor could.

As she was observing Connor, she heard a commotion from the clearing. IceHeart had managed to push her father backwards, making his sword arm fall out of rhythm. IceHeart struck Scott's sword, sending him tumbling backwards onto the ground. The king lunged again, but Scott deflected it with his sword right before it hit him. Rainee could see that her father's shirt was ripped, and dried blood clung to the frayed fabric. That didn't look like a battle wound, it was too even and purposeful.

Sapphire and Axel rushed in, but Scott waved them back. They both stayed ready, though, just in case. What was he doing? They could end this.

CHAPTER 69
SCOTT

Scott hadn't used a sword in an actual fight in years, something that he never thought he would regret. He'd given up his Realm Guardian position to raise a daughter, thinking that he wouldn't ever need those skills to protect her.

Now, he was on the ground, his sword pressing against Syren's, trying to regain leverage. He felt Axel and Sapphire close in, but something inside of him said this wasn't their battle to fight. He held up a hand, telling them to stop. They did. He wondered how he had assumed all this power over ex-realm assassins. But he was glad they listened. He had one more card to play before an all-out war broke out.

He pushed as hard as he could from his position on the ground, and it was just enough for IceHeart to stumble backwards. "Syren, please just listen to me," he pleaded, quickly getting to his feet. "I never wanted this to be a war."

Syren stared at him, a flicker of understanding in his eyes, but it disappeared as he spoke. "Scott Bennett. You were once a great ally to our realm. Then—" He raised his sword again. "—you fathered a demigod's bloodline, and you turned my own soldiers against me." He smiled bitterly. "Those treasons aren't easily forgiven."

Scott swallowed. He sounded like Kai. The betrayal in his voice, like the day Scott had gone to talk with Kai. Had Syren been there? Did Scott just not remember?

"None of my actions were meant as attacks against the Fire Realm." Scott said. "If your brother would have let me explain, you would know that already," he added, his voice slipping into a bitter cadence that twisted at his heart. He missed Kai. The Kai that he had been before the council had introduced the Line Severance Decree.

"Lies," IceHeart spat, his sword arm shaking. His eyes flickered again, like he was fighting internally.

Scott watched him carefully, his sword still drawn.

He spoke again, but the voice wasn't Syren's. <You *knew* what you were doing. She was a *demigod*, Scott.>

Scott stiffened. *It can't be.* He lowered his sword slightly. "Kai?" he whispered, the hurt bleeding into his voice.

IceHeart looked at him, a cold smirk on his face. <Nice of you to finally see me, old friend.>

The voice was unmistakably Kai's. The clearing was deafly silent. Scott thought his chest was going to cave in.

"How long?" Scott murmured, looking into his eyes. "How long have you been doing this, Kai?" His voice sounded broken, despite him trying to level it.

Syren-Kai laughed. <How long have I been dead?> he asked, like it was a perfectly normal question.

"Eighteen years, Kai." Scott searched his eyes, trying to catch a glimpse of the friend he once knew. But his eyes were black. "Have you been puppeteering Syren this entire time?"

Kai smiled coldly. <Syren is spineless,> he uttered. <He was never fit to rule the Fire Realm. I came back to *help* him.>

His eyes flickered again, this time with fear, and that was when Scott realized that Syren was still trying to fight against Kai. Had he been fighting this whole time, being constantly shoved aside by Kai's aggressive nature? Or had he let Kai in at one point, under the guise of brotherly advice?

There was one thing Scott was sure of now. His friend was gone. The Kai smiling back at him through Syren's teeth was someone else. Someone dark and twisted. A corruption of who the real Kai was.

"You..." Scott started. "You went through all of this...just to get back at me?" His voice caught. Every wound that hadn't quite healed in his heart burst open. "You hated the demigod bloodlines so much that you had to ensure their erasure?" He swallowed hard. "Did my actions...actions that I made out of love...really warrant this?"

Kai smirked back at him. <Not only was it warranted then, but I plan to finish it now.> He threw himself at Scott, fury in his eyes. <You, your daughter, and every traitor here,> he hissed through clenched teeth. <I'll destroy this whole realm if I have to.>

Scott caught him with his sword, keeping Kai's blade inches from his chest. He stared into the cold obsidian pools that were his eyes and whispered, "This isn't you, brother."

<I am more me than I ever was before, I assure you,> Kai stated.

Scott's chest ached. That wasn't true; he knew it wasn't. The Kai he knew wasn't evil. Stubborn and vindictive, but *not* evil.

Kai reared back to swing his sword, but it wobbled slightly. His eyes lightened momentarily, and Syren's voice whispered, "I'm sorry." Then Syren was gone, his eyes darkened by Kai's rage again as he brought the sword down, clashing against Scott's.

Finally, a few soldiers charged forward, having made their decision to fight for the Fire Realm. Scott's heart ached for them, but not as badly as it ached for Kai. For Syren.

Axel and Sapphire made quick work of the small wave of soldiers, while Scott fought for his life. He didn't know how much longer he could do that for.

Kai parried one of his strikes, sending Scott stumbling backwards momentarily. Kai took the opportunity to pounce, bringing his sword down in a move that would have killed Scott if he hadn't blocked it, just barely, with the edge of his sword.

"Scott, watch out!" Axel's voice cut through his concentration. Scott hadn't noticed the soldier sneaking up behind him. He did his best to avoid both the soldier and Kai, but it proved to be almost impossible. As his sword clashed with Kai's, he felt the distinct sting of a blade slice through his calf, nearly to the bone.

Axel's knife connected with the soldier's neck, mere seconds too late. Scott crumpled to the ground with a yell, his sword faltering. He heard two arrows, one right after the other, whiz past Kai's head and lodge into a nearby tree. Of course, *this* was the one time that Finn missed.

Kai prepared to swing the final blow to Scott, who was unable to recover in his current position. Then suddenly the clearing was flooded with spotlights and the sound of helicopters. Scott exhaled heavily. *About time they showed up.*

Kai looked around, realizing that he'd been trapped. He was surrounded not only by Scott's army of rejects, but also the human military. Even he couldn't handle that.

"Syren IceHeart, put your hands up and drop the sword," came a gruff voice. Scott could feel the guns trained in their direction. Scott had never liked fighting with guns; he much preferred the finesse of swords and bows. But boy, was he glad someone had brought guns to a sword fight and that they were on his side.

Kai dropped his sword, a smirk on his face. What was he planning? As the military officers closed in, he gave Scott one last look. <This isn't over, brother.>

Scott opened his mouth to respond, but Syren's face contorted as he dropped to his knees. Black smoke poured from his nose, ears, mouth, and eyes like he was burning from the inside out. As soon as the smoke cloud cleared, Syren collapsed into a heap. Scott thought he was dead, until he saw his chest rising and lowering, just barely.

A human soldier rushed forward in full SWAT gear and yanked a dazed-looking Syren to his feet, shoving his hands behind his back and cuffing him. He recited his rights to him, both human and divisional, but Syren didn't seem to be listening. His haunted gaze was fixed on Scott. "I didn't know," he whispered, his voice hoarse.

"By order of the governing bodies of Earth as well as the Divisional Council, you are hereby under arrest for breaking inter-realm travel treaties and protection orders," the soldier said, shoving Syren toward a helicopter.

Scott wanted to jump in and explain, to try and help, but the minute he opened his mouth, Syren shook his head slowly. Scott clamped his mouth shut, the look in Syren's eyes telling him everything he needed to know. This man was done. He'd take whatever punishment came next, whether he was the one who deserved it or not. Scott's chest smarted again, and for a second, he caught a glimpse of the child he'd once known in Syren.

As he was watching, he felt someone pull him to his feet, his calf screaming in protest. "Scott Bennett. You're under arrest by order of the governing bodies of Earth and Divisional Council for breaking inter-realm protocol and for obstruction of justice," a different voice cited gruffly. The cuffs were cold against his skin, grounding him. He had known this was a possibility when he had alerted the military.

He heard Rainee before he saw her. "Dad?" She came running around the helicopter, the wind blowing her hair in different directions. "Dad, what's going on?" She charged toward him, only to be grabbed by Axel.

"It's okay, it's going to be okay," Scott whispered. He wasn't even convinced of that himself, but Rainee did stop fighting against Axel's grip. Scott could hear him trying to console her, explaining that the Divisional Council would have her executed if she interfered. It felt weird to admit it, but Scott felt the need to thank Axel, if he ever saw him again.

He looked across the clearing and made eye contact with Finn, who had descended from the tree and was entering the chaos. Take care of them, he thought, trying to make his eyes scream what he couldn't communicate otherwise. Finn stopped running and nodded, saluting Scott in a way that felt right. Then he was shoved roughly into the helicopter, his calf still dripping blood; but his mind was quiet. He'd protected Rainee the best he could, for eighteen years. It was up to the rest of them to take it from there.

CHAPTER 70
AXEL

Axel had acted on pure instinct, grabbing Rainee before she got to Scott. He didn't know much about the human military, but he knew about the Divisional Council, and they didn't have a reputation for going easy on people. If Scott had pissed them off, who knows what they would do to Rainee if she intervened.

    The helicopters took off, leaving the clearing dark. The Fire Realm soldiers stood in the shadows, their eyes wide. Finn needed to figure out what to do with them. And as far as he knew, the rest of the town had no idea what had transpired here, and they probably never would. He wouldn't be surprised if the human government had a tool to erase the memories of a large group of people in a single click. Considering that they had been hiding the actuality of realm travel, and representing gods in children's bedtime stories for centuries, it wouldn't be too far-fetched.

    Rainee turned to him, tears in her eyes. He didn't know what to say to comfort her, so he did the only thing he could. He pulled her into a tight hug, holding her like she might disappear if he wasn't careful.

    She buried her face in his bloodstained shirt as the first sobs wracked her body. His heart shattered. He grabbed her tighter and whispered. "We'll get him back. I promise. We'll find him." He had no idea how he was going to accomplish that, but he'd burn the world down to never see her like this again.

    He felt a hand touch his shoulder, and he turned to see Finn standing there, crossbow slung over his shoulder, his quiver misplaced during the battle. Axel knew there was more to come. He didn't need to know anything about IceHeart to know that what they had just witnessed wasn't normal. He had a feeling that Kai would be back for them.

"We need to figure out how to get them back home. They can't stay here," Finn whispered, gesturing toward the tree line.

Axel nodded slowly, still holding Rainee for dear life. She had her fist tangled in his shirt, making sure he couldn't pull away. "If they came here today, the tether should still be active." He took in a deep breath. "If only the holodisk we had synced with the Fire Realm channels hadn't been smashed to pieces by the demon king."

"About that," Connor interrupted, emerging from the tree line. He'd taken his helmet off, and his hair was matted to his forehead with sweat. "I think I might be able to fix it, but it's going to take me a few hours."

Axel had never been more grateful to see the kid. He had no doubt that if there was any hope of restoring the holodisk, it would be due to the expertise that Connor possessed.

"C-Captain FangSword…" A timid soldier that looked about Connor's age stepped forward. Finn noticeably shifted at the title but nodded for him to continue. "We don't want to go back there." His eyes were wide.

Finn stepped forward, addressing the boy. "We don't have a place here for everyone," he said, his voice hushed. "It would be best if we could get you home, where there's food and shelter."

The boy shook his head. "Have you not been back to the Fire Realm since the Water Realm raid?"

Finn looked back at Axel with a confused look on his face, then turned back to the boy. "No, our mission has been here." He searched the boy's eyes. "Has something happened?"

The boy shuffled uneasily, then nodded. "The riots have reached the capital. We could tell the minute we stepped back through the portal. Everything is on fire. The palace is the only safe place, and probably not for long without a king."

The boy sounded scared, but the way he delivered the news made him seem much older than he was. He was clear, and so were the circumstances. Axel knew there had been talk of riots throughout the realm, but none of them had gotten near the capital, which was usually an unspoken barrier for political protests.

"We might need the help here, Finn." Axel could hear Sapphire but couldn't see her. He tried to turn to listen, but Rainee gripped him tighter. Fine. He'd never move again if that's what made her feel better.

Finn looked back at Sapphire and listened. "Kai is still out there and—" She paused like she was searching for the right words. "—the gods still haven't made an appearance. I think we should try to figure out an arrangement. It's not every day you get a battalion dropped in your lap."

She was right. There was still a lot more to come, but Axel didn't want to think about that right now. He wanted to get Rainee back to the house, where she could be safe, and forget about all of this until the next day.

"We have some room at the house," Rainee murmured, her head still on Axel's chest as she scanned the clearing. "And we have a few tents that we can put in each clearing for now."

Finn looked at her, his eyes softening as he nodded. "I can help get everything set up." He looked back at the soldiers. "Just until we figure something else out." He sighed. "Until then, I need three groups of three to be in charge of burying the dead. And the rest of you, you'll be in charge of prepping the clearings for camp."

Finn's voice had shifted. He wasn't just telling them what to do, he was commanding it. This was the Finn of legend, Axel could see that now.

"Understood?" Finn asserted.

The soldiers saluted him with a confirmation of, "Yes, sir!"

Axel saw something in Finn at that moment. He was no longer the demoted soldier; he was a captain, and he was done pretending he wasn't.

Finn turned to him and flicked a hand toward the house. "Take Rainee home. Make sure she's safe." His voice was stern, but his eyes were distant, like he wasn't really hearing the words he was saying.

Axel nodded, taking a hand off Rainee's back to salute him. "Captain," he whispered. For once, it wasn't taunting. He meant it. Finn had earned it. A soft smile tugged on Finn's lips. He was meant to be there.

Axel moved to usher Rainee toward the house, his hand on the small of her back.

"And, Lieutenant Taylor," Finn added. Axel turned to look at him, his heart pounding. *Is this what we're doing now?* "Thank you for having our backs out there."

Axel nodded, a smirk on his face. He never thought he'd outrun the AxeClaw name, but he liked the sound of Lieutenant Taylor. Not just because he never thought he'd have a title like that, but because Taylor felt more befitting than AxeClaw ever had.

He turned back to Rainee and walked with her toward the parking lot on the other side of the trees. He didn't care what came next, as long as he had his new family.

CHAPTER 71
FINN

Finn was back in his element. The rush of adrenaline that had hit him during battle was still coursing through him as he directed soldiers and helped with the cleanup. He'd sent Sapphire back to the house to see if Scott had any extra tents. The three tents the boys had brought with them would only comfortably sleep four apiece, and he figured they could fit ten or so at the house, but it would be crowded.

He'd taken a head count of how many soldiers were left: forty-eight. All between the ages of fourteen and sixteen. That fact wouldn't have bothered Finn a week ago, but something about it made his stomach twist now.

He watched the boys work, burying the dead without so much as blinking. His chest ached for those they'd had to kill while they defended themselves, but he knew there had been no other option in that moment.

"Captain FangSword?" a voice asked from behind him. He turned to look at a young soldier. He was holding Finn's quiver in his hands. "We found this by a tree and thought you might want it back."

He nodded and took the quiver, gripping it a bit too tightly. He met the soldier's eyes and whispered, "That's Captain Mason to you, Private."

The words felt right, but it would take some time to get used to. FangSword had been his name for twenty-one years. It was a name given to nobles and diplomats in the Fire Realm. But Mason was his new lineage—one he could create himself.

The soldier smiled and ran off to tell some of the others about his interaction with the captain. Finn grinned to himself. *Captain Mason. Lieutenant Taylor. Private Shay.* Just unsuspecting enough to start a war.

He paced over to the tree where one of his arrows still stuck out, his grin disappearing. He never missed. How could he have missed the one shot that could have ended this?

He knew that wasn't a fair assessment, but it didn't stop the guilt that was washing over him. He knew that the government still would have shown up and taken Scott away. That was outside of his control. He also had a feeling that his arrow would have killed Syren, but whatever primordial being Kai was would have escaped through. It would have been another body to clean up with the same level of security they currently had. Still, the what-ifs played like movies in his head. Just a little to the left, and maybe they would all still be there.

He yanked the arrows from the tree, not even bothering to salvage the tips. He'd need new ones for the next time anyway. He hated that there would be a next time.

He took a deep breath and leaned his forehead against the rough bark of the tree. This was the first time he'd let himself breathe since the battle. The first time he'd let himself feel how tired he was. How hurt he still felt.

Finn had sent Rainee with Axel, knowing that she trusted him, probably more than anyone else on the battlefield. But the ache in his chest reminded him that he could have taken her home, too. *He* could have made sure she was safe, instead of setting Axel up to be her safety net.

He was needed there, though. He had a battalion to command, heartbroken or not. He would sooner die than let another person down.

Sapphire returned then, hauling three six-person tents with her. Where had Scott gotten all this stuff? Knowing Scott, it was probably some covert realm camping operation, and one of these tents was forged in the fires of Mt. Pilytos in the Fire Realm. Finn smiled at the possibility; he missed Scott already. Even if the man was constantly glowering at him like he wanted to murder him.

Connor was tinkering with the pieces of the holodisk under a nearby tree, his hands working faster than Finn thought possible. He'd already managed to reassemble the inner components and was battling with the outer shell that had shattered against the tree.

When they had first arrived in the human realm, he had wondered if Connor was going to get in the way. Fresh out of boot camp and not the best fighter, Finn recognized a potential liability from a mile away. Now, he could happily say he'd been wrong. What the kid lacked in battle skills, he made up for in intelligence and strategic analysis. He was the kind of asset you kept under lock and key. A secret weapon.

Finn crossed the clearing to help Sapphire with the tents, leaving his quiver by the tree. He gave her a quick nod of acknowledgment before unrolling the first one.

"Leadership looks good on you," she said after a few moments of silence, offering him a small smile.

He smiled back, threading a tent rod through its frame. "Yeah, and what makes you say that?" He liked leading. Being in charge was his comfort place, but he wondered what she meant by her comment.

"I've never seen you so sure of yourself," she answered, starting on one of the other tents. "You were always stoic, but your eyes looked like they were waiting for the next thing to go wrong." Finn stopped what he was doing and looked at her as she continued, "You stepped into this captain role, and suddenly your stoicism has a backing. You're a natural."

He didn't know what to say to that. All he had wanted since the Outer Coves mission was to regain his rank and prove that he was worthy of leading. Hearing the validation from someone, especially someone like Sapphire, made it all feel earned. It didn't matter that he'd given himself the title back, it only mattered that he lived up to it.

"Thank you," he whispered, returning to the tent in front of him.

CHAPTER 72
AXEL

Axel was sitting on Rainee's bed, waiting for her to shower. He'd grabbed a protein bar and some warm tea from the kitchen in case she needed them. He wished he knew how to cook better. His clothes were still caked with dried blood, and his hair was matted with sweat from that damn helmet, but he'd worry about that later.

He stood as the door inched open and Rainee entered, her hair in a towel and clean pajamas pulled over her body. He smirked. He couldn't help it; she looked good in any outfit.

"You sure your face isn't just permanently stuck like that?" she quipped, a smile on her lips.

His smirk turned into a full smile. "With you around, it's possible," he replied, his eyes still locked on her.

He offered her the tea, and she took it, taking a slow sip as she eyed him. "What?" he asked in a hushed tone.

She shook her head. "You look like a wreck," she said with a smile. "An attractive wreck, but still a wreck." She said the last part softly, but it was enough to make Axel's heart race.

He raised an eyebrow, trying his best to hide the shakiness in his voice as he asked, "Attractive, huh?" He didn't want to let himself believe the words.

She nodded and crossed the room, setting the mug of tea down on her dresser, then placing a hand on his chest. He had to stop himself from pulling her into a kiss immediately.

She looked up into his eyes and whispered, "You know, I thought you were gone." Her voice caught on the word gone, making his chest twist.

He tried his best to smirk, but he wasn't sure it came across as that. "It's going to take a lot more than IceHeart to get rid of me." He smiled. "I have too much spite left to die."

She smiled softly and looked down. Her eyes were full of unshed tears, and she looked like she was miles away. No one had ever looked at him like that before. As though he actually would have been missed.

"You know, it was worse because it felt like just the thing you'd do," she whispered.

His heart ached, but he couldn't help but feel confused. "What does that mean?"

She looked up at him, searching his eyes, the first of the tears spilling over. "You would die without admitting that you care about anyone."

That was it. That was the knife to his heart.

"If I don't care, then no one gets hurt," he whispered, feeling tears prick his own eyes. "Because everyone I care about gets hurt in the end." He stared at her sincerely. "I would never give you that death sentence."

She blinked, her eyes shifting to something that looked like sympathy. "You believe that?"

"I do," he said softly, noticing the way her lips puckered slightly as she was thinking. "There are a lot better men out there," he added. "Men that would die for you without dragging you into the flames with them." He could hardly breathe. He'd never admitted that out loud. He had never had a reason to.

She narrowed her eyes. "You mean like Finn?"

The question caught Axel off guard. He wasn't prepared to name names. But he nodded. "He's a good example, yeah." He gulped. "He'd definitely be safer. He would know how to do all this without the baggage." He looked away from her, studying the carpet on the floor. He hadn't wanted to say it, but it was the truth, and she needed to know that there were much better options than him, even if it killed him.

She grabbed his chin lightly and turned his head to face her. There was a determination in her voice as she said, "What if I don't want Finn?"

"Rainee…" he started. He couldn't let her do this.

"No, Axel." She searched his eyes. "I want this. I want *you.*" More tears filled her eyes as she added, "And I wish you'd stop trying to convince me that I don't."

Then, she leaned over and pressed her lips to his. His heart stopped, but he kissed her back. He had secretly hoped she would respond that way, even though he was sure he'd break her even if he didn't want to. He wrapped his arms around her and pulled her closer, deepening the kiss.

He pulled away after a few seconds, resting his forehead on hers. "I want you, too." He breathed, staring into her eyes. It felt good to admit it, but something inside of him was panicking. "But I don't know how to do this." *I don't know how to be wanted.*

She shook her head and gave him another peck on the lips. "Just stay, then. We can figure it out." She laughed slightly. "Along with everything else we need to figure out."

He nodded. "Only for you, static."

She smiled at the nickname. She was so beautiful when she smiled. He was about to lean in to kiss her again when the house shook violently. Alarms sounded in the basement, and the sky outside burned red. Screams erupted from outside, and the glow of portals was visible from the window. The war had begun.

Axel turned to look out the window, only to find everything on fire. The house shook again. He grabbed Rainee tighter and shoved her toward the door. "Go, we need to get out of here before the house comes down." They rushed downstairs as another tremor hit, raining drywall on them.

Rainee's necklace glowed white against her skin as they rushed to the back door. Axel fumbled with the latch, trying to yank it open, but the tremors had caused the door to come off its track. He finally managed to realign it and yank it open right as the next tremor hit. He reached for Rainee, but as he looked back, the house had already started to crumble.

No. Not like this. Not now, he thought, throwing himself in after her.

The End
Book 1

ACKNOWLEDGMENTS

Ashen is a work that has held a very special place in my heart since I was young. I wrote the first version when I was 11 years old. By 13, I had decided I wanted to self-publish it. The adults in my life never blinked, for which I am insanely grateful.

A special thank you to my mom and dad, who acted as the first editor of *Ashen v1* and championed figuring out how to get it published. My mom spent so many hours editing the work of a middle-schooler because she cared. I couldn't be here without her. And my dad always believed I could do it.

I also want to acknowledge the impact of the educators who were in my corner, particularly my 6th grade English teacher, Mrs. Weaver, who allowed me to read my first draft aloud to the class and write during independent reading time. You saw a spark, and you decided to kindle it. I'm forever thankful.

A big thank you to the first readers of this book, including the ones who read *Ashen v1* all those years ago. Thank you to my Beta readers: Kyle, Ariah, Katie, and Zoey for taking a chance on the draft version of this novel. Your insights helped me improve immensely.

And thank you to my incredible Editor, Jen Jilany, who spent weeks editing and leaving thoughtful and encouraging feedback throughout the novel. This book could not be what it is without your contribution.

Thank you to Ariah Gilbert for creating gorgeous cover art, and the realm logos that were used in promotion. You really know how to make a creator's dream come true.

And finally, thank you to the little girl who started this dream. Thank you for never letting me give this up. It may have been a long trip to get here, but we made it.

ABOUT THE AUTHOR

Jade Wilson (Formerly Jade Davis) is a writer who began her career when she was only 11, publishing the first version of *The Destroyed Trilogy*. Currently in her 20s, Wilson lives in the Saint Louis area, where she continues to write. Her latest project includes remastering *The Destroyed Trilogy* and giving the realms the attention she always wanted them to have. She writes books for people who understand that emotions aren't always pretty and decisions have consequences.

Outside of writing, Jade has a dual bachelor's degree in accounting and information technology from Saint Louis University and works as a technology auditor. She's also in graduate school for her master's in MIS at Southern Illinois University – Edwardsville. She spends her free time chasing her toddler and finding the best reading spots in the St. Louis area.

Social media:

Instagram: @JadeWilsonAuthor

Substack: thedestroyeduniverse.substack.com

www.ingramcontent.com/pod-product-compliance
Lightning Source LLC
LaVergne TN
LVHW010308070526
838199LV00065B/5488